What We Did This Summer
by
Katie Taylor and Marta Westfall

Once upon a time there were two little girls named Katie and Marta. They didn't know each other, but they were still sisters. Twin sisters! Katie lived with her mom, Leah Taylor, and Marta lived with her daddy, Riker Westfall, and they all lived in the same town but in different houses. Then one day Katie went to the store with her mom and Marta went to the store with her daddy and it was the very same store! Then the cereal boxes fell over and Marta and Katie met and then Leah and Riker met and, after that, a bunch of stuff happened.

First, Katie didn't like Marta, but then she did. And then Marta didn't like Katie, but then she did, too. Riker liked Leah and she liked him back, but they pretended they didn't until the twin sisters went off to summer camp and decided it was time they all got to be one big happy family.

And that's what we did this summer.

THE END

(But really, it's only the beginning....)

Dear Reader,

I'm often asked where I get the ideas for the stories I write. Well, for this book, it happened to be a dream. I know that sounds bizarre, but one night I dreamed about a daddy who was holding the hands of his two daughters and trying to keep them together. When I awakened, the dream stayed vividly in my mind and I knew this was one idea that wasn't going away. It had to be written.

So Katie and Marta were born and their story evolved into the love story of their parents, Leah and Riker. The book was first published in 1991 and I am thrilled that it's being reprinted this year. *A Perfect Pair* is one of my own special favorites and I hope you'll enjoy this *dreamy* story as much as I enjoyed writing it.

Happy reading!

Karen Toller Whittenburg

KAREN TOLLER WHITTENBURG

A Perfect Pair

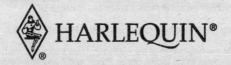

HARLEQUIN®

TORONTO • NEW YORK • LONDON
AMSTERDAM • PARIS • SYDNEY • HAMBURG
STOCKHOLM • ATHENS • TOKYO • MILAN • MADRID
PRAGUE • WARSAW • BUDAPEST • AUCKLAND

ISBN-13: 978-0-373-36129-8
ISBN-10:   0-373-36129-7

A PERFECT PAIR

KAREN TOLLER WHITTENBURG

Karen Toller Whittenburg is a native Oklahoman who fell in love with books the moment she learned to read and has been addicted to the written word ever since. She wrote stories as a child, but it wasn't until she discovered romance fiction that she felt compelled to write, fascinated by the chance to explore the positive power of love in people's lives. She grew up in Sand Springs [a historic town on the Arkansas River], attended Oklahoma State University and now lives in Tulsa with her husband, a professional photographer.

For my grandmother, Lois Gideon.
Thanks, Granny,
for all the special memories we share.
And a special thanks to Linda and Sommer
for allowing me to use the "star" story.

Chapter One

He had the last one.

Leah jammed her cart against the freezer case while she considered the produce aisle and the man with the banana pepper. It was the last one. She could see that from here. And he was handling it as if he couldn't decide whether or not he really needed a banana pepper.

She needed it...in the worst way.

A smoldering pout was burning a hole in her back and with a sigh, Leah glanced over her shoulder at her daughter. Katie still straggled behind, two aisles back, the ten-minute-old pout still fixed on her six-year-old face. Reluctantly Leah nodded. Katie's disposition improved noticeably in the two seconds before she darted down aisle number four, where colorful, overpriced cereal displays promised vitamin-enriched sugar and a cheap surprise inside every box. Katie would look at every brand before selecting the single, most disgusting and least nutritious form of breakfast food to be found in the store.

Leah had promised herself she wouldn't give in this time but...well, it was one of those days and if a box of cereal, expensive though it was, would put Katie in a more tractable mood, it seemed a small enough bribe to pay. Especially considering that in two hours and some-odd minutes, Leah was supposed to serve a dinner she hadn't as yet begun to prepare and there was at least thirty minutes of picking-up before the house would be presentable enough for her former in-laws' visit. Meanwhile, Leah still needed a banana pepper.

She looked back at the man who stood between her and a successful evening. Should she just ask him if she could have the pepper? He looked nice enough. No. Wrong. He looked better than nice. She ran a quick, assessing eye along the tanned, sinewy length of his forearm, to his muscled shoulders covered in a neat, perfectly fitting polo knit shirt…blue, every man's favorite color in polo knit. His jeans were stone-washed, new but snug fitting. His facial features were lean and strong, no subtle curves or angles. His face was tanned, too. Or perhaps the skin tone was natural, owing more to heredity than sun. He was blond, though. Dark blond with just a hint of red in his eyebrows and a clearly discernible reddish tint in his neat moustache. If he ever grew a beard, it probably would be red. Blond men often had reddish beards…all of this was getting her nowhere. This man didn't have a beard. What he had was the last banana pepper in the store.

She could drive across town to another grocery, but that would take time and…

The man looked up, caught her gaze and fascinated her with the slow, winsome smile that began first on his handsome mouth and eased upward into his very blue eyes. He lifted his shoulders in a perplexed shrug and indicated the pepper in his hand. "Do you know anything about these?" he asked.

She knew better than to chat with strange men in the supermarket, despite her friend Susannah's assertions that the place to find a good man was in the produce aisles of America. But he looked so sincere. How could she not feel some compassion for a man who'd picked up a banana pepper and didn't know what to do with it? She edged her cart closer to his. "I'm not an expert, but I do have a recipe that calls for banana peppers."

The man seemed doubtful. "A recipe for what?"

"A stuffed pepper casserole with three different kinds of peppers. Sounds awful, I know, but it's really pretty tasty."

His smile deepened, revealing an indentation on one side of his chin. Not a cleft, exactly. Certainly not a dimple, but attractive, all the same.

"Stuffed pepper *casserole*? I shudder to imagine what my

daughter would have to say about that." He held up the pepper for closer scrutiny. "What does this do for a salad?"

"That all depends on the salad," Leah said, wondering if she should pluck the thing out of his hand and rush off to the checkout counter, or if a little diplomacy would work just as well in this situation. "I prefer green peppers for salads. They're a little crisper than those." She eyed the yellow vegetable in his hand. "Would you mind handing me another—" Pausing for effect, she glanced at the empty bin behind him and said, "Oh. I guess you got the last one."

"What?" He looked at the stainless-steel bin, then looked back at her. "Oh, here, by all means, take this one. I just thought I'd try something different. Change my life by experimenting with a new taste—you know how it is…" He placed the pepper in a plastic bag, tied it with a twist tie, and offered it to her. "It's all yours, and I know if my daughter were standing here, she'd thank you for taking it."

Leah felt a little ashamed of herself for having coerced the pepper from him. He was being so gallant. "You're sure you don't want it?"

Again the smile. Again the purely sensual charm of his gaze. "I've seldom been more certain of anything."

Leah was more intrigued by the elusive cleft in his chin than she wished to be. And something about his eyes made her feel warmly wrapped and far too comfortable. "Well, thank you," she finally managed to say. "You've just saved my dinner. Stuffed pepper casserole would be nothing without the banana pepper."

"Sort of like split-pea soup without the peas, I would imagine."

"Something like that," Leah said with a smile. "You see, it's my former mother-in-law's recipe, and if any ingredient is missing…"

"She notices right off, does she?"

Leah nodded. "And I'd never hear the end of it."

"That would be bad." He leaned his forearms on the handle of the shopping cart. "Especially since you referred to her as a *former* mother-in-law."

There was a question in his voice and it sent a whisper of caution wending its way through Leah. "Yes, well, it's kind of an odd situation."

"In-law situations always are. Are you making the casserole for her or do you follow her recipe as a matter of principle?"

"She and my ex-father-in-law are coming for dinner tonight. Left to my own devices, I probably would toss the infamous recipe in the trash. I know my daughter would be thrilled to see it burn. She refuses to touch any food with green in it, no matter whose recipe it is."

"That casserole must create quite a stir at your house." His eyebrows lifted in a smooth question. "Do your ex-in-laws visit you often?"

"Only once a year, thank goodness."

Thoughtfully, he pursed his lips. "Do you think I could have that recipe? I have some distant relatives who visit all too often and they hate green stuff, too. Maybe I could serve your casserole and get them to come only once a year."

Humor lifted the edges of Leah's mouth. "I can't promise stuffed pepper casserole will work for you."

"I'll take my chances." His smile conveyed his enjoyment of their lighthearted exchange, and his gaze revealed a flattering interest in her. "I did mention that I was thinking about changing my life, didn't I?"

Leah liked him. She really did. But…well…nothing was this easy. "Do you always come to the grocery store when you want to change your life?"

He made a face. "Not usually, no. I just picked up my daughter from her dance class and happened to remember that we needed bread and milk and trash bags and some other small necessities of life. As a matter of fact, this is the first time I've been in this particular grocery store." His smiled returned to her. "I didn't realize what I was missing."

Leah smiled. "Best banana peppers in town. You'll have to try this store again the next time you want a change."

"Do you come here often?"

"I try to keep it to a maximum of five or six trips a day. Grocery shopping isn't my favorite—"

With a cardboard rumble, a display at the end of aisle four, two rows back, toppled to the floor. Sounds of boisterous activity followed close behind and suddenly all Leah could think of was Katie. Katie trying to climb the shelving and pulling it over. Katie buried under a ton of sugar-sweetened cereal. Katie in the center of all that commotion.

Spinning on her heel, Leah raced toward the noise, hoping Katie was uninjured, praying that she was all right, silently vowing never to let the child out of her sight again. As she turned the corner, Leah was aware of the man following close behind her. She realized, too, that other people were coming to see what had happened. But her attention soon focused on the spill of cereal boxes across the aisle, and on Katie, who sat squarely in the midst of it all…and squarely on top of another little girl.

Leah swallowed her dismay and rushed forward to pull her daughter up and away from the other child. "For heaven's sake, Katie, what happened? Are you all right?"

Katie turned around, her baby-blue eyes filling with instant tears. "She made me mad, Mom, so I gave her a little push. It wasn't my fault she knocked over that stuff."

That was Katie. Straightforward and stubbornly honest, even in the face of certain punishment. From the corner of her eye, Leah noticed the man from the produce aisle helping the other little girl to her feet. With a muffled cry, the child buried herself in his arms. *His daughter.* Leah knew it had to be. Not only was he holding the girl, but he was soothing away her tears, murmuring to her as only a parent can murmur to a child. Tender affection was in his voice, and his concern was evident on his face.

Leah turned the same attention to her child, but Katie wasn't big on sympathy. After one hug, she was ready to see what was going on, who would clean up the aisle and whether or not she would have to help. Her wide eyes moved from store clerk, to cereal boxes, to curious bystanders. Leah straightened, wondering if Katie would every outgrow her need to be center stage. Leah looked over at the man, hoping he wasn't going to make a fuss, knowing she would have been furious if it had been his little girl sitting on top of Katie instead of the other way around. But the man wasn't looking at Leah and she could find no anger in his expression. He was just staring at Katie in the strangest way.

Protective instincts rose like a tidal wave in Leah. Okay, so Katie had too much energy and a little too much mischief in her nature. She wasn't malicious and, as far as Leah knew, she'd never physically fought anyone before. Maybe the other little girl had provoked her into pushing. Or maybe…

"This is your daughter?" the man asked, his voice hoarse and so quiet it made Leah nervous.

She pulled Katie protectively to her side as she nodded. "I don't believe she meant to hurt your child. She's never acted like this before and I can't help but think…"

He continued to stare at Katie and a deep discomfort churned in Leah's stomach. Katie was just a baby, really. Six was hardly the age of accountability. Why did he keep staring? Why did she, Leah, have this sudden, dreadful feeling of calamity?

The man lifted his dark blue eyes to meet Leah's brown ones and she saw disbelief and a myriad of questions in their depths. "I'm Riker Westfall," he said as he grasped the child's shoulders and slowly turned her around. "And this is my daughter, Marta."

The child blinked teary lashes over eyes as blue as…Leah swallowed. Those were Katie's eyes. From thick, sooty lashes to dark, feathery brows. Leah searched the wide forehead, the short, slender nose, round cheeks and gamin mouth that wore an exact duplicate of Katie's pout. She didn't know what she was looking for. A difference, maybe. Something, anything to quell her rising sense of panic. But, whatever it was, Leah didn't find it. Marta Westfall didn't just look like Katie Taylor, she was a carbon copy. And Leah was suddenly, unaccountably frightened.

"But…?" was all she could say. She glanced back to the man, Riker Westfall. As they exchanged a long look, she knew it was all she needed to say. Whatever she was feeling at this moment, she knew he had experienced the same blend of impossible emotions. It was a mistake. It had to be. No two children could look so much alike.

And then someone, a clerk maybe, or a nearby shopper, voiced the impossible. "Oh, look, they're twins."

Twins. The words ricocheted in Leah's brain like a deflected bullet. Her heart began to pound like a handball off the wall of the court. *Thud. Thud. Thud.* This wasn't possible. Katie didn't have a twin. It was a trick of the light. Grocery stores were notorious for having poor lighting. And besides, Marta's hair was a little longer than Katie's. And she wasn't as tall as Katie, either. And there were other differences. There had to be.

"Mom?" Katie slipped her small hand into Leah's. "Let's go. Everyone's looking at us."

Leah glanced down at her daughter and, as she grasped the seeking fingers, she grounded her erratic thoughts. "I think you owe someone an apology, Katie."

Katie frowned, tapping her foot, then turned to the store clerk who was picking up cereal boxes. "I'm sorry," she said.

"Apologize to the little girl," Leah said, giving Katie's fingers a meaningful squeeze, but avoiding letting her gaze return to Riker Westfall. She didn't want to see her confusion mirrored in his expression. She didn't want him to see how vulnerable she felt. In fact, all she wanted was to get herself and her daughter out of this place as fast as possible.

"I'm sorry." There was a touch of sincerity in Katie's voice and Leah let it go at that. With a helpless, fleeting glance into Riker Westfall's indigo eyes, she tugged on Katie's hand, turned and walked quickly down the aisle. Her grocery cart was still sitting by the vegetable bin where she'd left it. Leah abandoned the banana pepper in the wire basket without hesitation. She didn't have time now to think about recipes, or tonight's dinner, or anything else. She only knew she had to get Katie home.

Halfway out the door, she heard someone call to her. Her first impulse was to break into a run but she hesitated a second too long and Riker Westfall caught her just outside the doors.

"Wait, I—" In two strides, he stepped around her and stopped, effectively blocking her way. Quickly, as if he knew she was bent on escape, he pulled a business card from his bill-fold and scribbled something on the back before offering it to Leah. "I don't know your name," he said. "But you can phone me. I think, perhaps, we should talk."

Leah almost didn't take the card, but she had the feeling that if she didn't, he would find some other way to contact her. And she didn't want that. The whole thing was crazy anyway. A mistake. She grabbed the card and stuffed it deep into her skirt pocket as she walked away. It would stay there, too. She had no intention of phoning him. There was nothing to talk about. Yet, even as the reassurances marched through her brain, Leah knew Riker Westfall was a threat to her. And she knew it wasn't only because his daughter bore an uncanny resemblance to her daughter.

Leah kept walking, grateful for Katie's unusual quiet, glad the uncomfortable moments in the store were over. It must have been her imagination. Marta didn't look all that much like Katie. Maybe she was the same age and their coloring was similar. That was it. The resemblance wasn't that great, Leah thought. Not really.

"I'm sorry I pushed her, Mom," Katie said, skipping once and swinging Leah's hand. "I just didn't like her looks."

"Katie, that's not a reason. That's not even a good excuse."

Dark hair fell forward as Katie dropped her chin to her chest in a moment of repentance...a very brief moment. "Did you see her, though, Mom? She was ugly. And she kept staring at me."

Leah didn't know what to say and began scanning the parking area for her car. "Let's go, Katie. Grandma and Grandpa will be upset if we're not home when they arrive."

"Why don't they visit us some other time? Why is it always now? They're retired. They could visit at Christmas or during the summer. Why do they come when I have to go to school?"

Leah wished she had some answers. She couldn't explain to Katie why her daddy had left when she was eighteen months old. She couldn't explain why he hadn't contacted them in five years. She couldn't explain why his parents continued to act as if she, Leah, had been the motivating force behind their son's irresponsibility. And now she couldn't explain why that other little girl had looked so much like Katie.

"In you go," Leah said as she opened the car door and held it while Katie scrambled onto the front seat. "Buckle up."

"Mom?"

Leah waited for the next inevitable and unanswerable question.

"What did that man give you?"

It wasn't what she'd expected Katie to ask and Leah fumbled for an answer. "Nothing, sweetheart."

"He did, too. I saw him. It was a card. He wrote on it. Are you going to call him?"

"No." Leah shut the door. "No, I'm not going to call him." And she wouldn't. But what should she say to Katie in the meantime? Should she let her see the card, then tear it up to show it meant nothing? Her hand crept into her pocket and found the stiff business card. She traced the embossed print with a fingertip. Riker Westfall. She'd liked him when they were only talking about banana peppers, but now…

Leah walked around the back of the station wagon and, concealing her actions from Katie's ever-watchful eyes, she took the card from her pocket.

WESTFALL'S, the printing read in bold, block letters. In the lower left-hand corner was a name, Riker Westfall, and in the lower right-hand corner there was a phone number.

Leah scraped the pad of her fingertip along the edge of the card. Everyone in Bartlesville knew what Westfall's was. A department store of high quality and personal service. Leah had shopped there as a matter of course before Jonathan had left her. But, if Riker Westfall was the man behind Westfall's Department Store, what had he been doing on this side of town? And in a grocery store to boot?

Katie tooted the car horn in an impatient summons and Leah started at the harsh sound. She started to take a step toward the driver's side of the car and stopped. Then, despite her better judgment, she turned the card over. Her breath froze in her lungs.

The message was brief, but went straight for Leah's heart and squeezed tight. He'd written a date on the back. Nothing more. A sequence of numbers that would have meant nothing…if it hadn't been the date of Katie's birth.

Chapter Two

"Well, I survived the weekend." Susannah Davis reached across the drawing table and picked up the box of pastels. "In spite of a perfectly disastrous blind date, a hangover, and a Sunday morning phone call from my mother. Top that, if you can."

Leah arched her eyebrows at her friend and co-worker. "Mildred complained Friday evening until this morning, when she and Bill finally left. She dusted everything from the baseboards to the top of the refrigerator. She swept cobwebs from the corners and threw out a bunch of canned food. It's contaminated with aluminum, you know. She criticized my cooking, defended Jonathan at every opportunity, placed the blame for his disappearance solidly on my doorstep, and used all my aspirin tablets." Leah sketched in a rough outline of the ad on which she was working. "Katie was wound as tight as a corkscrew and, needless to add, Mildred had plenty to say about my parenting ability."

"I think my blind date beats your ex-mother-in-law, but I'm willing to call it a draw." Susannah puffed at a few particles of pastel chalk. "We each had a washout weekend, so let's go out for lunch."

"No lunch for you two. Not today." Tom Milbanks entered the drafting room, cast an assessing eye over the back-to-back art tables and his two artists. "Susannah, if that ad doesn't go out before three this afternoon, I'm in trouble with a major client and you're in line for unemployment. Now, quit distracting Leah from her work and let's put this shop in the black." He walked to the opposite door. "I'll bring sandwiches and coffee in at twelve. BJ's okay?"

"Are you sure you can afford to feed us?" Susannah offered with a sugary smile.

"BJ's is fine," Leah said. "Make mine a turkey on wheat."

Susannah sniffed. "You're too easy, Leah. Why sell your lunch hour for a scrawny turkey sandwich?" She leveled a glare at Tom. "Make mine a BJ's super deluxe with fries and a large lemonade. Extra ice."

"You finish that ad, sweetheart, and I'll buy your dinner, too," Tom said as he left the room.

"Buy my dinner, ha! I'd rather take my chances with a nine-teenth-century dentist."

"Tom's a nice guy, Susannah. He has a lot of good qualities."

"I'm sure he does, *Mildred*."

Leah rubbed out a line of ad copy with her finger and wondered if she should just start all over. "All right, all right. I'm sorry for the unsolicited opinion. Mildred's voice is still ringing in my head, I suppose. If she mentioned Jonathan's good points once, she mentioned them a hundred times."

"How can she defend that worthless son-of-a-buffalo? After he left you and Katie high and dry without a word? When he just drove out of your life on his way to the supermarket and hasn't bothered to send so much as a postcard in the past five years?" Susannah erased lines fiercely. "Jonathan's the kind of man only a mother could love. Do you think Mildred and Bill know where he is?"

"Of course. I'm sure he's in touch with them regularly. I'm even more sure that their yearly visits to my house are for the sole purpose of finding out whether or not I've hired a detective to look for him. But I don't care where he is and I certainly don't want him to ever come back. At least he waited to leave until after Katie's adoption was final." Leah had a memory flash of Riker Westfall and his daughter standing in the grocery store aisle staring at her and her daughter. She shoved the recurring flashback aside. "I'm divorced from Jonathan, I have Katie, and he has no claim on her. I couldn't ask for more than that."

"As I said, Leah, you're too easy. Jonathan left you with a

bunch of bills and a ton of responsibility. Even if you don't want him back, you should get even."

"He's not worth the fuss, Susannah. No man is."

Susannah laid down her pencil and rolled her eyes. "Oh, please. Spare me the platitudes. Regardless of what you think, you need a man in your life worse than I do...and I need one pretty darn bad." Susannah sighed at her own weakness. "Besides, Katie needs a father figure. You've read the studies about children who grow up without a male influence and Katie's already a handful. What are you going to do when she gets older?"

Leah would have liked to protest and defend Katie's often rambunctious, always imaginative behavior, but she knew Susannah was right. Katie *was* a handful and Leah didn't know what to do about it. On the other side of the coin, though, there was no reason to believe a man would know any better.

"You know what she did this weekend?" Leah smiled as she remembered the incident. "She got into Mildred's luggage and put on one of her grandma's brassieres, which she modeled for us. Along with her grandpa's jockstrap. Mildred and Bill were not amused."

"I wish I'd been there to see that. Katie took their disapproval in stride, I suppose?"

"She didn't blink, not even when she explained how she'd learned the proper way to wear a jockstrap." Leah shaded-in the shoes she'd drawn. "She spent the evening in her room, which was no great punishment for her. I only wish *I'd* thought of modeling their underwear. I would have loved to spend an evening in my room rather than with Jonathan's parents."

"Tell them to cancel the yearly visit," Susannah suggested. "You don't enjoy it. Katie doesn't. You could find a better way to spend Easter weekend."

"I wish it were that easy."

"It is. All you have to do is put up some resistance. Fight for your rights."

Leah nodded, but the truth was she was tired of fighting. Since Jonathan had left, she felt as if she'd crawled hand over hand up the side of a mountain. She'd been totally unprepared. Suddenly, overnight, her secure, stable life-style had turned into a rollercoaster ride of uncertainty. One minute she'd been enjoying the daughter for whom she and Jon had waited so long. The next minute, Jon went to the store and never came back. At the time she'd been incredulous, hurt, humiliated, and angry. She'd gone from blaming Jonathan, to blaming herself, to blaming him again. She'd put up a brave front, told people she was doing great even when she'd felt like giving up. But in the end, she'd done what had to be done. For herself. For Katie.

And now she didn't want anyone or anything to rock her boat. She wouldn't allow it. She couldn't afford to.

"You want me to fix you up with my cousin?" Susannah asked as she stepped back from the table to get a different angle on the magazine ad. "He's not bad looking and he does drive a Porsche, even if it isn't in the best shape. And it really wasn't his fault he got fired. You could do worse, Leah."

"Without any help from my friends. Thanks, Susannah. I appreciate the offer, but I'm not interested in dating."

"Okay. Just thought I'd ask. You seem pretty down in the dumps today. More so than usual, after a visit from the *out*-laws."

Again, the image of Riker Westfall came clearly to mind... smiling, as he asked her about the banana pepper...frowning, as he introduced his daughter. She could still see the questions in his eyes and his voice when he'd handed her his card. She thought of him all too often. He had looked so nice, so sincere...as if that had anything to do with anything.

During the weekend, she'd gone over and over the encounter, tearing her thoughts from the warmth of his smile and forcing herself to consider the incredible possibility that Katie and Marta were twins. But where did that put Riker Westfall? Was he Marta's biological father, and by some inexplicable twist of fate, Katie's father, too? Or was Marta also adopted? And where was Marta's mother? And how could any of this be happening? Her hand shook and the shading pencil streaked across the layout.

Should she tell Susannah? Ask her advice? No. Susannah was wonderful. A dear friend. But she didn't have children and she'd never understand Leah's fear. Leah wasn't sure she understood it herself. If Katie was one of a set of twins... Well, why was that frightening? And what was it about Riker Westfall that scared her? Leah had no answer, but her heart beat faster at the mere thought of him.

So, okay. She wouldn't discuss it with Susannah. Or anyone else. Who could possibly understand? Except perhaps, Riker himself.

No. She would not call him. Even if there was nothing to be afraid of. Even if there was no chance that... No. Riker Westfall might be the most attractive man she'd met in the grocery store, but she wasn't going to call. That would be asking for trouble.

And if there was one thing she didn't need more of in her life, it was trouble.

"HOLD STEADY THERE, Marta Grace," Riker said as he stepped into the studio. Marta was positioned for her portrait while Augusta Westfall fussed with a splotch of Christmas Red on the canvas. "How are my favorite artist and my favorite model this afternoon? Looks like we're making progress."

Marta crinkled her nose. "She's never going to be through."

"No criticism from the mannequin, please." Augusta, Riker's mother, said, frowning furiously at the bright streak of unerasable red. "Oh, dear. I think I may have made a fatal mistake here. These acrylics dry faster than I can make up my mind, but oils take forever." Augusta stepped back to observe first the canvas and then an impatient Marta. "No, never mind. I believe I know just how to fix it."

"Gussie!" Marta pushed her cupid's bow mouth into a solid pout. "I don't want to sit anymore. Please?"

Riker couldn't resist the plea and walked over to scoop his daughter up and into his arms. He gave her a kiss on each cheek and hugged her tightly. "How's Daddy's girl?"

"Fine." Marta hugged him back, then squirmed to be free. "I don't want my picture painted anymore. It's not even pretty."

"Marta, your grandmother is working hard to—"

"She's right," Gussie said, shaking her crop of short, flyaway carrot-colored curls. "It isn't pretty and it doesn't look much like Moppet here, either. Maybe I should go back to painting fruit bowls."

"They didn't look like fruit," Marta pointed out candidly.

Gussie turned her vivid, green eyes to the child. "I was experimenting. Not all apples have to be red, you know. Or round."

"They shouldn't be purple." Marta slipped from Riker's embrace and latched on to his hand. "Can I skip dance class today, Daddy? I don't feel like going."

"*May* I skip dance class," Riker corrected. "And, no, you may not. Run on upstairs and get ready to go."

Marta pushed out her lower lip, dropped Riker's hand like a hot potato and, with nose in the air, stalked out of the room. Riker watched her go, feeling torn between what he thought was the right thing to do and what his daughter wanted. The feeling was as familiar as it was frustrating. "Do you think she's ever going to *like* dance class?" he asked his mother.

"No. Do you?" Gussie mixed colors on a palette and stepped back for a new perspective on her art. "I could make this an abstract painting. What do you think?"

Riker stepped behind her to look at the picture. It was awful. Great blotches of color that more closely resembled the Rorschach inkblots than a portrait of his daughter. He placed his hand on Gussie's shoulder. "You've always liked abstract art," he said.

She nodded. "I'll go back to the bowl of fruit. Or maybe I'll try sewing. I don't believe I've ever done that. Would you like for me to make you a suit, Riker?"

"Isn't that a little ambitious for a first project, even for you, Gus? Maybe you shouldn't give up on the portrait so soon."

Gussie reached up to pat his hand. "There's no need to be diplomatic, Riker. I tried painting. I'm not good at it. I'll go on to something else."

His mother had been "going on to something else" as long as he could remember. She was a square peg in a round hole, a nonconformist, and a truly free spirit. While other children played in the park, he'd accompanied his mother to protest marches and peace rallies. When he'd been ten years old, she'd joined the Peace Corps, leaving him to the care of his father. A year later, she was home, filling his life with stories of faraway places. When he turned twelve, she took him out of school and they traveled around the world. He'd had to repeat the sixth grade, but she had deemed that a small price to pay for the adventures they'd shared. He supposed she'd been right. With Gus, it was sometimes hard to be sure. She was always so confident of her decisions...at the moment she made them.

The truth was, she *wasn't* good at painting...or at many other things. But no one was better than Augusta Westfall at living.

"I appreciate all your help with Marta," he said. "I couldn't have made it without you."

"Nonsense, Riker. You're a strong person like your father was. You thrive on trouble and challenge. For some reason, it makes you feel better for me to be here, so I'm staying. But the minute you want some space, I'll be happy to give it to you."

An understatement if he'd ever heard one, Riker thought. Gussie was chafing at the bit to go back to her gypsy life-style, to get on to that elusive "something else." "I know you're not comfortable in the role of live-in grandmother, but Marta needs a female influence. She doesn't have many friends. She hates dance class and riding lessons and school. I'm worried about her."

Gussie began cleaning her brushes. "You worry too much, Riker. Just like your father did. Marta's going to be fine."

Riker wished he were as confident as that. Since her mother's death two years before, Marta has become increasingly self-contained. Not to the point that anyone else seemed to be concerned, but Riker noticed the change. And he worried.

"Something odd happened the other day," he began and then stopped. He hadn't meant to tell Gussie about the woman with the little girl who looked like Marta. He'd gone over those moments in the store again and again, until he was worn-out from unanswered questions. He could remember the woman vividly. Her dark brown hair waving around a face that he could have described as interesting or simply pretty, the sparkle of mischief in her brown eyes, the hint of mystery at the edges of her smile. She came clearly and often to mind, along with her daughter, Katie, who looked too much like his daughter to be a coincidence.

"Is that when Marta saw her twin sister?" Gussie draped a

cloth over the canvas and matter-of-factly put away her paints. "Marta told me all about it."

"She did? What did she say?"

"Oh, something about being pushed and how funny you acted and how she didn't know why. Did any of it really happen the way she told it?"

Riker drew a deep breath and ran a hand through his hair. Maybe he did need to talk to Augusta about this. Who else would understand? "Unless I'm greatly mistaken, Gus, that child is Marta's twin."

Gussie stopped what she was doing and turned around. "What? But that's impossible. Marta made it up. It's like her imaginary friend, Becky B. She was just pretending."

With a heavy sigh, Riker sat on the high stool his mother sometimes used when she painted. "The child is real. Whether or not she pushed Marta, I don't know, but there's no doubt in my mind that the resemblance is more than coincidence. The mother of the other child saw it, too. She was as astonished as I was."

Gussie sank to the floor, her lips pulled tight with a frown. "What did she say? The mother."

"Nothing. Not to me, anyway. I gave her my business card and asked her to call so we could talk. I don't think she will."

"I can't think of any reason she would. My God, Riker. That couldn't happen. Twins aren't separated in adoptions. Are they?"

"No. At least, I don't think so." Riker stared at his clasped hands. "I don't even know where to begin asking questions and it seems sort of pointless if the mother of the other child won't even talk to me."

"It has to be a mistake. You just thought the girl looked like Marta."

"It wasn't a mistake. Even a stranger standing nearby commented that the two girls were twins." He tapped his index fingers together and decided to make a clean breast of it. "Do you remember about a year ago when the three of us went to the movie and another child came up to Marta and called her Katie? I didn't think much about it then. But one day I went into the drugstore by Marta's dance studio and the pharmacist said hello to Marta. Only he called her Katie. He looked very surprised when we didn't respond. Then this happened. I don't know how or why, Gussie, but it does seem to add up to the possibility that Katie and Marta are twins. Identical twins."

"Maybe you should contact the lawyer who handled Marta's adoption."

"I've already tried. He's no longer practicing law in Oklahoma."

"I guess you'll just have to try to find that woman, then. Does she live in Bartlesville?"

Riker shrugged as he slid from the stool to his feet. "She shops here. But I'm not sure she wants to be found. I'm not sure it's the right thing to do, in any case."

"Right or not, you won't let this rest, Riker. You know it as well as I do. You've never been able to tolerate riddles. If you have to stake out that grocery store to find that woman and ask your questions, that's what you'll do."

Gussie's observation was blunt, but accurate. He'd already been thinking about going back to the store to look for the woman with the pretty brown eyes. She'd had a pretty voice, too. Soft and confident and warm. And she made a casserole from banana peppers.

"What are you smiling about?" his mother asked. "You know I'm right."

He tucked away the smile. He had no business thinking about Katie's mother that way. He needed to consider Marta and the ramifications to her if he pursued his questions to their conclusion.

"Daddy? I'm ready to go." Marta stood in the doorway, all dressed in a pink leotard and tights.

His heart swelled with love for this tiny elfin child. "Have you got everything?" he asked with a smile. "Tap shoes, ballet slippers? Becky B. didn't forget anything this time, did she?" Becky B. had been Marta's imaginary friend for years.

"There isn't any Becky," Marta said, twisting the strap of her ballet bag as she turned away. "Her name is Katie."

Riker looked at Gussie, then back to his daughter. If he hadn't been positive before, he was now. He had to find some answers, for Marta's sake as well as his own.

No matter what Katie's mother might think about his tactics.

"'AFTERNOON, Mrs. Taylor."

Leah adjusted her sunglasses and nodded guiltily at the stockboy. "Hi, Roger," she said as she hurried toward the back of the store and the bread display.

It was ridiculous to feel like a criminal in the neighborhood supermarket where she'd shopped for years, but that didn't stop her from slinking from aisle to aisle. She'd avoided the store all week, going out of her way to conserve the staples and buying necessities at the Quik-Stop store on her way home from work. But today she'd forgotten and there was no bread for Katie's lunch tomorrow.

Riker Westfall wasn't going to be in the store, anyway. He'd undoubtedly come to the same conclusion she had. They'd made a mistake. She would never see him again. Which was exactly what she was trying to do.

"Isn't it hard to see with those dark glasses on?"

Her hand closed too tightly on the loaf of bread, but her tension had nowhere else to go. "Not at all." Immediately she wished she'd ignored him, pretended she didn't recognize him, walked away without a response. Clutching the bread, she turned on her heel and proceeded belatedly with that plan.

"Wait...please," Riker said as he came after her, determination in every syllable, every step. "I must talk to you."

"We've talked about banana peppers. That's the only conversation I intend to have with you."

"You can't tell me you haven't been asking yourself the same endless string of questions I've been asking."

Leah kept walking, fighting her compelling urge to stop and hear what he had to say.

"Look, tell me your daughter isn't adopted. Tell me Jerry Hillman didn't handle the adoption. Tell me Katie doesn't have a star-shaped birthmark on her right thigh. Tell me she wasn't born in Tulsa at Mercy Hospital at nine forty-one in the evening of June eighteenth." His voice pushed ahead of Leah and overcame her need to escape. "Tell me I'm wrong about any one of those statements and I won't bother you again."

He was right on every count but one and Leah turned to confront him with it. "Nine twenty-nine," she said. "Katie was born at nine twenty-nine."

Over the intercom, someone paged a sacker. A woman in a red sweatsuit pushed her cart past shelves of pasta, rice and beans. Leah stepped out of the way, but kept her attention on Riker. His blue eyes locked with her sunglass-shaded gaze in a moment out of time. She was aware—acutely aware—of his height and imposing physical presence. Riker Westfall was not a man who would go unnoticed anywhere. And he was staring at her, sharing with her, in those few, long seconds, a bond she did not want to share. There was power in him, strength and determination and Leah felt a stirring attraction. A stirring she quickly stifled because there was no room in her life or in this moment for such feelings.

"I don't know what to say." She cradled the mangled loaf of bread in her hands and tried to plump the compressed slices.

"I don't know, either, but I think we should make an attempt."

An attempt at what? Leah couldn't imagine where this was leading, or where it might end, or what she ought to do. She looked away from his intense blue eyes, then brought her gaze back, maintaining a steady, serious regard. "I'm divorced, Mr. Westfall. Katie is all I have and I'm not letting you or anyone else disrupt her life."

"I only want to talk to you." His hands swept wide in a pleading gesture. "We have to try to piece together what has happened. For Marta and Katie."

For Marta and Katie. The words seemed somehow inseparably linked and Leah felt a new wave of uneasiness. "I'm late," she said. "I'm supposed to pick up Katie."

"Have dinner with me. Tomorrow. I'll meet you at Benito's. Is that all right?"

Leah didn't want to say yes. But she couldn't quite bring

herself to say no. "Tomorrow," she said. And with that ambiguity, she turned to go.

"Seven," he called after her.

"Seven," she repeated dutifully and hurried to the checkout with her loaf of mangled bread.

Chapter Three

Leah toyed with the silver salt and pepper shakers because there were few other distractions on the tables at *Benito's*. She hadn't meant to arrive early at the restaurant. She hadn't *meant* to be there at all. Since last night, she'd thought almost nonstop about Riker's invitation to dinner. She'd gone over all the questions she had and decided she could live without knowing the answers.

And then Katie—precious, unpredictable Katie—had forced her to reconsider.

Riker entered the restaurant and, after a brief exchange with the hostess, started toward the table where Leah sat. His expression was serious, yet she had the distinct impression that he was happy, eager to reach her. She looked away, focusing on the salt shaker in her hand, refusing to watch his approach. One glance had told her more than she wanted to know. There was something so relaxed about his movements, so self-possessed, so commanding that it made Leah uncomfortable. For her, the situation was unnerving at best. The fact that he approached it with such aplomb bothered her.

And the way he looked at her bothered her even more. Why did seeing him create this unsettling tingle at the back of her neck? And what caused the swirl of anxiety in her stomach? She did not like the smooth way he maneuvered across the dining room, looking only at her, yet never missing a step or bumping into a chair.

He was alone. Leah had spent several of the past fifteen minutes wondering if perhaps Marta's mother would be present at this meeting. A feeling of relief filtered through her nervousness and Leah pushed it away. She had no room for relief. And no reason. No reason at all.

"I hope you haven't been waiting long," Riker said as he pulled out the chair opposite Leah and seated himself. "I'd planned to be here before you arrived." He paused and a slow, careful smile tipped the edges of his mouth. "Actually I wasn't sure you'd come at all."

Leah placed the salt shaker beside the pepper shaker in the center of the table and clasped her hands together. Her heart beat like a trip-hammer now that he was here. She was half afraid to meet his gaze for fear he'd see her distress she was desperate to hide. "I—uh—I thought I should hear what you have to say."

There, she'd formed a complete sentence, a coherent sentence. Bolstered by that thought, she raised her gaze to meet his. A mistake, she realized as his smile filled its promise in his eyes. Riker possessed a calm self-assurance that was both soothing and unsettling. Leah knew that while she might admire his confidence, she also needed to guard herself against it.

"Have you ordered?" He picked up the menu and glanced over his shoulder for the waiter. "Would you care for a drink first?"

"No." She wondered why she felt as if he'd asked if she wanted one last cigarette before being blindfolded and shot. After all, she was only going to talk with the man. That hardly constituted facing a firing squad. "On second thought, I would like a glass of wine. Something white and dry."

"Certainly." Riker turned to the waiter and ordered not only the wine but dinner as well. He glanced at her for approval of his selections, and she felt that with him it was more than a mere courtesy.

As the waiter walked away from the table, Riker smiled at her again...as if they weren't there to discuss a matter of deep importance...as if they'd simply met to enjoy each other's company.

A shiver of awareness ran through her. He was an attractive man. She couldn't deny that...or her reaction to him. But she couldn't afford to notice the masculine appeal of his impressive physique and well-defined jawline. She couldn't let his charm or his ease of manner impress her. She was here for one reason: to protect Katie.

"I hadn't planned to meet you tonight," she said, trying to keep a defensive tone out of the words. "I'm not convinced I should be here even now."

"I understand." His voice softened, his expression conveyed empathy, his blue eyes encouraged trust. "What did Katie do to change your mind?"

"Katie?" Leah tried not to look surprised at his perception. "Why would you think Katie had anything to do with my decision?"

"Simple deduction, I suppose, and the fact that Marta's behavior during the past few days greatly influenced my decision to find you again."

Leah sighed. "Why couldn't you have left well enough alone?"

The remainder of his smile faded. "I can't pretend that your daughter doesn't exist because I'd prefer not to deal with this situation. Ignorance is one thing. Deliberately ignoring known facts is another. Marta and Katie have met now. There's nothing I can do to change that. Nothing you can do about it, either. But the way we handle this from now on will affect both of them for the rest of their lives." He paused to draw a deep breath. "By some strange twist of fate, you and I are the parents of twin daughters and—" the corners of his mouth lifted in a wry smile "—and I don't even know your name."

"Leah," she said softly. "Leah Taylor."

"Leah." The sound rolled off his tongue with an inflection of warmth and liking. "I've never known anyone named Leah…but if I'd imagined someone by that name, she would have looked like you."

The atmosphere seemed suddenly very close and personal and Leah sought a way to gain equal ground. "I've never known anyone named Riker," she said and then purposefully added, "or Marta."

"Jean chose the name. She had it picked out months before we knew whether or not we were going to get a baby." Riker paused as the waiter placed the glasses of wine on the table. He nodded his thanks and lifted the goblet to his lips before he continued speaking. "Jean was my wife and Marta's mother. She died two years ago."

"I'm sorry." Leah tapped a restless fingertip on the tabletop. There was a question she had to ask, had to get out in the open. "You and your wife *adopted* Marta. She isn't your...or your wife's...biological child."

Riker looked puzzled. "No. Why would you think...?"

"It's just something that worried me. I didn't think of it at first, but later I had this horrible idea that you might be—that maybe, for some reason, you and your wife didn't want two children and so...Katie was placed for adoption." Leah licked dry lips. "It sounds dumb, I know, but I couldn't help wondering, worrying, about it. If you were the *biological* father..." She let the sentence drop, feeling the implications wound her all over again.

"Jean's health was never good and we knew when we married that she could not bear children. Adoption was our only bet for the family we wanted and when Jean heard about Jerry Hillman, we didn't waste any time getting in touch with him. It was less than six months later that he brought Marta to us."

"He *brought* her to you?"

"We drove up to Tulsa. The mother had relinquished her parental rights beforehand and so Jerry brought her from the hospital to his office where we picked her up. She was five days old and so tiny I was almost afraid to hold her."

Leah took a drink of her wine, hoping it would fortify her, wishing it could make this complicated situation simple. "Katie was only four days old when Jerry called to say we could pick her up. We lived in Tulsa at the time and I was so thrilled I could hardly remember how to get to his office." She set down the glass and raised a troubled gaze to Riker. "Why wouldn't he have told me Katie had a twin? I would have taken them both. Why did he separate them?"

"I don't know, but I'm going to find out."

Those words scared Leah more than anything else that had

happened or been said during the past week. "You don't think the adoptions were...illegal, do you?"

"I don't see how they could be. Unless Jerry stole the babies and I can't believe he did that."

"He didn't. He couldn't have."

"It's possible that the birth mother wanted the girls placed separately."

Leah couldn't imagine why, but stranger things had happened. Her own presence in this restaurant with this man was living proof of that. "So you don't believe Jerry did anything illegal? I've always worried that Katie's adoption would be challenged."

Riker nodded his understanding. "That's every adoptive parent's nightmare, I suppose. I've spent my share of the past six years worrying about that, too. Especially after Jean died."

"Adoption brings its own set of problems, doesn't it?"

"And its own set of joys. I can't imagine my life without Marta."

Leah pushed away a stray lock of silky brown hair. "My days would be dull without Katie, that's for sure. Some days would be less dull than others, you understand, but I do enjoy her. High energy and all."

Riker leaned forward. "Tell me about Katie. What was she like as an infant? Marta was restless and didn't sleep very well for the first six months. Then she did a complete turnaround."

"Katie too," Leah said before she thought. "I walked the floor more nights than I like to recall."

"Marta was only content when there was someone else nearby. I guess she was lonely."

Leah remembered thinking much the same thing about her own infant daughter. *Lonely.* Suddenly the word had a new meaning. "You don't think they...missed each other, do you? I mean they were so young."

"Now that I know about Katie, it seems logical to believe Marta knew something...someone...was missing. Someone who was supposed to be with her and wasn't." Riker picked up his glass and turned the stem with his fingers. "We'll never know what they were feeling then. Our problem is figuring out what they're feeling now."

The waiter arrived with dinner and, despite the aromatic smell and the aesthetic arrangement of the food on the plates, Leah knew she couldn't eat.

Riker watched her contemplate the food in silence. A lock of hair fell forward against her cheek and she brushed it back absently. Her expression was a blend of indecision and discomfort, making him wish there was some way to reassure her. But how could he make her understand that he was no threat to her or her daughter? Especially when he had every intention of becoming a part of their lives?

Marta needed Katie. He'd seen that within hours of accepting as fact that the two were indeed, identical twins. Riker had never been one to waste time on denial. When presented with a problem, he moved as quickly as possible into the decision-making process. He saw no reason to sit around wishing problems didn't exist. This situation, though hard on the emotions, had to be dealt with.

"I expected Marta to ask questions after that day in the grocery store," Riker said conversationally. "But instead of displaying curiosity, she'd become quieter, more introspective, and…she changed the name of her imaginary friend to Katie." Riker watched to see how that bit of information affected Leah. For a moment, he thought she was going to ignore it.

She toyed with the food on her plate and then set the fork along the china's edge. Her lips pursed, relaxed, then pulled tight again. "Katie's asked a lot of questions. Not all of them having to do with Marta. I've ignored some of them, tried to answer others, but today she—" Leah looked up and he saw a spark of humor amidst the concern in her soft brown eyes. "According to the principal, Katie instigated a protest of the cafeteria food. In layman's and parent's terms that means she started a food fight."

"A food fight? Isn't first grade a little young for that?"

"Katie's always been on the cutting edge of precocious," Leah said with a sigh. "Last year, in kindergarten, she spent almost as much time in the principal's office as she did in the classroom. My phone number was on automatic dial on the office phone, right after police, fire and ambulance."

"You're exaggerating. She couldn't have been in that much trouble."

Leah's mouth curved in a rueful smile. "Katie loves to be the center of attention and she isn't overly afraid of consequences. But from the time she was old enough to talk, she's never denied doing something that she actually did...even when she knew she'd be punished for it."

"Until today," Riker said with sudden understanding.

"Until today," Leah agreed. "She told everyone, even me, that she wasn't in the lunchroom throwing turkey nuggets. It was her twin sister, Marta."

He bit back a smile. "Turkey *nuggets?* If Marta had been there, I'm sure she would have been throwing those, too."

"But Marta wasn't there. Katie was and she insisted that the blame belonged to Marta." Leah picked up her fork and laid it down again. "That's the reason I decided to meet you tonight. I have to give Katie some answers."

"You know it isn't as simple as that, Leah."

She raised startled eyes to his and he was struck by the richness of emotion in their depths. A man could lose his reason in eyes like that, Riker thought. Reason? Hell. A man could lose his soul to a woman like Leah Taylor. This situation would have been easier for him to handle if she were a little less feminine and a whole lot less vulnerable.

"What do you mean it isn't that simple?" Leah asked. "Katie has questions and I'm going to answer them. That's the only reason I'm here."

"Katie has a sister. She doesn't belong completely to you. Marta doesn't belong completely to me. They have a relationship that goes back farther than their relationship with either of us. Now you can accept that or you can fight it, but that won't change the facts and it won't change the relationship."

"And I suppose you've simply *accepted* all of this?"

Riker reached for his wineglass. "Let's say, I've accepted that they are identical twins. That doesn't answer all of my questions, but it does give me some direction."

"Direction?" Leah repeated. "What are you planning to do, Riker?"

He liked the way she said his name. Even with an edge of defensiveness in her voice, the spark of challenge came through in her tone. "I think Marta and Katie should be allowed to be sisters," he said.

Leah almost got up from the table at that point, but she stopped herself and Riker watched her turn her fear into anger. "No," she said. "They are not sisters. They share the same biological parents. That's all. A matching set of chromosomes does not make a relationship."

"Don't be naive. Marta has already incorporated Katie into her life through her imaginary friend. Today at school, Katie gave you an example of the way she's going to handle it. We can't make this go away, Leah. It's here now, and if we don't do something about it, these two girls will come to us one day and want to know why."

"We'll explain that they were too young. They'll understand. Katie would, I know."

Riker leaned back as he studied the flush on Leah's cheeks, the sable darkness in her eyes. "I don't think so. Not when there's no valid reason to keep them apart."

"What about simple common sense?" Leah crumpled her napkin and laid it on the table. "When I adopted Katie, her records were sealed. That reassured me that no one was going to come along and lay claim to my child. That reassured the biological mother that she could get on with her life. You're playing with fire, Riker."

"No." He leaned forward, his voice soft but intense. "Tell me, Leah. When you adopted Katie, did you find out everything about her? Did you know, for example, if there's any illness inherent in her biological family?"

Leah straightened her shoulders. "I knew everything of importance."

He nodded. "But if Katie developed an illness because of some genetic problem, would you pretend it doesn't exist and say you'll explain it later and Katie will *understand?*"

Leah's gaze held his, never wavering, although he could see her struggle for an honest answer. "That's not the same."

"Isn't it? Katie had a sister when she became your child.

Maybe she could have lived her entire life without ever knowing about Marta. Maybe they might have ended up in the same place at the same time ten years from now. The point is, they met at age six. They have to be allowed to choose what happens now.''

''Well, I'm not about to let Katie *choose* to—'' Leah's voice broke and she looked down at her plate. ''I can't do that.''

''I'm not asking you to give up your daughter, Leah. I'm not asking you to give up anything. I just want what's best for Marta. And I feel that, in this instance, Marta is the only one who can know what's best. She and Katie have to come to terms with each other and build whatever relationship they will or won't have in the future. You and I can only observe and support them in that decision.''

''What if they hate each other? Or what if one of them wants to be sisters and the other one doesn't? That's going to be pretty difficult to handle, don't you think?''

''No more difficult for them than an adult game of 'let's pretend this never happened.' Life hands out some tough lessons and you can't always protect Katie. I can't protect Marta from being hurt. What I can do, what I'm trying to do, is to ease my daughter through a sticky situation without lies and deceit. And that's where I have to ask for your help.''

''I'm not getting involved in this.'' Her words were strong, her expression definite, but Riker thought her resolve was weakening nonetheless.

''You're already involved and, if you need proof, I'm sure Katie will provide some within the coming weeks.'' He watched that sink in before he continued. ''Come to my house one evening. Just you, by yourself. Meet Marta and my mother, who lives with us…at the moment. Reassure yourself that Marta and I represent no threat to you and Katie. Then think about letting the two girls get together. Maybe they won't like each other at all. Maybe they'll hit it off immediately. But at least, they'll know about the other and they'll have had an opportunity to explore their unique relationship. That's all I'm asking, Leah.''

''That's too much.'' She stood with firm decision. ''I can't allow—I just can't.'' She planned to walk away, but something stopped her and she looked at him "Thank you for dinner. I...wasn't very hungry."

"Leah?" He knew he held her attention, so he didn't hurry his words. "Where is Katie's father?"

Distress washed her expression before she could control it. "I don't know. He left a long time ago. He never looked back, and neither have I." With that, she spun on her heel and left him alone at the table in the middle of the restaurant.

He was suddenly sorry he'd asked. He'd known about Jonathan Taylor. The produce manager at the grocery store had told him...with only a small amount of encouragement. It was quite a story. He'd simply walked out on his wife and baby daughter with no warning and no apparent regret. He'd left behind a legacy, though. Leah Taylor was cautious, protective and very guarded. Riker supposed she had every right to be. But she'd find out he didn't give up easily. Not when what he wanted was so important. Marta would have her chance to know Katie. How could Leah think for a minute she could keep the two girls apart?

Leah, he thought. Leah and Katie and Marta. The names felt comfortable and familiar in his thoughts. He had a feeling they were going to be there in his mind a great deal of the time from now on.

Leah and Katie and Marta.

Chapter Four

The cookies were gone.

Every last one. There was hardly a crumb left in the jar.

There were, however, crumbs scattered just about everywhere else. Leah set the jar on the counter and followed the crumb trail to Katie's room. When Leah tapped at the door, Katie looked up from her tea set. A stuffed bear, a frazzled doll and a matching pair of old sock monkeys sat at the table. Leah knew the routine. Katie shared tea with her toy playmates and scolded them for having such bad manners. It was one of her favorite games.

"Hi, Mommy. Do you want some tea?"

"No, thank you." Leah pushed aside the maternal impulse to smooth the willful dark hair away from her daughter's eyes. "Did you take the cookies from the cookie jar while I was doing laundry in the garage?"

"No." Katie straightened her teddy bear and pushed him to a more upright position in the child-sized chair. She paid no attention to Leah.

"What happened to the cookies, Katie?"

The child sighed sadly. "I told her not to do it, Mom, but she won't listen to me."

Leah's heartbeat quickened with annoyance. "Who are you talking about, Katie?"

"Marta. She's so naughty."

Leah sighed. "Marta isn't here, Katie."

"She is, too. She's hiding behind the mirror because she knows you don't like her."

Leah's patience snapped. "Stop it, Katie. You took those cookies, so don't try to blame someone else."

Big blue eyes widened and began to fill with shimmering tears...an effective weapon and one Katie used rarely. "It wasn't me, Mommy. It was Marta. She's a bad girl." Katie sniffed and the first teardrop trembled on her lower lashes. "It's not fair if you get mad at me."

Leah battled a desire to threaten Katie with all kinds of punishment if she didn't tell the truth. But so far, no reasonable punishment had managed to prevent Katie's attempts to shift blame. Lately, Katie could do nothing wrong. Everything was Marta's fault. And Leah had never been more frustrated and confused about how to handle her daughter.

The situation had been going on for more than a week now. At school and at home. And Leah was at her wit's end.

"I want you to tell me the truth." Leah moved into the room and knelt beside Katie's chair. She glanced at the cookie crumbs evident on the tiny china plates and then, eye to eye, she willed her daughter to honesty. "What did you do with the cookies?"

Katie dropped her chin to her chest. "I ate them," she whispered.

At last. Leah reached out and brushed aside a straggly strand of dark hair from Katie's face. "Don't you feel better when you tell the truth?"

"I feel kind of sick." Katie's voice quivered, then firmed with a new thought. "Marta's the one who should be sick. She brought them in here. I wouldn't have eaten them if she hadn't been so naughty."

It was obviously pointless to press the issue further. So now, Leah faced her parental dilemma. Did she let the crime go unpunished, rationalizing that there were mitigating circumstances? Or did she discipline Katie here and now for taking the cookies and then lying about it? And if she doled out punitive action, did she have the energy to withstand the cries of indignation Katie was certain to give?

"Brownie Bear wants to give you a kiss, Mommy."

Leah gave a wan smile as the threadbare teddy nuzzled her

cheek. Score—Katie, one…Mommy, zero. "Katie, we need to talk."

"Not again." Katie used her most adult voice as she stuffed the bear into the chair again. "You're just going to tell me that Marta's not here. But she is. She's always getting me into trouble when I'm trying to be good. And it's not my fault you don't believe me." Katie leaned across the table and swatted one of the sock monkeys. "Bad monkey. You drink your tea and leave Brownie Bear alone." She rolled her eyes at Leah. "Leonard has no manners. He's always trying to get Brownie Bear into trouble. I think he ate some of the cookies, too, Mom. Maybe you should talk to him."

Leah rubbed her forehead, where a headache throbbed. Time to drop back and punt, she decided and, drag out a time-honored line of defense. "I have to finish the laundry. We'll discuss this later, Katie."

"Okay, Mommy." Katie, with offense to spare, happily went back to her tea party.

Leah closed the bedroom door on the cozy scene of child and toys and leaned her shoulder against the wall. What was she going to do? She couldn't allow this imaginary companion to absolve Katie from punishment, but she couldn't bring herself to call her daughter an out-and-out liar, either. Especially since Marta wasn't exactly imaginary.

"Katie has an active imagination," the first-grade teacher had said just yesterday in the parent-teacher conference. *"It does complicate our learning environment, though. And she's so bright, too."*

The teacher had made it sound sad, as if Katie's imagination somehow negated her intellect. And Katie did well in school…when she felt like it. When *Marta* wasn't getting her into trouble.

Leah pushed away from the wall. The truth was Katie had been a handful before her "evil twin" entered the picture. Now she'd simply found a handy excuse, a wonderful new way to manipulate her mother. And Leah responded like any other red-blooded American parent…she felt guilty.

"Have you considered therapy for Katie?" the school prin-

cipal had asked yesterday after the teacher left the meeting. *"We do seem to be seeing an escalation of inappropriate behavior. You both might benefit from professional counseling."*

Leah had taken the name and number of the local youth counseling service graciously, but she'd wanted to stamp her foot and tell the principal that Katie was bored with the ABC curriculum and the 1-2-3 method of learning. It was the school's fault, not Katie's.

But she might as well blame Marta.

As she stepped into the musty air of the one-car garage, Leah mentally shuffled her options and hoped one would fall into her mind clearly and succinctly as "the answer." She could make an appointment with the counseling center or she could phone Riker Westfall.

Now, which of those two options would be the wisest course of action for Katie and for her own peace of mind?

Twisting the starter knob on the washing machine, Leah decided to forget her own peace of mind. God had probably never meant for single mothers to enjoy that state, anyway. Okay. So what was best for Katie? Meeting Marta again? Or one-on-one sessions with a psychologist? It was possible that the counselor might recommend allowing Katie to develop a relationship with Marta. It was possible he or she might recommend years of therapy for Katie and Katie's mother.

Leah poured in detergent and stuffed dirty clothes into the tub. She hated to consider cost, but circumstances dictated expense as a definite consideration. Her budget had to stretch too far already and even at a reduced rate, therapy would be an expensive undertaking. Of course, if she believed that Katie would really benefit...

But she didn't believe it. Katie was capable of figuring out just what a counselor would want to hear. Whether or not she'd say it was another matter. The point was, therapy would most likely just bring out Katie's confusion over Marta Westfall. Then it would have to be dealt with. Just as Riker had said.

Leah sighed as she picked up a laundry basket full to overflowing with towels warm from the dryer. All paths seemed to lead to Riker Westfall and the phone number Leah had pretended to forget.

Was life ever going to be simple?

THE VOICE on the other end of the phone sounded like Katie's.

Leah gripped the receiver tightly. "May I speak to your father, please?"

"Who's calling, please?"

What should she say? Would Marta know her name? "I'm a...friend."

The phone clunked in Leah's ear. "Daddy! Daddy! It's for you."

"Hello?"

She almost dropped the phone at the sound of his deep voice. "Riker?" She cleared her throat. "Riker Westfall? This is—"

"Leah."

"—Leah Taylor."

His voice overlapped hers, giving a nuance of pleasure to her name.

"I was afraid you weren't going to call me." He made it seem personal somehow and Leah grappled with the impulse to dump her every problem into his lap.

"I'm calling about Katie," she said determinedly. "And Marta."

"Yes, I know."

"I wondered if...if maybe I could..." This was harder than she'd expected. "Is your offer to visit still open?"

"Of course. Did you want to come now?"

"No. No. I just thought we could, maybe, set up a time that would be convenient."

"What about tonight? You could join us for dinner."

"No, not tonight." She wasn't prepared and she still wanted to talk to Katie about this afternoon's misbehavior.

"Tomorrow, then. One o'clock? Two?"

"How about three?"

"Great." Again, that personal note of pleasure. Again, that unsettled restlessness around Leah's heart.

"Okay." She made the commitment reluctantly, wondered if

something that felt so risky could possibly turn out to be right. "I'll see you, then."

"Would you like for me to pick you up?"

"I'd prefer to drive."

"Let me give you directions, then."

It was simple. He delivered instructions the way he seemed to do everything…clearly, concisely and with utter confidence. And Leah knew there was no backing out now. "Thank you," she said, anxious to conclude the disturbing call. "I'll be at your house tomorrow at three."

"I'm looking forward to it, already."

She couldn't hang up without asking one more question. "What are you going to tell Marta?"

His hesitation was brief. "I'll tell her you're a new friend…and Katie's mother."

"Oh." Leah's throat tightened. "Do you think that's wise?"

"I wouldn't do it if I didn't, Leah."

He sounded so sure, so incredibly sure. "Goodbye, Riker."

"Until tomorrow, Leah."

She put down the receiver, closed her eyes and prayed that she hadn't just ruined her daughter's life.

THE HOUSE was planted on the side of a hill, a study of angled rooflines and cedar. Decking stretched across the front, providing a ski-lodge appearance for the house and a bountiful view for the occupants. Leah almost missed the driveway and had to back up several feet before she could maneuver her car through the stone pillars and down the slope to the house. There was no gate, but she felt as if one clanged closed behind her and she'd never get out of this place.

What would a therapist make of that, she thought as she stalled to put off the moment of reckoning. She locked the doors of her car and then unlocked them because she didn't want to fumble with her keys in case she had to leave in a hurry. She wouldn't stay long. Just long enough to confirm her impressions about the Westfalls's life-style and the kind of parent Riker was.

Pulling her courage up past her knees, Leah faced the house.

It was worse than she'd imagined. Beautiful. Unpretentious. Homelike. And huge. Katie would love it on sight.

Leah felt sick. She and Katie got by, made do, sacrificed little luxuries for the sake of necessities. Obviously the Westfalls didn't have to choose between the two. Unless the interior of the house was a mess, it would reflect the same standard of living as the exterior. A high standard. One Katie would embrace enthusiastically if—and that was rapidly becoming a big if—Katie met Marta again at all.

"I've been watching for you." The door opened at her approach and Riker greeted her with a guileless smile. "I was afraid you wouldn't find us. The house isn't exactly easy to locate."

"You gave good directions," Leah said and cleared her voice of a nervous quiver. "I didn't have a bit of trouble."

He held the door wide, gestured her inside. "Where's Katie this afternoon?"

"I didn't bring her," Leah said quickly. "She's staying with a friend."

"Marta's upstairs."

Leah raised her troubled gaze to meet Riker's incredibly blue eyes. "Did you tell her?"

"That you were coming? Yes. I try not to spring surprises on her. She's not good with the unexpected."

"Katie isn't, either. She pitched a fit to know where I was going and why she had to stay with Susannah."

"Did you tell her?"

"No. Not yet."

"You could have brought her along. I wouldn't have minded."

"I didn't *not* bring her out of some meaningless courtesy, Riker. She's not…she and I aren't ready for this. I'm here, because I've got to do something and this seemed to make the most sense. At the time. Now, I'm not so sure it's—"

"Riker, are you going to keep our guest in the front hall all afternoon? Be polite. Ask her to come in and sit down. I'll bring out the hors d'oeuvres."

Riker made a face. "My mother. She's anxious to meet you."

Someone else to face. Someone else she'd have to explain to

Katie later. "Sure," Leah said, because there didn't seem to be anything else she could say.

Riker led the way up a trio of Italian-tiled steps and into a high-ceilinged room. In one assessing glance, Leah took in the plate-glass windows of one wall, the bookcases and brick fireplace on the other. Stairs on the other end of the room angled toward an open hallway on the second floor. One area flowed to another…living area to dining, dining to kitchen, upstairs to downstairs…all a blend of earthy colors and pastel tints. It was understated luxury at its best and seeing it firmed Leah's resolve to hold herself and her daughter at a distance.

"Welcome, welcome. I'm Augusta Westfall." The woman who approached Leah was dressed like a gypsy. Her caftan was colorful and unironed. Orangey-red curls escaped the bandanna tied around her head. Bangle bracelets clanged out with metallic enthusiasm and her smile…Leah had never felt so warmed, so welcomed by a smile.

"I'm Leah Taylor." She smiled in helpless response and offered a handshake. "It's nice to meet you, Mrs. Westfall."

"Gussie, please. Or Gus. Or Augusta. I don't care. If I'd been born a few years later, I'd have kept my maiden name when I married and gone by Ms. I was a feminist before the word was invented. So…won't you sit down? I'll get the food."

"Please," Leah protested as she settled on the edge of a chair, "don't go to any trouble."

"Save your breath. She's unstoppable. And cooking is her new hobby." Riker moved to the center of a large sectional sofa and sat. "You'd be more comfortable over here. That chair is a little stiff."

"It's fine, really." Leah set her purse on the floor and scooted back in the chair. It was stiff and not very comfortable, but she was not going to rearrange her position or her life at his suggestion. "You have a beautiful home."

"Thank you." He draped his arm along the wealth of couch cushions and smiled at her. His blond hair was swept back from his forehead in a neatly trimmed, casual sort of style. His moustache was equally neat and added a touch of machismo to his rugged good looks. In another place, under different circumstances—at the supermarket, for instance—Leah might have thought about him from a purely female and physical point of view. There was no way to avoid his sensuality. He wore it like some sort of expensive cologne. But forewarned was forearmed and she'd do well to remember that in another place, under different circumstances, she'd never have visited him in his home at all.

"I could hardly wait for you to arrive, Leah. We haven't had any decent conversation around here for weeks." Augusta returned with two trays of appetizers, which she placed on the coffee table. Then she sat, cross-legged, on the floor. "Riker never invites anyone to visit. He's so backward when it comes to social calls. Here, Leah, have something to eat. I made these myself. I hope they're good."

"They look…great." Leah accepted the plate Augusta offered and tried to appear hungry. She wasn't. For one thing, she was nervous. And for another, the hors d'oeuvres weren't like any she'd ever seen before. She took a small plate and helped herself to a black-edged cracker. She nibbled carefully and tasted the conflict of chocolate, cheese and poppy seeds. "How long have you lived in Bartlesville?" Leah inquired politely as she put the cracker down on her plate.

"Off and on…forever." Gussie sighed. "I was never able to persuade my late husband to move on to new horizons. Riker, unfortunately, is just as obstinate as his father."

"Someone has to run the business." Riker's lips curved affectionately as she spoke, obviously at ease with his mother's complaints. He turned his smile to Leah. "Gus likes to think the world would run perfectly if there was a lot more love and a lot less responsibility."

"I'd like to think she was right." Leah politely reached for another appetizer.

"I'm so glad I like you," Augusta said with a smile. "It would have been awful if you'd been hateful and rude and completely unlikable."

Leah sought Riker's gaze and she wondered if he were thinking the same thoughts as she. What if he had been different? What if circumstances had placed him on the other end of the financial spectrum? What if Marta's homelife left much to be desired? What then? Would Riker still want to allow the girls to establish a relationship? Would she, Leah, have fewer objections…or more?

If she accepted that Marta was Katie's sister and, therefore, a part of her life, then she supposed she had to be grateful that Marta had a family who loved and cherished her as much as Leah loved and cherished Katie.

It seemed an odd thing to be thinking about.

"Daddy?"

At the tentative question, Leah looked up and was startled to see Katie standing on the stair landing. But, of course, it wasn't Katie. It was Marta.

"Come on down, Marta Grace," Riker said, turning toward his daughter. "Join us and have some of your grandmother's snacks. Mmmmm, are they good."

Marta wrinkled her nose in answer, but her wide blue gaze fastened on Leah and stayed there. It was as if she were asking Leah's permission before joining the adult gathering. Leah didn't know what to do.

"Don't you look pretty," Gussie said. "Look, I saved the cracker with the biggest glob of cheese for you. Better hurry before I eat it myself."

Marta took her time, navigating the remaining stairs with deliberate steps. Katie would have skipped, jumped, or hopped, Leah thought. She might even have tried to slide on the banister. But she would not have walked. No matter how many strangers sat in the living room. In fact, the bigger the audience, the more she liked it. Obviously Marta was not quite so uninhibited. The child walked sedately to the sectional and sidled up close to Riker. And not once did her gaze stray from Leah's face.

Riker put an arm around Marta and pulled her close to his side. "Marta, this is Mrs. Taylor, the new friend I told you about."

"Hello, Marta." Leah's throat was cottony dry. Her palms were moist from perspiration. Her heartbeat echoed in the cavernous uncertainty of her thoughts. "It's nice to see you again."

The child's gaze swerved to her father's face for reassurance or instruction, and at his nod she turned again to Leah. "Hello, Mrs. Taylor. I'm pleased to meet you."

It was startling to hear Katie's voice utter such polite words and Leah was glad that Augusta created a diversion by calling Marta's attention to the trays of goodies. Marta looked skeptically at the cheese-covered crackers and Leah studied the child's every movement. Katie would have picked out the crackers she wanted immediately upon entering the room and then, depending on whether or not she liked the taste of each, she would either grab two or three more or put them all back on the plate...whether she'd tasted them or not. Leah had corrected her numerous times about that sort of thing, but she could always count on Katie to do something to claim everyone's attention. Even if the attention was negative.

Marta seemed shy and conscious of the possibility of making a wrong choice. Of course, she might just be overly familiar with Gussie's lack of culinary skills. Finally she selected an hors d'oeuvre and nibbled at it while her gaze sneaked back to Leah. "Are you Katie's mother?" Marta asked candidly.

"Yes."

"Where is she?"

"She's visiting one of her friends this afternoon."

"Who?"

Leah wasn't offended by the child's curiosity. Katie would have asked the same questions, only sooner. "Katie is spending the afternoon with Susannah Davis."

"Does Susannah look just like me, too?"

Riker frowned. Gussie's forehead wrinkled with concern. Leah swallowed an uncomfortable knot at the back of her throat. "No, Susannah is a grown-up friend. Katie enjoys staying with her once in a while."

"Oh." Marta took another dainty bite of cracker. "May I go swimming now, Daddy?"

"Even with the heated water, it's going to be a little cool in the pool, Marta Grace. Are you sure you want to swim?"

Marta nodded vigorously. "I'm ready. See?" She lifted the hem of her dress over her head to reveal a pint-sized bikini underneath. Leah smiled. Katie would have done exactly the same thing. And how she would love to wear that blue bikini.

"Would you like to sit by the pool and watch Esther Williams here swim?" Riker asked. "I'll see that she keeps the splashes to a minimum."

"I'm not worried about getting wet," Leah said. "I'm basically wash-and-wear, anyway."

"You might be drip-dry before the afternoon's over," Riker said, pushing himself up from the sofa and offering a hand to his mother. A hand, Leah noted, that was blithely brushed aside as Augusta rolled agilely and independently to her feet. "Get a towel from the mudroom, Pumpkin, and meet us at the pool."

Marta skipped away, a duplicate of Katie in almost every way. Her hair was curled and neat while Katie's seemed always to need a brushing, but Leah knew if the girls were standing side by side, facing away from her, she wouldn't be able to tell them apart. That was a scary thought.

With a sigh, Leah rose and followed Riker's smooth gesture and Augusta's glib chatter through the dining area, the kitchen, and the breakfast area beyond. Riker opened French doors onto a deck that nipped and tucked its way around the odd angles of the house and encircled a large, oval pool. A retaining wall marked the end of the landscaping and the beginning of the wooded area behind the house. It was all quite beautiful and yet it looked and felt lived-in...like a home, instead of just a house.

And the pool had a slide. Katie would love that.

Whoops. Katie most likely would never see the pool. Or this house. Or Augusta. Or Riker. Or Marta. Leah was becoming firm on that point.

"Look at me, Daddy!" Marta grabbed her nose and jumped, feetfirst, into the water, sending chlorinated spray all over the pebbled surface of the pool enclosure.

Riker waved and then suggested they move the deck chairs well away from the target area. Once settled, with Marta chattering and splashing, with Augusta fussing over her crackers and cheese, with Riker concentrating his attention on his daughter, Leah began to relax. She accepted a glass of minty iced tea and sipped it as she enjoyed the easygoing camaraderie of this unusual family.

"You'll have to bring your daughter over some afternoon to swim." Augusta adjusted the bandanna on her head and then, impatiently, pulled it off and finger-combed her copper-penny curls. "Marta would love the company. Right now, she plays mainly with her imaginary friend. For the longest time, all we heard was Becky B. this and Becky B. that. Then all of a sudden, Marta changed her friend's name to Katie and—" Augusta made a face. "Oh, that was tactless of me, wasn't it? But then, I guess you know about the name change already. Anyway, Marta would be thrilled to have a real live playmate."

"Marta has playmates," Riker said defensively.

Augusta sniffed. "Not many."

Riker cast a quick frown in Gussie's direction before changing the subject. "Has Katie taken swimming lessons?"

"No. I've taught her. She doesn't get the opportunity to swim very often, but she does seem to have some natural ability."

"Marta's taken lessons for the past three summers," Riker said. "But she doesn't care much for them. And, as you can see, her swimming skills consist mostly of jumping or sliding into the water, getting out and jumping or sliding again. Maybe if she and Katie took lessons together, it would help."

Leah's complacent relaxation crumbled around her. She wanted to keep Katie's life uncomplicated. But Riker was obviously going to keep pushing. And for what? He had a beautiful daughter, already. So Marta had an imaginary friend named Katie. So she needed a way to overcome an innate shyness. Was that enough reason to drag Katie into an emotional and potentially damaging situation? Leah sighed and set her glass on the table. "I don't think Katie and Marta will be taking lessons of any kind, together. I haven't even decided if I think it's all right for them to meet."

"They've already met," Augusta pointed out benignly. "Of course, I'm not big on lessons, myself. Children have a big enough job just being children without taking *lessons*."

Riker shook his head. "My mother and I have a fundamental difference of opinion on childhood. I see it as a time to widen experience and seed a wide range of interests. Gussie thinks children should just be allowed to play to their heart's content."

"Katie would love that philosophy," Leah commented dryly. "If she could play instead of going to school, she'd be one happy young lady."

"Not enough challenge in the classroom, I'll bet." Gussie said and Leah was surprised at the older woman's perception.

"That is a problem for Katie. She has too much imagination and energy to sit still for long periods of time. Consequently she gets into trouble more often than not."

"The food fights," Riker said, his smile taking any hint of censure or judgment from the words. "I can't help wishing Marta had a little of Katie's sauciness, just a hint of an adventurous spirit. But she'd die of embarrassment if she got into trouble at school."

"Count your blessings," Leah advised. "It's not much fun to receive a frantic phone call from the school principal, telling you your daughter has just swallowed a star."

"A star?" Riker and Augusta chorused the word.

"She swallowed a star?" Riker asked.

Leah nodded. "In kindergarten. She was wearing one of those plastic dangle bracelets with little stars and moons. Someone told Katie she shouldn't put it in her mouth, so of course, she did."

"And she swallowed a star." Augusta laughed. "She wasn't hurt, though?"

"Oh, no. But she did create quite a stir in the principal's office. By the time I got to the school, she'd swallowed a penny, too."

"I like Katie already," Gussie said. "She obviously knows no limitations."

"Yes, well, it makes being her parent somewhat difficult."

"Parenting *any* child is difficult. Ask Riker. He makes raising Marta look like the building of the pyramids...only harder."

"I guess there are no easy answers." Leah's gaze turned to the elfin child in the pool. With her dark hair slicked back from her forehead and the excited expression on her water-dappled face, she looked more like Katie than ever and Leah's heart twisted with indecision. "Does Marta make good grades in school?"

"Straight A's," Riker said with pride. "I think she spends too much time worried about lessons and tests and not enough time on developing social skills, though. She's not exactly outgoing."

But Katie was…to the detriment of lessons and tests and other such practical matters.

"What other lessons does Marta take?"

Gussie cleared her throat to show her disapproval, but Riker ignored her and answered Leah's question. "Dancing lessons…tap, ballet and jazz. Riding lessons at the Oakhurst Stables. And then the swimming lessons in summer. She's going to go to camp this summer, too, so there'll be arts and crafts and canoeing, although I guess those aren't actual lessons."

Leah raised her eyebrows, inclined to think Gussie was right. Marta had too little time to just play. "Running her back and forth must keep you hopping," Leah said. "Katie plays soccer in the spring and fall and it's all I can do to shuttle her back and forth to practice and the Saturday games. I can't imagine trying to fit in lessons as well."

Riker crossed his ankles and leaned back in the lounge chair. "I probably try to work in too many activities for Marta, but what can I say in self-defense? I operate mostly on gut instinct and guilt, trying to give her every advantage, trying to make up to her for the mother she doesn't have."

"An impossible task." Leah picked up her tea glass, set it down again without drinking. Her thoughts drifted to Jonathan and she jerked them back. "Katie hardly remembers her father and she doesn't seem to mind not having him around."

"Survival skills," Augusta said with a knowing look. "Children pretend not to care because it hurts too much. Death and divorce are hard blows for a tiny heart to take."

That was depressing, Leah thought. Riker caught her eye, offered a reassuring smile. "Don't listen to Gussie. She gets on this soapbox occasionally and forgets that Marta's tiny heart has more love than it can hold. I'm sure Katie's heart is as full as it can be, too." He lifted one shoulder in a gentle shrug. "We do the best we can, don't we, Leah?"

She was trying. God knew she was trying.

"Daddy! Gussie! Mrs. Taylor!" Marta yelled from the end of

the slide, calling their attention to her swan dive into the pool. Bellybuster. Marta splashed flat on her stomach and sank, rising to the surface a minute later, laughing and sputtering.

Leah laughed, finding the child's gaiety irresistible and charming. Katie would love to perform bellybusters. She'd adore having the attention of three adults and one child. She'd play it for all it was worth and have more fun than… Leah didn't want to continue that line of thought or she'd be rationalizing why Katie should have a chance to swim in the Westfalls' pool. But how could she agree to bring Katie over to swim, to play with Marta, without opening Pandora's box?

"Can your little girl do this?" Marta called as she clamored up the rungs of the slide and slid, belly down, into the pool.

"She'd love to try," Leah called back, knowing Katie would do everything in her power to take over Marta's "star" status. If the girls swam together or played together, the competition would most likely be fierce. Leah hated to think of Katie trying to outdo Marta in the pool, in the playroom, in school. Wait a minute…school? The thought was followed by immediate rejection. A selfish idea. Leah wouldn't put Marta in a position to be used by Katie. That would only lead to disaster.

Or would it? If Marta spent too much time on study and Katie spent too much time on not studying, would one influence the other into a happy compromise? If Marta tended to be an introvert and Katie was a blatant extrovert, could the two of them together strike a trade-off in personality traits?

"What do you think, Leah? Isn't it obvious we're going to have to let the girls get together?" Riker's incisive regard made her fumble for an answer.

"I'm not sure it will work," she said. "Katie won't be satisfied with superficial answers. She'll want to know more about Marta than you know. She'll ask questions until you go nuts trying to answer her."

"But she has a right to ask, Leah. Marta is so full of questions she's refusing to ask now, that I'm afraid she may need therapy."

"Oh, please," Gussie interrupted. "How will she fit therapy in between dance class and riding lessons?"

"Be quiet, Gus, unless you have something insightful to add to this discussion."

"How about an hors d'oeuvre? At the rate these are going we'll be eating them for months to come." She turned a clear, green gaze to Leah. "Would Katie eat these? You could take some home to her, if you'd like."

"Thank you. Katie eats practically everything."

Riker smiled. "Except turkey nuggets and anything green."

Leah nodded agreement. Already they had a history, she and Riker. He knew things about Katie. She knew things about Marta. As much as she hated to admit it, Leah knew she was fighting a losing battle. "Maybe we could let the girls get together next weekend."

"You mean it?" Riker straightened in his chair.

Gussie clapped her hands together in delight. "Oh, Marta will love it. I just know she and Katie will be good for each other."

Leah only hoped they wouldn't actually harm each other. "Sunday is generally pretty quiet at our house. How about then?"

"Sunday's great." Riker was obviously pleased.

Leah quickly added what she considered the most vital condition. "Instead of meeting at one house or the other, why don't we go on a picnic? Neutral territory, you might say."

"Good idea," Riker responded immediately.

Leah ran her finger over the rim of her glass and went on, "We'll need to have some sort of explanation ready. About their being twins and not having the same parents. We probably ought to be consistent about that. If I tell Katie one thing and you tell Marta something else…"

"We can each work on that and I'll call you later in the week to discuss it. Okay?"

What else could she say? "Okay. So, I guess that's settled. I'd better get home."

"Stay," Augusta pleaded. "We've hardly had a chance to visit. Do you sew by any chance?"

"Don't leave, yet." Riker smiled persuasively. "Marta will be disappointed if you don't let her show you her room. It's her pride and joy."

Leah didn't want to stay. She didn't want to talk about sewing. And she didn't want to inspect Marta's room. But to say no would reveal how unsure she was of her decision. How odd that in order to appear in control of herself and her daughter, she had to share a kinship with this family that she did not want to share. "Well, if she cleaned it especially for me…"

"You should be honored," Gussie said. "Marta thought of it all on her own. With no parental prompting." The red curls bobbed in Riker's direction. "Believe it or not, she hasn't had any lessons on cleaning her room."

"Gussie—" Riker began with a fierce scowl that was all too masculine and appealing.

"Daddy, look!" Marta's shout claimed his attention and Leah watched as the scowl immediately softened to tender affection. She found herself wishing he might someday look at her that way.

But it would be foolish to think about Riker in any way except as Marta's parent. It could be altogether too dangerous to let herself dwell on his personally attractive qualities, even though he had several.

Under different circumstances, perhaps she and Riker might have—

No. Leah drowned the supposition in a long swallow of minty tea. Under the circumstances, Riker Westfall was off limits to her.

Under any circumstances, she ought to be grateful for that.

Chapter Five

"I'm not going to like her." Katie punctuated her statement with a slam of the car door.

Leah sighed, clenched her hands deep in the pockets of her khaki shorts, and regarded her daughter with exasperation. "I told you, Katie, you don't have to like her. You don't even have to meet her if you don't want to. Say the word and we'll get back in the car and go home."

"Nope." Katie's stubborn little chin emphasized her determination. "You've already told them we were going to be here."

Leah wondered if she and Katie would ever be on common ground. First, Katie had refused flatly to meet Marta. Then she'd changed her mind. Changed it back. Changed it again. She would. She wouldn't. She would. It wasn't hard to decipher the underlying message. Katie was too curious about Marta *not* to want to see her again, but she didn't want Leah to know that. So she tried to pin the blame and any resulting consequences on someone else—Leah.

"I'm going to swing," Katie said decisively. "Tell me if that kid shows up."

Leah put a hand on Katie's shoulder, then bent to her daughter's eye level. "Katie, for the last time, her name is Marta. You don't have to like her, but don't be rude to her. You never know, you might even like having a…a look-alike friend."

Katie's eyes were big and blue and serious. "I won't like her."

Leah rose with a nod, acknowledging Katie's opinion and affirming her own fear of the imminent encounter. It was going to be a disaster. She'd been unsure of what to tell Katie, when to tell Katie and how much to tell Katie and subsequently, she'd fallen back on weak adjectives like nice and look-alike and friendly. She'd avoided words like sister, twins and adoptions. She and Riker had disagreed about that. Leah reassured herself that she hadn't actually lied. Unless omitting a few details constituted a lie. But she hadn't been able to look Katie in the eye and state irrevocably that Marta Westfall was not just a look-alike friend, but Katie's twin.

"Push me high, Mom," Katie pleaded. She'd pumped her legs furiously, but the swing responded far too slowly to suit her. "I want to see if I can loop over the top."

It never seemed to occur to Katie that if she did manage to flip herself and the swing over the top bar in a full loop-de-loop, she'd undoubtedly fall. Leah gave her a push, knowing there was no danger of her allowing such a thing to happen.

Oh, no, the only danger lay in coming to this park today in the first place.

"They're heeeerre." Katie dragged out the words as she dragged her white tennis shoes in the dirt to stop the swing. "She's wearing a Minnie Mouse shirt, Mom."

Disaster already, Leah thought, and Riker and his daughter weren't even two steps inside the park boundaries yet. Of all the material possessions Katie craved, Minnie and Mickey Mouse items were at the top of the list—a list Leah couldn't begin to afford.

"Hi," Riker said as he and Marta approached the swing set hand in hand. Marta was dressed in a matched outfit, a big Minnie Mouse on the shirt, a tiny Minnie on the cuff of her shorts. There was a big lavender bow in her hair, a pair of socks with lace trim at her ankles, and a pair of lavender sandals on her feet. Compared to Katie, in her cute but well-worn denim jumpsuit, with her hair already coming loose from her usual ponytail, Marta was a fashion plate. But there was no disguising their uncanny resemblance.

"Hi." Leah stepped close behind Katie, who had stopped the swing and stood with her hands clasped on the chains, her feet poised to push off and soar toward the sky at any moment. "Katie, this is Mr. Westfall and…Marta."

"Hi," Katie said with a sniff.

"Hi." Marta offered a tentative smile, but held tightly to Riker's hand. "It's very nice to meet you."

"Well," Riker said. "Isn't this a beautiful day for a picnic?"

"It's gorgeous." This situation was even more uncomfortable than she'd imagined. "Spring has been so pretty this year. Warm, too. My rosebush is already starting to bloom."

Riker's mouth curved in a smile that sympathized with her efforts to ease the awkward situation. "Let's set out the picnic. This kind of weather makes me hungry. Anyone else ready to eat?"

"That's a good idea," Leah said. Any idea would be good compared to standing around, talking about the weather and watching the two little girls size up each other in appraising silence. "I'll get our things from the car. You go ahead and play, Katie. Marta? Do you want to swing? I can give you a push."

"You should push me, Mommy," Katie said, staking her claim clearly and concisely. "*He* can push her."

"Marta doesn't need pushes, do you?" Riker looked down at his daughter and, with a squeeze of her hand, he turned her loose.

"I know how to pump," Marta said as she walked to the swing on the other side of Katie, positioned herself in the rubber strap that served as a seat and then pushed herself into motion with her feet.

"I know how to pump, too." Katie immediately rose to the challenge and shrugged off Leah's assistance.

Leah watched for a moment in dismay before she walked to where Riker stood. "Off to a great start, aren't they?" she muttered under her breath.

He turned with her toward the cars. "You didn't really think they'd fall all over each other with affection, did you?"

"No, but…"

"Give them time, Leah. As strange as this all is to you and me, it's got to be worse for them."

"I don't see how it could be any worse. I hardly slept at all last night, worrying about this."

"Me, either. I was up at two, four and five-thirty, each time wondering why Marta and Katie were separated in the first place, how they were going to deal with having a twin thrust on them, and whether I could face going through with this meeting today."

"You weren't sure?" Leah paused to look at him, to note the sincere look in his eyes, the concern on his face, the uncertain set of his mouth below the moustache. "I thought you were positive this was the right thing, the *only* thing, to do. You never acted as if we had any choice."

He lifted one shoulder in a rueful shrug. "I don't think we did. But that doesn't mean I don't worry about the outcome and how it will affect Marta's life. And mine."

"Katie didn't want to come today. She's been a real bear all morning."

"Marta's been quiet. I'm sure she was worried, too."

Leah shaded her eyes against the noonday sun and watched the back-and-forth motion of the swings. Katie was in the lead, now, outdistancing Marta by a foot or more. But Marta was trying to catch up. Her thin little legs were pumping back and forth in obvious effort. The competition was on, Leah thought. "I hope they don't end up hating each other."

Riker followed her gaze to the girls. "They're too young for that. They'll have to test the situation out for a while, but eventually I think we'll have trouble prying them apart."

"I think you're being overly optimistic." She sincerely hoped he was. *Pry them apart.* The idea made Leah shudder. The thought of sharing Katie with Riker's family, even for short periods of time, already had her on the defensive. What would she do if this relationship *took*? Leah turned to her car, opened the back door and lifted out the paper sack she'd packed with hers and Katie's lunch. Before she'd fully gotten the sack balanced in her arms, Riker had taken it from her.

"Here. Let me carry that. Where do you want to picnic? That table, or on the grass by the tennis courts?"

"It doesn't matter. Wherever you like." Leah felt funny. She could hardly recall the last time a man, or anyone for that matter, had carried something for her. At home, she carried in the groceries and carried out the trash. She carried laundry back and forth from the garage. There were times, even now, when she carried Katie. The lunch sack wasn't all that heavy, but she felt oddly pampered that Riker was carrying it for her.

"The girls would probably prefer the grass," he said. "I brought a blanket. We'll spread it out and lie in the sun while they play."

"You're joking." Leah pushed a strand of flyaway hair away from her face. "You don't honestly think those two are going to play happily without our constant attention, do you? Katie's good for about ten minutes, then she wants me to watch whatever she's doing. Regardless of what I might be doing at the time."

His smile tugged at Leah's heart, made her want to like him more than she knew was prudent. Was there no end to the pitfalls in this situation?

"Let's give it a try, anyway." He took a blanket from the back of his Wagoneer and started for the grassy knoll just this side of the tennis courts. "We'll plead age and exhaustion if they give us any trouble."

Leah wasn't sure but that she might prefer the company of a couple of six-year-olds. Riker was too attractive a man for her to lie beside on a blanket without stirring up some sort of trouble. She wasn't that old and she wasn't that exhausted. But she followed him, anyway, and helped spread the bright blue blanket over the thick green grass.

"Sit." Riker commanded—politely, but firmly. "I'll get the rest of the stuff from the Jeep. Is this everything from your car?"

"Unless you count the paperback novel in the back seat."

"You brought a book?" His smile warmed her more than the overhead sun. "Now who's the optimist? Or did you think I'd be that boring? Never mind. Don't answer. I'll be back in a minute."

Leah settled herself on the blanket and let the sun's heat caress her body, easing a little of her tension. Katie and Marta had stopped swinging. Marta was on the slide. Katie hung upside down from the jungle gym. Leah waved, hoping against hope that she appeared normal. Like any mother who took her daughter on a Sunday picnic. Like any parent meeting another parent in the park so their children could play together. Katie dropped one hand from the bars and waved randomly in answer. "Mommy," she called. "Watch this."

In seconds, she'd done a sort-of back flip, completed a monkey walk on the underside of the gym cage and pulled herself upright to sit on the cross section of the bars. Then, flushed with triumph, Katie turned toward the slide and stuck out her tongue at Marta.

"Oh, Katie." Leah said it softly, wondering if there was any way to undo the damage already done. Wouldn't it be better if she just took Katie home now and pretended that none of this had ever happened?

Unabashed, Katie climbed off the jungle gym, skipped over and dropped onto the blanket. Leah reached out and brushed the tangled hair away from her daughter's flushed face. "Having a good time?" she asked.

"No." Katie shook her head vigorously. "I told you I wouldn't like her, Mom. She's wearing a purple bow in her hair."

Katherine Hepburn couldn't have said it with more disdain. "Some people like ribbons, Katie," Leah said. "Some don't."

"I asked her if she wanted to throw sand on the slide so it would be slick and we could slide on it, but she said she'd get her hands dirty." Katie tossed a disgusted look across the playground. "I wish Braden had come. He's a lot more fun than *her.*"

Leah leaned back, bracing her upper body on her elbows. "Braden throws sand in your hair, Katie. Last time we went to the park with him, you said you were never going to play with him again."

"I didn't say that."

Of course not, Leah thought. Katie was the queen of fickle. And she was confused about Marta. So, at the moment, anyone would be a better playmate. "We'll be ready to eat in a few minutes. Are you hungry?"

Katie's ponytail bobbled as she shook her head dramatically from side to side. "Not for sandwiches. Yuck."

"I don't suppose you have to eat." Leah's attention swung toward the black Wagoneer. Riker's hair gleamed with red highlights in the sun. His arm muscles rippled smoothly as he picked up the wicker hamper with one hand and closed the Jeep's rear window with the other. Since her divorce, Leah usually noted a particularly good-looking man with the same lack of enthusiasm she reserved for a rise in the price of coffee. She liked to think that one day, when Katie was grown, she might find a man whose companionship she enjoyed. She hadn't been sure, though, she'd ever again feel that stirring of sexual attraction she'd once experienced.

And here, of all times, in all places, it was stirring. She turned it off immediately by turning her thoughts back to Katie. "It's a pretty day to play in the park, isn't it, sweetie?" she said as she tried to corral the escaping ponytail.

Katie shook her head, negating Leah's efforts. "You've said that a hundred times, Mom. Can't you think about anything else?"

"I can think about lunch. Mmmmm. Delicious peanut butter and strawberry jam sandwiches. Your favorite."

"I'd rather have General George's Chicken-In-A-Bucket."

Leah sighed, sensing she could do nothing to please her child today, wondering why she kept trying.

"Did Marta wear you out on the swing, Katie?" Riker asked as he set his picnic basket beside the blanket.

Katie didn't answer. She just looked up at him with the intimidating assessment of big baby blues and that "you-must-be-kidding" expression only six-year-olds can get away with. Leah nudged Katie toward courtesy with the heel of her hand. Katie shot her mother a frown. And Riker opened the basket to pull out a bucket of General George's Chicken.

"Do you like fried chicken, Katie?" he asked.

Katie, never slow to answer opportunity's knock, sat straighter and positioned a shy smile on her lips. "General George is my fav'rite. May I have some?"

"We brought sandwiches, Katie," Leah reminded.

"Oh." Katie's smile dimmed a fraction and her voice held the tiniest hint of disappointment, but she was the picture of compliance. "That's right. Peanut butter sandwiches."

Leah was half-charmed at her daughter's acting abilities, half-inclined to warn Riker he was being manipulated. But then he turned his smile toward her.

"You don't mind if Katie has chicken, do you? In fact, there's more than enough for everyone. I brought hot rolls, potato chips and baked beans, too. Does that sound good?"

He might have been speaking to Katie, or to the world at large. But Leah felt as if he were asking her permission, tempting her to share his lunch, encouraging her to sit back, relax, let him take care of her needs. How did he do that? How could he say something so *ordinary* and make *her* feel special? She must be getting too much direct sun.

"I'll eat a sandwich, thanks." Leah turned away from Riker's steady gaze and felt Katie's shoulder push against her knee. Katie raised her eyebrows and rolled her eyes toward the bucket of chicken. Leah got the message. "But it's all right with me if Katie wants chicken."

"Good." Riker took plastic plates from the hamper. "General George is Marta's favorite, too." He looked across the playground to the slide where his daughter still sat. "Marta Grace! Let's have lunch."

"Marta *Grace*?" Katie made a face. "Does she *like* that name?"

"Why don't you ask her?" Riker handed Katie a plate and offered the bucket of chicken. "Do you like your name?"

Katie pulled out a drumstick. "I guess so. It's really Katherine, not Katie. Katherine Anne Taylor. Why did you name me that, Mom? I forgot."

"Katherine for my mother. Anne because it's my middle name, too."

With a nod, Katie looked to Riker. "I'm adopted," she said.

Riker stopped in midmotion, a spoonful of baked beans halfway between the carton and the plate. The pause was infinitesimal, but it pounded in Leah's ears. "Yes, Katie," Riker said. "I know you were adopted. Marta was, too."

"We couldn't be twins if she wasn't." Katie said it simply as she bit into the chicken leg with enthusiasm.

Leah's eyes flew to meet Riker's, and her heart thudded rapidly against her chest. For a moment, they shared a common fear. What to say? What to do? Then, with an almost imperceptible shake of his head, Riker turned away. But somehow, his look, his small, quiet smile calmed her, reassured her that everything would be all right.

"Hi." Marta joined them on the blanket, taking care to sit opposite Katie, but not too far away. Unobtrusively she picked up a wet paper towel and wiped her hands. Then she smiled at Riker. "May I have some chicken, please, Daddy?"

As he responded and fixed a plate for Marta, Leah noticed that Katie, quietly, put her chicken on her plate, picked up a wet paper towel and wiped the dirt from her hands. It was a small gesture, but a significant one, and for the first time, Leah knew that, for better or worse, Marta was in Katie's life to stay.

"THEY'RE SO MUCH ALIKE, I can't get over it." Riker matched his stride to Leah's as they walked along the perimeter of the park. "If they were standing side by side, dressed alike, with their hair done the same way, I think I could tell which one was Marta, but I'm not absolutely certain."

"I could pick Katie out," Leah said unequivocally. "She'd give me that look and I'd know."

Riker smiled, as much for himself as for her, Leah thought. Their arms swung with the steady rhythm of their walk and occasionally, his fingers brushed hers in passing. She had begun to wait for that to happen, anticipating the warm tingle the touch would create along her arm.

Had it really been so long since she'd had the undivided attention of an adult male? Was she so lonely for a masculine point of view that she was exaggerating how much she liked Riker Westfall? And what difference did it make, anyway? She could hardly claim his *undivided* attention. Katie and Marta were not far away and were constantly calling for attention. His and hers. So why did she get this funny, little, shivery sensation every time Riker's blue eyes met her brown ones?

"For a first encounter, it seems to be going very well," he said. "Gussie will be happy to hear that."

"She seems very nice. Gussie, I mean." Leah stopped swinging her right hand and slipped it into her pocket. "Has she lived with you long?"

"Just about a year. Marta and I managed to survive the first year after Jean's death on our own, barely. Gussie's been a tremendous help to me since she arrived. Marta really needed a woman's influence. She was so young to lose her mother."

"Yes." Leah knew this pain. Jonathan hadn't died, but Katie had lost him just the same. "Katie was too young to remember when Jonathan left, but she's old enough now to miss him, for all the good that does. The odd thing is, I'm the one who feels guilty."

"I understand that." Riker's voice was deep and soothing. "Being an only parent is laden with guilt feelings and agonizing decisions. And being an adoptive parent seems to make it worse. There's always the crazy idea in the back of my mind that, somewhere out there, sometime when I least expect it, Marta's biological mother is going to walk up to me and tell me what a poor job I'm doing as a father."

"You do that, too?" Leah was surprised and, strangely pleased to discover she wasn't the only person who worried about that happening. "I've even dreamed about it. This woman shook her finger at me and accused me of ruining her child. I woke up crying and saying, she's my child. My child." She gave a shiver, trying to shake the doubts and the memory. "Don't you think it's odd that the biological parent we worry most about is the mother? I guess in our society that's normal, but I sometimes wonder if a man who claimed to be Katie's biological father could cause me as much concern as a woman, who claimed to be her mother."

"What we know about their backgrounds seems sketchy, doesn't it?" Riker regarded the two girls as they teeter-tottered in the middle of the small park. "Especially when I think I know Marta so well."

"This has been a frightening experience for me," Leah confided. "Finding out that Katie has a twin has brought out all my protective instincts in full force. I hate to think what kind of emotional state I'd be in if her biological parents showed up."

"What would you do if your ex-husband showed up again?"

"Put a big red *X* on an appropriate part of his anatomy and then kick it." She glanced a little sheepishly at Riker. "Actually I'd be more civilized than that."

"You'd put a target on his forehead and turn him loose in a firing range?"

She laughed. "I never worry about seeing Jonathan again. He went to so much trouble to get lost, I don't think he has the courage to be found. If only I could get rid of his parents, as well."

"The banana-pepper casserole didn't work, huh?"

"The effects last only a year. Then they're back for more." She answered a wave from Katie with a smile and a wave of her own. "But Katie does love her grandparents. My parents both died before she was born, so Bill and Mildred are the only ones she has."

"Life isn't easy for you, is it, Leah? Your husband left. Your parents are gone. How do you manage?"

Immediately, somehow, she saw Riker's interest as personal, having nothing to do with Katie and her relationship to Marta. This was a man making a discovery about a woman, finding a vulnerable spot. And Leah didn't want him to know how vulnerable she was.

"I manage quite well, thanks." She opened her stride a bit, hoping that somehow she might outdistance him and his curiosity. "I have friends, a wonderful daughter, a good job, and lots of outside interests."

Riker let the subject drop. He admired Leah's positive attitude, but he knew friends and a job and outside interests couldn't take away her burden of responsibilities. He knew from discreet inquiry that Jonathan Taylor had left behind debts and probably other problems. If it had been left to Riker, he'd have hunted the man down and done more than kick his butt.

"Riker? What have you found out about the…adoption?" Leah's voice was softer, more tentative now and Riker had to stay an impulse to put his arm across her shoulders to comfort her.

"Not much. I told you that the attorney who handled it, Jerry Hillman, is no longer practicing law in Oklahoma, didn't I? I haven't found him yet, but if he's still in the U.S. and still a member of the American Bar, he'll turn up on a list somewhere or other. I can't help wondering if he made a profit from our adoptions. Do you know what your expenses were?''

Leah shook her head, sending her brown hair bouncing and curling around her face. "Jonathan handled all that. I understood that we paid hospital expenses and legal fees only, but I couldn't prove it. I never found any record of the transaction after Jonathan had left."

"You have the adoption papers, though?"

"Yes, of course. I went tearing through Jon's files as soon as I realized he wasn't coming back. Those were the worst couple of days of my life. As soon as I had the adoption decree in my hand, everything seemed all right. I don't know why that was so important at the time. I'm sure I could have gotten a copy from the state records office, but I didn't think of that then. I was just petrified I'd lose Katie."

His heart broke for her. No one should have to face that kind of emotional upheaval alone. "I don't think we're in any danger of losing our daughters, Leah, no matter what facts come to light about their separate adoptions. Look, it appears they may even be starting to like each other."

Leah looked. The girls were standing together, head down, as if they were in a huddle, plotting the next offensive play. But somehow Leah didn't think they had suddenly become friends. Her answer came on the heels of the thought. In the distance, the sound of a tinkling bell drifted on the afternoon air. "Heads up," Leah said. "The Mr. Goody Ice Cream Truck is coming our way."

"Mommy!"

"Daddy!"

Across the park, Katie and Marta ran at top speed, brown hair flying out behind, arms chugging at their sides. They even ran alike, Leah realized. Even down to the way Katie dipped her chin toward her chest. The realization brought an unexpected feeling of affection...for Marta.

"The ice cream man!" Katie slid to a stop in front of Leah.

"The ice cream man!" Marta grabbed for Riker's hand.

"The ice cream man?" Riker tossed the question to Leah.

She furrowed her brow in a frown. "Is that like a snowman? A man made of ice cream?"

"Mommy," Katie said, jumping up and down. "He's coming now and if you don't give me any money, I'll miss him. Please? Please, please, please?"

"Please, Daddy? Can we have some ice cream?" Marta raised her voice over Katie's.

"Katie," Leah began. "You know I don't like for you to—"

"Here." Riker already had his billfold in hand and was in the process of extracting two crisp dollar bills. "A dollar for each of you. Now, be careful to wait on the grass until he's completely stopped his truck, okay?"

The dollar bills and the girls were gone in the blink of an eye. "Okay, Daddy," floated back, but it was programmed politeness, nothing more. Leah watched Katie's ponytail swing as she ran and then she turned to Riker. "I wish you hadn't done that."

"What?"

"Give them…I mean, given Katie money for ice cream."

"Is she allergic to it?" He sounded suddenly concerned.

"No, but I don't usually let her have treats like that. They're overpriced and there's no telling how old the stuff is."

"One ice cream bar isn't going to hurt her."

Leah lifted her chin. "That's really not your decision to make, Riker. And besides, I don't appreciate your giving her money just because she asked for it."

His eyebrows went up. "Don't be so touchy, Leah. It was just a dollar."

Just a dollar. She envied him the ability to shrug aside the amount as insignificant. She couldn't afford to do so. And that made her angrier than the idea that he'd usurped a small portion of her parental authority. "I'm very protective of Katie, Riker. And this sort of thing puts me on the defensive. I don't want you giving Katie money. It sets a…a bad precedent."

"Don't be ridiculous. I'm not going to do anything to hurt Katie. I can't believe you even think it's necessary to mention it."

"That's the reason it has to be said, Riker." Her voice shook a little with emphasis. She suddenly felt threatened from all angles. It *had* been only a dollar and only one ice cream. But still, she couldn't stop the overwhelming urge to put him in his place, away from Katie, away from her. "I don't think you'd do anything intentionally to hurt Katie, but this whole situation is fraught with hurts and heartaches. I wish I hadn't agreed to come today. We shouldn't have tried to force the girls into a relationship."

"We're not forcing them, Leah. We're providing an opportunity for them." Riker sounded exasperated, upset because she was upset. "An opportunity, I'll point out, that they would have created for themselves one way or another. No matter what you and I did or didn't do."

Leah said nothing else. It seemed pointless. Besides, she didn't trust herself to say more without revealing how very scared she was. Riker probably knew, but she saw no sense in taking away any doubts he might have. She'd never felt more helpless, less in control of her life. Even after Jonathan had left her, she'd been able to plan, to take action. But with Katie and her newfound twin, Leah didn't know what would happen next or from which direction the heartbreak might come. She wanted to be prepared for Katie's sake. But she didn't know which way to turn.

"I'm sorry, Leah." Riker put a hand on her shoulder. His very blue eyes expressed his interest and concern. "I didn't mean to step on your parental toes. Next time, I'll ask first."

"It's all right," she said, reassured that she'd made her point. "But I would appreciate being asked next time."

"Done." His lips slanted into a slow smile. His hand stayed warm on her shoulder. "Let's get the wet-wipes out of the hamper. I have a feeling we're going to have some major cleanup work after the twins finish their ice cream."

Referring to Katie and Marta as "the twins" hardly eased Leah's remaining fears. But she decided to ignore it. That might be the only way she'd survive the rest of this day.

Her tension stayed high until she had Katie belted in the car and they were on their way home. "It was a pretty day to be at the park, wasn't it, Katie?"

Katie wasn't fooled for a minute. "I told you I wouldn't like her, Mom," she said in her most irritating adult voice. "When we get home, can I go over to Braden's house?"

"We'll see," Leah said as she tried to quell the swift rush of relief that washed through her. Braden, boy-terror of the neighborhood, suddenly seemed a perfect playmate for her precious little Katie.

Chapter Six

"Mommy? Can I spend the night with Marta?"

Katie's question caught Leah off guard and sent her complacency borne of the past two days' quiet into a tailspin. She stopped nursing the stubborn timer of the washing machine and gave it a sharp twist, which turned the machine into a shuddering mass of grinding gears. Leah restrained the expletive that almost made it past her lips and forced herself to calmly, slowly pull out the knob and reset the cycle. This accomplished, machine under control, she glanced at Katie, who stood in the doorway that led from the garage into the house.

"I thought you didn't like Marta," Leah said, recognizing her own naïveté even as the words left her mouth. "You said you'd rather be friends with Braden."

"Braden's stupid and he's a boy and I can't spend the night with him and I never said I didn't like Marta."

This rush of fickle logic might have made Leah smile under different circumstances. But she didn't feel like smiling now. "You have to be invited, Katie. You can't just decide to—"

"I am invited," the child insisted. "Marta's on the phone right now. She asked me to come over to her house on Friday and spend the night. Can I, Mom?"

Leah grabbed a handful of dirty socks and stuffed them into the washer. "I'm busy right now, Katie. We'll discuss this when I've finished with the laundry."

"But that'll take forever. And Marta's waiting for me to tell her."

"Tell her you'll call her back." The smell of laundry soap and bleach almost choked Leah. Or was it the renewed threat of complications that made her throat tight? "We'll talk about it as soon as I come inside the house."

"Mommmmeeee." Frustration rang in Katie's voice. "Why can't I go? You like Marta. You know her daddy. And her grandma. I'll be safe. Remember, you said you didn't mind if I wanted to be friends with her. You said I could go to her house sometime."

"Katie." Leah tried not to let Katie's barrage of objections distract her from the issue at hand. All the parenting manuals cautioned against arguing with a child. But Katie was so good at instigating these things. "We'll talk about this in a minute. Now go to the phone and tell Marta you'll have to call her back."

"You are so mean." Katie shut the door on any reprimand her mother might see fit to give and Leah was left with her usual dilemma. Punish Katie for mouthing off. Or rationalize it into an understandable childish behavior.

Leah checked the load of clothes in the dryer and took out a few of the permanent-press items to finish drying on hangers. Because Marta hadn't been mentioned in the two days since the picnic, Leah had lulled herself into thinking the worst was over. The girls had met. They didn't like each other. The possibility of a relationship was over...for the time being, anyway. Since that day at the park, Katie hadn't even blamed her troubles on her evil twin, Marta. And now....

Damn Riker Westfall. What did he think he was doing letting Marta invite Katie without discussing it first. Katie had no business being with his daughter at his house. Leah could only imagine what Katie would have to say about Marta's pretty pink-and-white bedroom, Marta's wall of toys, Marta's closet full of frilly dresses. Leah crossed that worry off her list. Katie would not be impressed by frilly dresses. But the toys, the dolls, the pure luxury of Marta's life would leave a lasting impression on Katie. And knowing Katie's appetite for material things, how could Leah blithely agree to let her spend even one night at the Westfall home?

The answer was, she couldn't. Not without creating a new

crisis. Damn Riker Westfall, anyway. He had so much. Why did he want to include her daughter?

"Mommy?" Katie opened the door and offered a conciliatory smile. "Mr. Westfall is on the phone. He wants to talk to you."

She didn't need this. Where was her fairy godmother when she needed protection? Where was the common sense she needed to dispel this sudden, ridiculous rush of nervous excitement? It wasn't as if Riker Westfall wanted to talk to her for any reason other than to persuade her to let Katie spend the night. And this time she wouldn't be persuaded even if he turned on his charm full strength.

"Well, that might be all right," she vacillated a few minutes later. She'd lost ground the moment he'd said, "*Hello, Leah. How have you been?*" in that husky, personal tone of voice, as if he were really interested in what had happened to her in the past couple of days. Was that a quality that came from being a successful businessman? Or was he successful because he had the knack of putting people at ease? And what difference did it make? He'd moved from personal interest to Marta's interest with just as much ease.

"—so Marta thought it would be fun to have Katie spend the night. I know I should have talked to you before letting her make the invitation…" He paused, waiting a few seconds before he continued. "If you're uncomfortable with an overnight, maybe you could bring Katie by for a couple of hours on Friday evening. You'd be welcome to stay, too."

For the couple of hours or overnight? "Actually, Riker, I'm not thrilled with either choice—" She broke off the words when she looked up and saw her daughter's finely tuned pout. As Riker had once said, the girls had met now. There was nothing to do but move forward. "Maybe you could bring Marta over here instead. We could have hot dogs and the girls could play for a couple of hours."

Katie's pout softened just a little with interest. Leah knew Katie would prefer to play house guest instead of hostess. But life was full of compromises.

"What time should we be there?" Riker asked.

"Is six too early?" Six would put Leah into a mad dash to

get home from work and get ready, but she'd rather start early and end early…if at all possible. "Then you could pick up Marta around eight-thirty or nine? Okay?"

"We'll be there. Do you want me to bring anything? Sodas? Snacks?"

"No. Marta can have supper with Katie and me. Thanks, anyway."

"No. Thank you, Leah." His voice took on that throaty, personal quality again. A shiver tickled the backs of her knees. "I know what a sacrifice this is for you. For Marta's sake, I appreciate it."

She didn't know what to say.

Katie did. "Mommy? Let me talk to Marta, again. Tell Mr. Westfall I need to talk to Marta."

With mixed reluctance and relief, Leah relayed the request and turned the phone over to her daughter. Sacrifice, she thought. Was she really making a sacrifice for Katie's sake. Or had she just succumbed to the opening volley in a battle she was destined to lose?

"YOU GOT CHILI with beans." Katie set the can on the countertop with disgust. "Don't put any on my hot dog."

"I wouldn't dream of it." Leah gave Katie a push out of the kitchen. "Please, Katie, go to your room and straighten it before your company arrives. I've asked you twice already."

"Okay, okay." Katie scuffed her feet on the carpet as she went. "If you'd let me go to Marta's house like I wanted to, we wouldn't have to clean house at all. Marta's house has a housekeeper. She doesn't have to clean her room."

It was a rhetorical accusation, meant to make Leah feel guilty. Other children didn't have to clean their rooms. Only Katie was forced to perform such a menial chore. Leah opened the refrigerator and placed the container of apple juice on the top shelf. Katie had requested soda pop, but this naturally sweet substitute would have to do. She hoped Marta wouldn't turn up her nose at hot dogs and apple juice.

A knock at the door interrupted her thoughts and Leah jumped as if someone had set off a packet of firecrackers in her kitchen.

"I'll get it." Katie bounced down the hall, her energy and enthusiasm allowing her to outdistance Leah without effort. "Hi," Katie said as she opened the door. "Come on in."

Leah hovered in the kitchen doorway, wiping her hands on a dish towel, waiting for Riker to look up from greeting Katie and see her. When he did, she was unprepared for the nervous jump her stomach made. Their eye contact lasted five seconds, maybe less, but there was something so intimate about it that Leah immediately dropped her gaze. "Hello, Marta," she said.

"Hello, Mrs. Taylor." Marta released Riker's hand and stepped hesitantly into the living room.

Leah wished she'd had more time to dust. She hoped Katie had finished straightening her room. She wondered if Riker had been this nervous when she'd visited him at his house.

"Come on, Mart." Katie was through with amenities and she motioned for Marta to follow her into the kitchen. Leah stepped aside so the two girls could pass. "My mom bought chili with beans in it," Katie said. "But you don't have to eat it. I already told her not to put any on my hot dog."

"Chili?" Marta's voice imitated Katie's to the last nuance of disgust. "With beans in it?"

Leah shook her head and walked to the front door where Riker stood, hands in his pockets, waiting as if he expected an invitation to stay. Maybe, she thought, he needed reassurance about Marta's well-being before he could comfortably leave her for the next couple of hours. "I'm sure they'll be fine," Leah said, continuing to wipe her hands on the dish towel, even though they were long since dry. "Even with the wrong kind of chili."

"I prefer chili with beans."

"So do I. But Katie has a mind of her own."

"Marta, too. With the two of them ganging together, you may be forced back to the store to get chili without beans."

"I'm pretty easy to get along with most of the time, but they can complain until the roof falls in before I'll go back to that store tonight."

He smiled. "Rough day at the office?"

"A typical Friday."

"Complicated by worries over how Katie and Marta would get along tonight, I'll bet."

"No, I—" She broke off the denial and with a sheepish shrug, she admitted the truth of what he'd said. "Actually I have worried some. Thanks for not letting either one of them bulldoze us into an overnight situation. The picnic didn't go that well and there's no telling how this second arranged meeting will turn out. Anyway, I think dinner and a couple of hours of playing together ought to suffice, don't you?"

"We won't give them a choice."

She nodded. Smiled. Waited for him to leave. Wondered why she didn't just come out and suggest he do so.

The crash came in the lull between thought and action.

"Marta! Look what you did!" It was Katie's voice, verging on panic.

Riker looked toward the kitchen. Leah spun around. Acting on the same impulse, they hurried to the scene of the crime— Leah's pretty blue-and-beige kitchen. Well, it had once been pretty and most of it was still blue and beige. But the center of the linoleum floor, the front of the dishwasher, the doors of the lower cabinets, and both little girls from the knees down were splattered mustard yellow.

"She did it, Mom." Katie's finger pointed unerringly at Marta. "I was standing way over there."

Obviously. Leah glanced "over there" where the stains were hardly visible to Katie's legs which were polka-dotted with mustard globs.

Marta blinked in wide-eyed worry and held up the nearly empty jar of mustard. "I didn't break the jar," she said.

"It's plastic." Leah managed a reassuring smile. "The lid probably wasn't on tight."

"Stand still." Riker moved into action even as he commanded his daughter not to budge. "Do you have any paper towels?" he asked. "Stand still," he said again as Katie took a step toward the doorway. Miraculously Katie obeyed.

"I'll get an old towel." Leah turned toward the pantry.

"Better get several."

"I didn't do it, Mommy." Katie's plaintive voice followed Leah into the closet. "It was Marta's idea to get the mustard."

"Katie, Marta is your guest. Don't blame her for dropping the mustard jar."

"But, Mommy—"

"Katie." Leah spoke sternly as she tucked the old towels under her arm and closed the pantry door.

"She's right, Mrs. Taylor." Marta's voice was small and apologetic. "It's my fault. I dropped the jar. Don't scold Katie."

Katie's attention swung to Marta and Leah noted the glimmer of respect in her daughter's expression. "Don't scold Marta...either, Mommy," Katie said. "She didn't mean to make this mess."

"I know that," Leah said. "I'm not angry with either one of you."

"No one's in trouble here. It was an accident." Riker deftly stepped around the spilled mustard, picked up his daughter and set her on the clean countertop beside the sink. Then he caught Katie around her waist and put her on the opposite side of the sink. "Now, let's get you two clean before you end up with permanent polka-dots on your legs."

"Oh, Daddy." Trauma already forgotten, Marta laughed and stuck her legs straight out for cleaning. Katie laughed, too, and copied Marta's action.

Leah tossed him a towel, wondering if Katie's whining about getting in trouble had convinced Riker that as a mother, she was a terrible tyrant. Why did Katie do things like that? Just when Leah especially wanted to make a good impression. She decided not to analyze *why* she wanted to make a good impression and dropped to her knees to begin scraping mustard from the floor.

Riker finished washing the twins and boosted them, one at a time, over the kitchen floor to the doorway and a living room full of clean carpet. Katie scampered off with Marta in tow and Riker bent beside Leah. "Any towels left?"

She nodded toward the pile of limp and yellowed rags on the floor. "You might try rinsing them, but I'm afraid they've given their all to the cause."

"Where's the mop? Maybe I can get up the rest of the stain with some soap and water and a little muscle power."

Leah cast him a skeptical look. "With a lot of muscle and plenty of scouring powder, maybe. It would be easier if I simply redecorated the kitchen."

He smiled, liking the way she'd handled the situation, liking her sense of humor and the way her nose crinkled with thought as she evaluated her options. He liked Leah. Which was kind of odd, since he hardly knew her. She was Katie's mother and Marta needed Katie and, therefore, he liked Leah. It was simple. But as he crouched beside her, balancing on the balls of his feet, resting his forearms on his thighs, his hands hanging idly a couple of inches above the floor—close enough to touch her hands if he'd wanted to—Riker knew it wasn't that simple at all.

Leah Taylor appealed to him on a level that had nothing to do with being anyone's mother. She was pretty, no doubt about that. And when she smiled, he felt a funny little curl of tension deep in his stomach. He recognized it for what it was, an elemental attraction, a bit of sexual chemistry that either did or didn't happen between a man and a woman. So, it happened for him with Leah. He could handle chemistry.

But being in the small, shiny kitchen, watching Leah wipe mustard from the floor, he admitted there was more to this than sexual attraction. He admired Leah Taylor. Despite her small stature, she packed a lot of character. She was strong, independent, brave and determined. Life may have dealt her a low hand, but she was calling the bluff and playing out the game. He liked that about her. He liked her spirit. And it was that attraction that bothered him most.

"The mop's in the garage," she said, her dark eyes questioning his delay. "It's hanging just inside the door."

"The mop." He pushed his thoughts and his body into gear and retrieved the mop. He had no business thinking about Leah this way. She was Katie's mother. He was Marta's father. Wasn't that enough for them to deal with at the moment? At anytime?

"You really don't have to mop the floor," she said. "I can do it."

"So can I." He squeezed excess water from the sponge and applied wet mop to blotched linoleum. "I took lessons."

"Your mother taught you."

He looked up with a grin. "My mother doesn't know which end of the mop to squeeze and which end to push. She's not your basic domestic goddess."

Leah pushed a bouncy strand of brown hair behind her ear, and ignored it when it promptly escaped. "So, who gave you mopping lessons, Riker?"

"Believe it or not, my father. He was pretty handy around the house and a darn good cook, too. Lucky for me. If Gussie had had her way, I'd have grown up in a grass hut, eating bean sprouts and rutabagas. She was the quintessential earth mother, minus a few 'quintessents' here and there."

Leah laughed. "My mother was the down-to-earth, pot-roast-on-Sunday type, and if my father had ever stepped into her kitchen, he'd have lost a foot. We were your basic traditional family." She leaned her hip against the cabinet and her expression went soft with memory. "I always thought my life would follow the pattern of my childhood. I thought I'd have a husband and two or three children, a picket fence, cookouts with my next-door neighbors…" She glanced up with a self-effacing smile. "I think I may have gotten lucky and missed out on all that."

"You are lucky. How many times did you ever see Donna Reed cleaning mustard off her kitchen floor?"

"I've only seen reruns of her television show, but I don't think she ever mopped."

"Trust me," he said. "It takes a professional. Look at this floor." With a wide gesture of his hand, he invited her to inspect his handiwork. "No mustard marks…and you can see your reflection in that linoleum."

"Just what I always wanted to see," Leah said, taking the mop from his hand and putting it away in the garage. "Now," she said when she returned. "I'd better get the hot dogs cooked before Katie and Marta start screaming for General George's Chicken."

"I could go get some chicken."

"Don't be so nice, Riker." She said it quietly, in a light tone, but he heard the underlying distress and knew she was warning him away. "Hot dogs will be just fine for supper."

"I'm only trying to help, Leah."

Her gaze lifted to meet his squarely, honestly. "I don't need help, Riker. And you don't have to try so hard to be my friend. That isn't a prerequisite for my allowing Katie to play with Marta."

His hand covered hers, there on the counter. He thought he felt her tremble, but maybe he imagined it. "It isn't taking any effort, Leah."

She lifted an eyebrow, flexed a finger against his palm. "What?"

"Being your friend," he explained. "I don't have to try hard. The feeling seems to be developing quite naturally on its own."

"Only because of the girls."

He heard the determination in her voice, recognized the vulnerability that she was trying hard to disguise. "Should I apologize because I like you, Leah? Doesn't it make it easier for Marta and Katie if you and I like each other? Doesn't that make this whole thing easier for us?"

"No. It—" She lifted her chin as she slipped her hand from his grasp. The corners of her mouth lifted to form a tiny smile. "None of this is easy, Riker. Let's just not complicate it any more than it already is. Of course we like each other. That's sort of a moot point. If I didn't like you, you and Marta wouldn't be here now." Her smile eased. "And unless you want hot dogs with chili *and* beans, I suggest you leave while the going is good. You might head on out to General George's Chicken and have your dinner there. If you take your time, you'll be able to stop back for Marta on your way home."

Riker watched Leah turn her fear into productive charm. She was worried about the situation. She was worried about him. She was worried that this friendship between them, young as it was, would inevitably collide with the attraction they both felt. He was a bit worried, himself. But right now, no amount of common sense was going to pry him out of her kitchen. "I'd better stay and help you eat the chili. We wouldn't want it to go to waste."

She sighed. "You don't have to stay, Riker. Marta will be fine. I won't let anything happen to her."

He lifted his shoulders and extended his hands, palms up, in a wry shrug. "I'm a single parent," he said. "I'm overprotective of my only child. You understand, don't you?"

"Oh, I understand." Leah turned to the refrigerator, her movements quick and graceful. "I don't think I could leave Katie alone with you and Marta." She glanced over her shoulder. "Nothing personal, Riker. I do *like* you."

She was almost flirting with him and he was fascinated by the idea. No, fascinated wasn't the right word. He was surprised and flattered and… Crazy. Leah was right. There were complications enough without this. He wasn't sure he wanted to get romantically involved with any woman. He'd loved Jean and lost her. That was enough loss for a lifetime. "I like you, too, Leah." He pushed back the sleeves of his shirt and picked up the can of chili with beans. "Now, point me toward the nearest can opener."

She gestured toward a drawer. "If you get heartburn, it isn't my fault."

Heartburn was exactly what he was risking, Riker thought, and if he were smart, he'd be at General George's Chicken Ranch at this very moment. Instead he said, "Tell me about your work. Advantage Advertising isn't it?"

"How did you know that?"

"You must have mentioned it."

"I didn't." She set the mayonnaise jar on the counter, and put her hand on her hip. "You've been investigating me, haven't you?"

"Investigating is a strong word. I asked around, found out a few things. That's all. I didn't get your last year's tax return or any medical records. Nothing really personal."

"Why did you do that, Riker? My life isn't any of your business."

"Maybe not. But what do you know about me?"

She paused. "I know where you work. I've been to your store several times."

"What do you think about it? I'm always looking for an objective opinion."

"Who wouldn't like Westfall's? I used to love to shop there."

He decided not to comment on the past tense. He had a good idea of why she no longer frequented his store. "So you did know where I worked?"

"Well, of course. Everyone's heard of Westfall's."

"Everyone's heard of Advantage Advertising, too. In fact, I think your agency does quite a few of our ad designs."

"Don't you know?"

"Where're the spoons? And a pot for this chili?" He followed her instructions to find the pot and spooned the chili into the pan. "I have an assistant who makes most of the advertising decisions. Since my wife died, I haven't been as…involved with the store as I was before. It's sort of like trying to make up now for all the time I didn't spend with Jean before."

"So you're spending it with Marta?"

He stirred the chili, even though it didn't need stirring yet. "I am spending more time with her, yes. But I'm taking time for myself as well. Sounds odd, I know. But when you lose someone you love, your perspective changes."

"Yes, I know."

Riker felt like a fool. Of course she knew. "This chili is off to a good start. Is there something else I can do to help you?"

"You might go and check on our daughters. Just make sure they haven't torn up the rest of the house while we've been busy."

"Good idea. You won't let this burn, will you?"

"Only the beans." She smiled and shooed him out of the kitchen with a wave of her hands.

Coaxed by her smile, he went. He tried to tell himself that the warmth he felt was a simple response to the homey setting and the situation. His daughter was here, having fun. It was right that he should be here, having fun, too. They were a team, he and Marta. Just like Leah and Katie. Two teams. Two players each. The rules were simple. Stay within the boundary lines. No passes. No personal contact. If he could manage that, Marta could have a beneficial relationship with her twin sister and everyone would be satisfied.

He hoped.

"WHEN CAN I COME to your house?" Katie asked Riker around a mouthful of hot dog…without chili.

"Katie," Leah began, knowing she should have been better prepared for this. "It isn't polite to ask something like that."

Katie swallowed the bite of hot dog. "But Mommy, Marta invited me."

Marta looked to her daddy. "It's okay, isn't it, Daddy?"

His blue eyes sought Leah's, sharing his pleasure and her concern, at the progress of the relationship of the two girls. "I think that's a great idea, Marta. Perhaps Katie's mother will come, too."

"She doesn't have to." Katie added extra emphasis to the words. "I go places all the time without her."

"Maybe she will keep me company while the two of you play," Riker suggested with a smile. "You wouldn't want me to have to play with you."

Marta smiled. "Yes, we would, Daddy."

"No, we wouldn't." Katie frowned at Marta. "We can play by ourselves. Just like tonight."

Leah still didn't want Katie to go to Marta's house. And she did not want to "keep Riker company." So, how would she avoid the trap and escape the consequences? "This is going to be a busy week, Katie. I'm afraid there won't be time to visit Marta."

Two elfin noses crinkled with disappointment. Two chins rose in nearly simultaneous argument. Two voices bombarded Leah's ears.

"But, Mommy…"

"Please let her.…"

"…it's not fair."

"…Daddy said it was okay."

Leah turned to Riker. "Is this what's meant by 'a double dose'?"

He laughed over the twins' escalating pleas. "Give it up, Leah. You're outnumbered two to one."

He was right. It was too late for prudence. The quicksand was rising rapidly. "How about next Saturday?" she said with a sigh.

Chapter Seven

"Will you sit down, Riker?" Gussie frowned at him over her needlework. "You're making me nervous."

"It isn't me, Gus. It's that embroidery thing you're working on." Riker turned away from the window and settled onto the plump and plush cushions of the sofa. "If you'd get your glasses, you wouldn't have so much trouble seeing how to stitch."

"I can see very well, thank you. And I can see you're on pins and needles waiting for Leah Taylor to get here."

"You're imagining things, Gussie." Riker tried his best to appear relaxed and totally unconcerned about his expected guests. "The idea of Leah and Katie being here does not make me nervous."

"I didn't say the 'idea' bothered you. I said you couldn't wait for her to arrive." Gussie clucked her tongue. "Now, see what you've made me do. I have to take out this whole row of stitches."

While Gussie fussed with the needle and thread, Riker pondered her use of the singular, "her." She meant Leah, of course. Was he so transparent that even his usually off-in-the-clouds mother picked up on his nervous excitement? And it was excitement. He'd tried to tell himself it was imagination. This was not a date. Not anything more than two parents spending a couple of hours together so their children could play. But the nearer Saturday came, the more plans he made, and the more he worried over whether or not Leah would like the meal, the swim, the visit…him.

It shouldn't have mattered. But the closer it came to four o'clock, the designated time of arrival, the more it did seem to matter. "Did you remember to put pop on ice?" he asked, suddenly recalling another detail. "I meant to do that as soon as I got back from the store."

"It's iced and probably half-frozen by now," Gussie said, pulling a long bit of thread from her canvas. "The chicken is marinated and ready to cook. The salad is in the refrigerator. There's barbecue sauce, salt and pepper on the tray beside the grill. It's all ready, Riker. I watched you put everything together. Now if you could only get yourself together."

He gave a deprecating little chuckle. "I don't know what you're talking about, Gus. This is just another Saturday afternoon and Marta is having company."

"Marta's *twin* is the company, which is a bit intimidating to me. And Leah is coming, too, which is a bit intimidating to you."

"You're imagining things."

"Maybe I am. You always could fib with a straight face, Riker. It's one of those exasperating traits you learned from your father. Now that you're grown, I guess it's safe to tell you I was never sure when you were telling the truth and when you weren't."

"I always told the truth. It's one of those exasperating traits I learned from you."

"Hmm." She sounded unconvinced. "Leah is a very attractive woman. I'd be ashamed of you, if you hadn't noticed."

Here we go, Riker thought. Feetfirst into the subject. "I noticed. But that's as far as I mean for it to go, Gussie. I put Marta's interest first and foremost. I'm not foolish enough to get involved with Katie's mother."

Gussie tried to guide her thread into the eye of her needle. "Just be sure you don't get involved for the wrong reasons, Riker. Katie's mother is not the woman for you. On the other hand, Leah Taylor might be just the woman you've been waiting for."

"I'm not *waiting* for any woman, Gussie. Jean's only been gone two years. I'm not ready for anyone to take her place."

"If you think someone can replace Jean, you're a long way

from being 'ready.' Life goes on, Riker. You need to go on with it."

"I know this lecture by heart, Gussie. You don't have to give it to me again."

"Your father never listened to me, either." Resolutely Gussie returned to her project. "This doesn't look much like a lighthouse. Maybe, when I finish the sky…"

The words trailed off into concentrated effort and Marta slipped quietly onto the couch beside Riker. She cuddled against his side and he hugged her with one arm. "Hello, Marta Grace. Where have you been for most of the afternoon?"

"In my room. I was pretending Katie was here and we were having a tea party."

"In a few minutes she will be here and you won't have to pretend."

Marta nodded and Riker wondered if she was nervous about Katie being in *her* room, Katie playing with *her* toys, Katie taking part of *her* father's attention. "Daddy?" she said. "Did you know Katie has a Brownie Bear, too. He's not just like mine, but she named him just the same as me."

"You and Katie have a lot in common, don't you? It's nice to have a friend like that."

"She's my sister, isn't she, Daddy?" Marta lifted solemn blue eyes to meet his. "When you adopted me, why didn't you adopt her?"

Riker's throat tightened, but he gave a smile his best shot. "I didn't know about Katie, then. If I'd known—"

"Katie said her daddy ran away from home and that's why I came to live with you."

"No, Marta. You were a baby, only five days old, when I adopted you. Katie's daddy…ran away…later. When you and Katie were older." He stumbled with the words, not knowing how to explain. "Katie's mother didn't know about you when she adopted Katie and I didn't know there was a Katie when I adopted you."

Marta seemed to understand, or else her attention simply strayed. "I'm going to go put on my swimsuit so we can swim as soon as Katie gets here. Okay, Daddy?"

"Okay." There was no way to hide his relief and the arch of Gussie's eyebrow told him she noticed it. "I'll keep a lookout for your friend."

"Sister," Marta corrected as she jumped off the couch. "Katie's my twin sister. Remember?"

"She seems to be taking this right in stride." Gussie made the comment as Marta bounced up the stairs in an exaggerated bunny hop. "I wasn't sure how it would work out."

"Do you think I did the right thing, Gussie? Is she too young to have to deal with a long-lost sister? Maybe I should reconsider counseling."

"Relax, Riker. It's done. Marta would be better off if you'd spend more time worrying about your problems than hers."

"Gussie." It was a warning, but as usual, Gussie paid it no mind.

"Back off, Riker. I'm your mother. I'm supposed to say things like that."

"You never did before."

"I know. I've stayed in one place so long I'm stagnating. Becoming an old granny who frets over her children like a mother hen."

Riker laughed. "Should I get your rocking chair, old Granny?"

"Someday, you'll be sorry you spoke to me that way. It hurts my—" Gussie stopped in midsentence and laid aside the needlework. "I think Leah and her daughter have arrived." Gussie stood and dusted her hands on the sides and front of her clothes. "Come on. I can't wait to meet Katie and you can't wait to see Leah." She linked her arm with his, drawing him up off the sofa and toward the door. "Don't be shy, dear. I won't let her know how anxious you've been."

Gussie was impossible, Riker thought as he accompanied her to the door. And too darn perceptive. He was sure that within the hour, Leah would be regaled with the story of his restlessness. Gussie would embellish it with threads of many colors and embroider it into a completely embarrassing picture. He'd have to find an opportunity to discount his mother's story and tactfully deny it. He only hoped he was as good with a lie as Gussie believed he was.

"Hello. Hello." Gussie held wide the door as Leah and Katie approached from the driveway. "You must be Katie. I'm Marta's grandmother. It's a pleasure to meet you."

Katie accepted Gussie's outstretched hand with some hesitancy. "Hello. Where's Marta?"

"She's upstairs putting on her swimsuit." Riker smiled at Katie, struck again by the fact that, if he hadn't known better, he might have thought this child was his Marta. "You can go on up, if you want. Her bedroom is the first door off the hall."

"Can I, Mommy?"

At Leah's nod, Katie walked through the house, taking in everything like a sponge soaking up water. Leah watched her daughter's progress with mixed feelings. She'd dreaded this moment all week and, now that it was here, she was almost relieved. If Katie fell hook, line, and sinker for the Westfalls' life-style, then Leah would counteract the effect with a good dose of philosophy. If Katie didn't fall, if she kept some measure of the principles Leah had taught her, then so much the better. Either way, the decision was out of her hands now. And she might as well look forward to a relaxing swim in Riker's pool.

"Hello, Gussie." Leah smiled warmly at Riker's mother, who was dressed in culottes and a flowing, silky blouse. Beads of all shapes and sizes hung around her neck and dangled on her arms. Large hoop earrings accented her ears and her mass of copper red curls. "It's nice to see you again."

"I've been looking forward to this all week. I can't believe…" Her gaze followed Katie up the stairs. "She's like a carbon copy of Marta."

"They're identical twins. What else could you expect?" Riker stepped forward and took the bag from Leah's hand. "Hello, Leah. How are you?"

Did she imagine the warmth in his voice, the welcome in his eyes? Was she smiling at him the same way he was smiling at her? Could Gussie sense the tension that spun through her just because Riker was nearby? "I'm fine, thank you." She managed to keep her voice even, her tone cool. "Katie's driven me crazy

today. She must have asked me a hundred times if it was time
to go.''

"Marta's looked forward to it, too," Riker said.

"Yes," Gussie agreed, casting a private kind of smile at her
son. "We've all been excited today."

Riker ushered Leah into the living room with what she thought
was a bit of haste. Gussie took a seat on the hassock and grinned
like the Cheshire cat. Leah thought she might fade into Won-
derland at any moment.

"If you want to change into your swimsuit, Leah, you can use
my bedroom." Riker motioned toward a hall leading behind the
stairs. "I think the girls are going to want to get out to the pool
as soon as possible and as the lifeguards, we ought to be ready."

"Yes, I'm sure you're right. Katie can't wait to swim. She's
been ready all day." Leah tried not to think about how skimpy
her own swimsuit was. She didn't want to dwell on where her
thoughts would turn when she saw Riker in swimming trunks.
"Gussie," she said. "Are you going to swim, too?"

The older woman shook her head. "Afraid not. I have a meeting of my Wildlife Society tonight. I'm the president and it's my
turn to bring the refreshments. I still have to stir up a few snacks
so…no time for a swim."

"You're not going to be here tonight?" Leah hoped the swirl
of panic in her stomach didn't carry up and into her voice. Alone
with Riker. This was not what she'd planned. "I was hoping you
and Katie could get acquainted."

"We will. I'm sure she and Marta will be spending a lot of
time together from now on. Today ought to be just for her and
Marta. They won't want 'old granny' at their tea party."

"Definitely no 'old granny.'" Riker stroked his moustache
and hid a smile. "If the truth were known, they'd probably prefer
to have no adults around at all."

Leah wondered how soon she could reasonably plead a headache and go home. If she wanted to take Katie with her…and
she did…she'd have to wait at least until after the swim. "I just
hope they get along okay."

"I just hope the two of you can find something to talk about
while they play." Gussie again offered that benignly mysterious

smile to Riker. "If you get bored, Leah, feel free to work on my embroidery project. It's not progressing as well as I'd hoped."

Leah took time to admire the needlework, even though there wasn't a lot to admire. But the few minutes she spent discussing threads and stitch count with Gussie gave her time to compose her rapid pulse and give herself a stern lecture on imagining tensions that didn't exist. Riker was cool and collected. Any interest he had in her was borne of politeness and the fact that she was Katie's mother. Anything else was imagination. Pure and simple.

"Mommy?" Katie leaned over the rail at the stair landing. "Can I wear one of Marta's swimsuits? She said I could."

Leah started to protest, but decided she wasn't going to spoil Katie's fun for a minor detail. "I don't care, Katie." She remembered Riker and turned to him. "Do you mind?"

"No, of course not."

Leah turned back to Katie, but the child was long gone and from upstairs floated down the trill of little girls' voices.

"I think they're happy to be together," Riker said.

"Yes." Leah handed the embroidery to Gussie. "That's very nice. I like pictures of barns." She glanced at Riker. "Maybe I should change now. If I know Katie, she'll be in the water before I even get my shoes off."

Riker held out the beach bag. "Don't worry. I'll stand guard. Take your time. It's going to be a rowdy afternoon and I doubt we'll have much opportunity for lying in the sun."

All the better, Leah thought. The more time she spent interacting with Katie and Marta, the less time she'd spend worrying about the sensations evoked by Riker's presence.

"It's supposed to be a lighthouse." Gussie's voice followed Leah into the hallway that led to Riker's bedroom. "Maybe it will look less like a barn when I get the sky finished."

IMAGINATION was a dangerous thing.

Leah had imagined a dozen scenarios during the past seven days. Each had dwelt far too heavily on Riker Westfall and the effect he seemed to have on her nervous system. But of all the scenes her imagination had created, none of them came close to the reality.

Leah enjoyed herself. She couldn't believe it was so simple. After her initial anxiety, she plunged into the pool and the fun with wholehearted enthusiasm. Riker looked great in swim trunks. His physique was even better than she'd imagined. And although she never was able to achieve a state of comfortable disinterest in his good looks, she was able to pretend it didn't matter.

They played in the pool until sunset, when Riker decreed that it was time for dinner. No arguments. He wrapped the girls in towels and pointed them upstairs to dry and change. He was a little more discreet with Leah as he suggested she could change first while he started the grill.

"There are extra towels in the bathroom," he said as he opened the French doors that led from the patio into his bedroom. "Help yourself. Take a shower if you want. Just be careful getting in and out. The steps go down. It's kind of unusual."

Leah had no intention of using Riker's shower. No matter how much she smelled of chlorinated water. She thought it was just too personal a thing to do.

But when she looked at the odd shape of the shower—the clear vinyl curtain curving across the front of the round, tiled stall, the shining chrome fixtures—an impulse urged her to immerse herself beneath the spray. Just for a minute. Just to see if it felt as wonderfully luxurious as it looked. Without giving herself time to reconsider, she turned on the water, stripped out of her swimsuit and stepped down into the steamy mist.

The water was hot as it pelted her and the warm moist vapors filled her lungs and stung her eyes. She could smell the soap Riker used to bathe. Funny. She hadn't realized she'd been close enough to him to become familiar with the scent of his soap. Or his shampoo. She'd never used the brand before, but as she poured a little into the cup of her hand, it oozed through her fingers, thick and shiny and familiar smelling. Lifting her hands to her head, she breathed in the steamy fragrance of clean hair, of Riker's hair. Then, with rough, sure movements, she massaged the shampoo into her hair and told herself she was being a damned fool. She had no business in this bathroom, no business using his soap, no business washing her hair with his shampoo.

It was nonsense.

It was stupid.

It was…dangerous.

Leah dried and dressed as quickly as possible. She spent a few minutes wiping down the shower, hoping she could erase any lingering inappropriate thoughts relating to her host. When she walked outside again and found Riker standing beside the grill, she gathered her composure and offered a smile. "I feel like a new woman," she said in a rush. "Mmmm, that smells good. I love to barbecue, don't you?" She tried to move closer to the smoke, hoping it would hide the evidence of her shower.

"We don't do it very often, but I like the mesquite flavor now and again." Riker adjusted the towel that hung across his shoulders and chest. Then he held out the long, barbecue fork. "If you'll take over for a few minutes, I'll take a quick shower, change and be back before the chicken is cooked."

"Sure." Leah had a momentary image of Riker getting into the shower she'd just vacated. "Take as long as you want. I can handle the food."

He nodded, but made no move to leave. "You found everything? Towels? Soap? Shampoo?"

She felt a warm blush highlight her face and bent over the grill for a handy excuse. "Thanks. Your bedroom is as lovely as the rest of the house."

"Gussie helped me redecorate last year. It took a while after Jean's death before I could bear to change the house."

"I repainted everything after Jon left. It seemed like the only sensible thing to do. I didn't want to continue living in rooms that reminded me so much of him, and I couldn't afford to move, so I painted."

"Life goes on. We have to go on with it." Riker couldn't believe he was repeating Gussie's exact words. Not so soon. Not to Leah. "Well, I'll be back soon. Just keep the chicken from burning."

Leah brought up the fork in a mock salute. "Will do, General George."

With a smile and a restless feeling, Riker turned toward the house, thinking how good Leah had smelled...all clean and damp and fragrant. The image of her in his shower, using his soap, brought to mind other images that he summarily dismissed. This was not the time nor the place for such thoughts. But as he stepped into his bedroom, he glanced back at Leah. She was watching him, too, but looked away the moment she realized he was looking. He could imagine the expression in her dark eyes— one of chagrin at being caught, mixed with one of determination not to let it show—he could only wonder what she might be thinking.

Which was probably for the best, considering that he found himself thinking about what might have happened between the two of them under different circumstances. What would have happened, he wondered, if the only thing they'd discovered in that grocery store was a common interest in banana peppers.

"CAN KATIE spend the night?" Marta asked after dinner. "We want to stay up late and watch television and play." With hope-bright eyes, she turned to Leah. "You can stay, too, Mrs. Taylor. You could share Gussie's bed."

Riker developed a cough. "You might want to check with your grandmother, Marta Grace, before you invite someone to share her bed."

"She wouldn't mind, Daddy. She likes to sleep on the floor, anyway." Marta swung around to face Leah. "It wouldn't be any trouble at all, Mrs. Taylor. I promise."

"That's very nice of you, Marta, but Katie and I have beds of our own at home. We'll—"

"But, Mommy..." Katie, who'd been quiet so far, jumped in with a high-pitched complaint. "Why can't I spend the night? I'll be good. I won't cause Mr. Westfall any trouble and I won't say anything to embarrass you. I promise. Just please, please let me stay."

Leah cast a helpless look at Riker, hoping against hope he might join her in a united front against this dual assault. "Not tonight, Katie," she said in a voice she hoped showed no sign of weakness. "Maybe some other time."

"That's what you said last week." Katie moaned as if she felt actual pain. "Didn't she, Marta? She said I could and then she changed her mind."

Marta didn't seem quite so reserved with Katie around. "Please, Mrs. Taylor," she begged. "I'll take care of her. She can wear some of my pajamas and Daddy will get a toothbrush for her. Won't you, Daddy?"

"I think there's a puppy loose in here, somewhere. Listen to all that whining." Riker frowned as he glanced around the dining room. "Did you two let a puppy in here?"

"A puppy?" Marta was easily distracted.

"A puppy?" Katie was a bit more cautious. "I didn't hear a puppy."

"Hmmm." Riker rubbed his jaw as if perplexed. "Maybe it was Brownie Bear I heard. I'll bet he's set out the tea party and doesn't have anyone to play with. Do you hear it, Leah?"

Conscious of Katie's skeptical gaze, Leah paused to listen. "I do hear something. Maybe you girls should run upstairs and find out what it is."

Katie pushed back her chair. "Come on, Marta. That means I can't spend the night."

Marta glanced at the adults, as if confirming the truth of the statement. Then a smile curved her cupid's bow mouth and she grabbed Katie's hand and leaned close to whisper. "I've got an idea."

Leah watched them race out of the room and heard the *thumpity thump* of their footsteps going up the stairs. "Thanks, Riker. I wasn't sure you would support me on this one."

He shrugged. "We do have extenuating circumstances in play, here. Katie and Marta are identical twins, not simply two children who are becoming friends. I understand your concern."

"I'm not sure you do. You…and Marta…have so much. Materially, I mean. And Katie is just as susceptible as any other child to wanting…well, more than I can comfortably provide." Leah hated this. She hated having to confess that there were many things Katie wanted that, financially, it was impossible for Leah to provide. But she felt she had to explain to Riker, if only to be fair. "One of the reasons I was hesitant about bringing

Katie over here was that I thought she might become jealous of all the extras Marta has. That could create problems for all of us. Katie especially. I don't want her to think she can ask you for a dollar any time she hears the ice cream truck. I don't want to offend you, but...."

Leah knew she was a little late in expressing this particular concern. Katie was here. She'd already been exposed to the lifestyle, to the idea that Marta had more material possessions. But Leah still needed Riker to understand and support her in this.

"The only way you will offend me, Leah," Riker said. "...is to deny me the occasional pleasure of giving Katie an ice cream. I won't try to buy her good will, if that's what you're afraid of, but I'm not going to say I won't sometimes offer your daughter a gift. Marta needs to learn about sharing as much as Katie needs to learn that material things don't always bring happiness." He paused, smiled. "You'll have to let go of Katie a little, Leah. She and Marta are going to want to spend time together. Eventually I'll have to entrust Marta with you and you'll have to entrust Katie with me. We can't continue to chaperon every visit."

"This is only the second one."

"Third, if you count the picnic."

Leah decided to end this uncomfortable conversation. "Well, she's not spending the night this time, if only because she whined and complained." Placing her napkin on the table, she pushed back her chair. "Let's clean the kitchen. Katie and I will have to leave pretty soon."

"You don't know what you're suggesting," Riker said, tossing his napkin on the table. He stood, offering his hand to Leah. "Gussie made her 'snacks' for the Wildlife meeting and the kitchen may never be the same again."

"Oh, I'm sure we can make it presentable." Leah placed her hand in Riker's and allowed him to pull her from the chair. If he held her hand a moment too long, she pretended not to notice. If her skin felt too warm from his touch, she decided it was a result of the exercise of the earlier swim. If her heart beat a little bit faster, she attributed it to worrying about Katie. "Gussie will appreciate coming home to a clean kitchen. There are days when

I'd mortgage my soul if only I could come home to find my house clean and the laundry done.''

A sympathetic smile curved his lips. "I guess Katie's a little young to help out much."

"I'm not sure Katie will ever 'help out much' around the house. She's much better at creating chaos than cleaning it up." Leah paused in the action of stacking her plate on top of Katie's. "That sounds like she's a terrible burden to me, doesn't it? I didn't mean it that way at all. She does help fold clothes and I insist she pick up after herself. Most of the time, she's really a delight to have around. It's just that sometimes her energy exceeds all known boundaries and I have a hard time keeping up."

Riker's laugh was slow and gentle. "Is that when she swallows stars?"

Leah smiled, responding to his warm, nonjudgmental tone. "And calls phone numbers she hears on television. And pulls the sheets off her bed and knots them together so she can be Rapunzel. There's no way to anticipate what Katie will do next."

"She and Marta are good for each other, Leah. I think that as time goes on, we're going to see that we made the right decision."

She hoped he was right. She sincerely hoped he was right. "Let's make the right decision now and wash these dishes before Gussie comes home and finds us yakking away instead of working."

"She wouldn't be more pleased one way or the other. Gussie is a free spirit, who believes everyone should do just what they feel like doing." Riker took the plates Leah held and set them back on the table. "Let's go out to the pool and put away the inflatable toys before it gets completely dark outside. Then, we'll turn our energies toward the kitchen."

"I could start on the kitchen while you take care of the pool," Leah suggested, as much in self-defense as for any other reason. "Then we'd be through faster."

"And you'd go home sooner. No, we'll tackle this together, one chore at a time." He slipped a hand into the back pocket of his jeans and regarded her thoughtfully. "You really don't have to help with either job if you don't want to. You can go in the living room and count Gussie's stitches, if you'd rather.''

It would be the safe and prudent thing to do, but Leah shook her head. ''I'll help. Just show me what to do. I'm not overly familiar with the care and maintenance of pool accessories.''

''I'll show you exactly what to do.''

When they reached the pool, Riker opened the stone and cedar storage shed and then turned around to fish an inflatable giraffe, a zebra, a crocodile and an inner tube from the pool. ''Flip the valve cover and squeeze until it's flat,'' he instructed as he handed two of the vinyl animals to Leah. ''When we've squished them into a manageable lump, we'll put them in the shed and, voilà! One chore done.''

Leah hugged the zebra as the air hissed from the valve, but she was still squeezing when Riker had the crocodile folded in a flat bundle. Determined to accomplish her end of the task, she resorted to sitting on the inflated areas and jumping up and down. She saw Marta and Katie in the upstairs window and waved, but they immediately disappeared from view.

''I wonder why Katie and Marta didn't come out to help us,'' she said to Riker as he stepped inside the shed and placed the shrunken pool toys on a shelf in the storage building. ''Jumping up and down on a giraffe is right up Katie's alley.''

''They're probably planning a new strategy on how to get you to let Katie spend the night.''

Leah followed him inside the shed, handed him the toys she held and brushed a couple of water droplets from her blouse. ''I'm sure you're right. Katie never gives up after only one attack. Usually she—''

The door of the shed creaked and then slammed shut as if it had been caught by a fierce gust of wind. Inside, dust flew and Leah sneezed. The only window was high on the back wall and without the light coming in through the open door, the room was dark and small.

''How did that happen?'' Riker moved past Leah, brushing against her in the darkness. ''Did the wind come up all of a sudden?''

Leah thought it was more likely that mischief had cropped up all of a sudden. Mischief in the form of two children. "Can you get it open?" she asked.

"I think so."

She could hear the sounds of his effort as he worked with the inside latch.

"Seems to be stuck. Was the key still in the doorknob when we came in here? I can't remember if I took it out."

"It was in the door." Leah could see the lock and key in her mind's eyes. It was hardly an intricate system requiring any great effort to secure. It was just a simple door with a simple lock.

And she and Riker were just simply locked in.

Chapter Eight

"I can't get it open." Riker sounded surprised. "I can't believe this. It's not supposed to lock on the inside."

"I'll bet this is the first time it's been tested." Leah wrapped her arms across her chest...not because it was cold, but because she suddenly realized how small, how close the little room was. "Maybe we should yell for help."

Riker glanced over his shoulder. She could just about make out the rueful lift of his brow in the dim light. "Who's going to hear us? Gussie's gone and the girls don't even know we're out here."

"They know."

"They might come looking for—" He turned around. "They know?"

"They saw us from the upstairs window. I waved. I wouldn't be a bit surprised if they weren't the 'gust' of wind that got us locked in here."

"Marta wouldn't do something like that."

Leah said nothing because she knew better than to ever say Katie wouldn't do something.

"You don't really think they would...?" The idea tripped from Riker's tongue like an erratic leak. He couldn't quite believe, but he was wondering, trying to determine if his Marta might have had something to do with their dilemma. "Why would they lock us in here?"

Leah sighed and tried to locate a place to sit. "If we're stuck out here, we'll have plenty of time to change our minds about letting Katie spend the night.''

"They're six, going on seven, Leah. Marta and Katie couldn't make such a premeditated decision. They wouldn't lock us in.''

"No, but they might shut the door, escape back to the house and wait for us to chase after them. And if we don't, they probably won't think the door might have locked. And they'll be afraid we're mad. And they won't take the chance of finding out for sure.'' Leah found a slatted wood box that felt sturdy enough to hold her and sat down. "When will Gussie be home?''

Riker rattled the door. "I don't believe this,'' he said. "Who knows when my mother will get here. And when she does, she might not even realize we're missing.''

Leah smiled, not excited about the prospect of being locked in the storage building for hours, but not really worried that they wouldn't be rescued. "I don't think those two little girls will be able to keep it a secret, Riker. Katie might dream up the mischievous idea of closing the door on us, but she'll begin to worry about me in a little while. When it gets good and dark.''

"So what do we do until the guilts sets in?''

"There's another box. You may as well sit down.''

He did and Leah was immediately sorry she'd suggested it. The close quarters brought his thigh into contact with hers. His arm lay close enough that she could feel the warmth of his body. She could smell the scent of his soap and his shampoo. That familiar, musky fragrance seemed to blend and encircle her. She should never have gotten into his shower. She should never have left the kitchen. She was going to strangle Katie for this.

"Got any cards?'' she asked.

"Only if you want to play Old Maid. I haven't played with a real deck of cards in ages.''

"Not much time for adults games, is there?''

"No. Who would have thought that being a parent could be so…confining?''

"Funny, Riker. If you had a screwdriver, you could probably take the door off the hinges.''

"The pivotal word there being 'if.' I don't keep any tools out here, only the pool supplies.'' He moved restlessly beside her then stood and paced one and a half strides to the door before he turned. "Want to play Twenty Questions?"

"As your mother said earlier, surely we can find something to talk about to keep from being bored."

"I'm not bored, Leah. I'm trying to get my mind off Marta and what I'm going to do to her when we get out of here."

She was glad to hear that note of impatience in his voice. It was good to know he sometimes lost a bit of his "cool." "Marta might not have had a thing to do with this, Riker."

"Do you honestly think Katie would have locked us in here by herself?"

Tricky question. "I don't think she meant to *lock* us in. I think she just meant to *shut* us in. There is a difference."

"Hard to appreciate it at the moment, though, isn't it?" He came back to where she sat, looked up at the small window. "Katie can't take all the blame for this. Marta is at least equally guilty."

"We may have created a monster, Riker, bringing the two of them together." The memory of the twins' identical smiles made Leah sigh. "You know, when I was a child, I used to think it would be great to have a twin. It seemed like it would be so much fun."

"And now you know."

"They didn't really mean any harm."

"You're sounding like a doting parent. Next you'll be telling me how cute they are."

Leah couldn't resist. "Have you ever seen a cuter pair?"

"After tonight, I may start looking." With a resolute movement, he resumed his place beside her. "Right now I'm not much in the mood to be a parent. Let's talk about something other than our children."

Leah felt safer talking about the girls, but she didn't say so. "You lead, I'll follow. Any subject except politics or computers."

His chuckle was warm and comforting and he smiled at her. "Religion okay?"

"I'm Lutheran. I don't think there's much else to say, unless you want to confess your affiliation."

"Presbyterian."

"See?" she said. "We've run out of subject matter already."

"We could always go a round of 'Truth or Dare.'"

"Thanks, but I'll pass. You really have a thing about games, don't you, Riker?"

"I was deprived as a child. My mother took me to peace rallies and protest marches instead of playing with me. It seriously affected my development."

"Peace rallies?" Leah found that interesting. "Gussie was a part of the sixties?"

"It was the best decade of her life." There was humor and tolerance and admiration in his voice. "No, I can't say that. Every decade, every year is the best one. She has a gift for living. Did you know she was in the Peace Corps?"

From there, it was an easy step into the story of Riker's year with his father and of the next year's trip around the world with his mother. Leah tried to visualize him as a twelve-year-old boy, tramping through the Andes and the Eiffel Tower, seeing things most people never got a chance to see. "What an adventure for you, Riker. You must have been so excited."

"I was too young to appreciate it. I've forgotten so much about what we saw. Mainly I have memories of Gussie. The things she said, not the 'big picture' she wanted me to see." He clasped his hands and leaned forward to rest his elbows on his knees. "Which goes to show that my mother had far more influence over me than anything else. I have only a vague memory of the Taj Mahal, but I clearly remember the story my mother told me while we stood in front of it."

"She told you about Shah Jahan and how he loved his wife so much he built the Taj Mahal for her burial crypt." Leah sighed with envy. "I would love to see it. I'd love to see anyplace. I'd like to go to Oklahoma City. As you may have gathered, I'm not what you'd call well traveled."

Riker turned his head to look at her. "Traveling's not all it's cracked up to be. The story my mother told me in front of the Taj Mahal was the one about when she got arrested for burning her bra."

"You're kidding."

"What? That she burned her bra or that she told me about it in front of the most beautiful building in the world?" He gave a throaty laugh. "There's never any reason to kid about the adventures of Augusta Bird Westfall."

"Her middle name is Bird?"

"Her maiden name. The mystery is how she and my father ever got together in the first place. I think my paternal grandparents each had a massive coronary when my father said he was going to marry her."

"But their marriage was happy, wasn't it?"

Riker seemed to consider that. "As happy as a far right conservative and a revolutionary can be together, I suppose. They had some tremendous fights. But they did stay together, and they loved each other. He died eleven years ago."

"I'm sorry."

Riker gave that little shrug people sometimes give when the hurt is old but not forgotten. "He had a good life, a happy life. It's been harder to rationalize Jean's death. She suffered. We all did. I don't ever want to go through that kind of loss again."

Leah heard the pain in his voice and this time, there was no shrug of acceptance. "It would be great if we could all simply pick and choose how we'd prefer to suffer."

The air went still, thick with memories and emotion. Riker challenged the silence first. "You and I have had our share of loss, haven't we? Whatever the religious beliefs, loss changes the way we live, our perspective, how we handle a crisis."

"A crisis like being locked in a shed with only a deck of Old Maid cards for entertainment?" Leah didn't want the talk to turn serious. The room was too small, he was too close, the intimacy of shared emotions was filled with hazard.

"I lied about the cards."

"It's probably just as well. We'd have to have a flashlight to play."

"So, I guess we're back to Twenty Questions. Or are we down to Nineteen, now?"

"I think we're ready for the next topic of discussion. What's it to be?"

"Education reform?" he suggested, then shook his head. "No,

too political. Let's mark off societal problems. They inherently lead to politics. How do you feel about sports?''

"As a whole? Individually? Or the politics of college sport programs?''

"You sound like Gussie. But she does love a good basketball game.''

"So do I. Katie plays soccer, so of course, I like that. Except for the early-morning games. What I wouldn't give to sleep in on a few of those Saturdays.''

"Those are the times you miss having the other parent around, aren't they? Someone to whom you can say, *Honey, this is your week to take her to soccer,* and roll over in bed and go back to sleep.''

"Just having someone to go with me to the games would be a help," Leah admitted. "And I sometimes wish I could share just a little of the responsibility. Although I can't really say I miss that, because I've never had anyone who would share. Jonathan was not big on responsibility, shared or otherwise.''

"Obviously." Riker's voice held impatience and poorly disguised contempt. "He's missed out on a lot of good things, Leah. He'll be sorry someday.''

"I doubt it." She picked up on Riker's skeptical look. "Really. Jonathan must have planned his escape for months. He had money stashed somewhere. And I found that most of his treasured possessions had disappeared, too. I felt like a total fool when I realized how efficiently he'd planned his departure and how blindly I'd ignored the clues. But he's not sorry he left." She paused. "Luckily, neither am I.''

"You sound remarkably composed about it. I'm afraid, under the same set of circumstances, I'd still be full of anger.''

"Anger is nonproductive and, in a lot of ways, it was a relief when he was gone." Leah ran a finger under the cuff of her shorts, smoothing the fabric, giving her hands something to do. "When I realized he hadn't been kidnapped or murdered or anything really awful, I was mad that he hadn't had the decency to leave me with some dignity, to end our marriage with some semblance of respect. I still get angry when I think about that and about what he's done to Katie. But after a while, anger takes too much energy. I need that energy for Katie and for surviving. You probably experienced more anger in dealing with Jean's death than I did through all of Jonathan's disappearance.''

Riker considered that. "I was angry off and on through her illness and for quite a while after she died. It wasn't fair and I hated it.''

Leah shivered. She didn't want to hear this. She didn't want to know about his grief. She didn't want to reveal hers. Riker had too great a hold on her already. "It's getting cooler. The wind must have picked up. Maybe if we yell, the girls will hear us and venture out to see what the noise is.''

"Maybe, but I doubt it. If you're cold, we'll just have to huddle close together.''

Before Leah could manage to voice a protest, Riker had scooted his box stool up against hers and put his arm around her. "Riker, I'm not—''

"This is an emergency, Leah. Don't take it personally.'' He settled his arm across her shoulders and closed his hand over her nearly bare upper arm. *Don't take it personally,* he said. As if she should just ignore the exaggerated rhythm of her heart and the indecent degree of warmth radiating from his body into hers.

"I'm not really that cold,'' she said.

"It has gotten cooler since the sun went down. It's still May, too early yet for those warm, Oklahoma evenings. No telling how long we'll be out here. We may as well stay as warm as we can for as long as we can.'' He squeezed her arm. "Don't worry. I don't mind being close to you.''

The understatement of the year, he thought as the words left his mouth. He was finding that being close to Leah was quite a pleasurable experience. Her hair brushed his cheek, momentarily catching on the early shadow of tomorrow's beard. He liked the feel of it, the spicy scent that clung to her, the softness of her skin beneath his fingers. A yearning to taste her stirred like a forbidden impulse inside him. He wondered what it would be like to kiss Leah, to pull her into the full circle of his arms, to press his lips against hers. He wondered what he was doing, thinking like that. It had been two years since Jean's death and in all that time, not once had he anticipated a kiss or wondered what it might be like. This was dangerous…and unexpected.

"How about a round of camp-fire songs?" he suggested because he needed a light, uncomplicated atmosphere. "I think I remember the chorus of 'Moonlight Bay.'"

"Feel free." Leah crossed her arms below her breasts, a protective gesture Riker recognized, whether she did or not. "I only sing in the shower."

"Pity. I think a few verses of 'Found A Peanut' might bring out the fire department."

She was going to need the fire department, Leah thought, if her body temperature didn't stop shooting up every time he made the slightest move. She ought to get up, walk around, cool down. If she were cold, surely there was a towel out here somewhere. This was a pool house, wasn't it? "Maybe you ought to try the door again. Maybe it's not locked anymore."

"You go ahead." He let go of her arm, but stayed close beside her. "Give it the old college try."

She was on her feet like a shot and rattling the doorknob a moment later. "Won't turn," she said. "I guess Katie hasn't had a strong enough attack of conscience, yet."

"We haven't been out here all that long, Leah. Probably twenty minutes at the most."

It seemed longer. And it was getting longer by the second. She rattled the knob again, pushed at the frame with her hip. "If we pushed together, we might be able to break it." A desperate measure, she knew, but…she was getting desperate. "You could fix the door later."

She heard the sounds of his movements but she was unprepared when he stopped so close to her. Closer than he'd been when they were sitting on the crates. Closer than she really wished he was. "Here," she said breathily. "Put your hands against the door and I'll put my…"

Where she'd intended to put her hands or hip or whatever seemed suddenly unimportant as his hands came to rest against the door, on either side of her shoulders.

"This won't work, Leah." His voice was low, husky, mesmerizing. His breath was warm and tantalizing on her lips. "You could get hurt trying to get out. And I don't want you to get hurt. We can wait."

His words flowed around her, warning of the danger, symbolizing something, meaning nothing...or everything. She couldn't breathe. She thought she might never be able to breathe again. "We can wait," she repeated without awareness of what she said. He was too close. And she was falling...

His head bent. Her chin lifted. A shallow sigh echoed in the narrowing distance between his lips and hers.

"Riker! Leah! Are you out here?"

Gussie's voice shattered the silence. Leah's heart jumped to her throat. Riker lifted his head and released his breath in a shuddering rush. "Gussie's home," he whispered, as if asking Leah whether or not he should answer his mother's call. A second ticked by. "We're rescued," he said.

"Rescued." The word formed on Leah's lips, but she couldn't quite manage the sound waves. She had almost kissed Riker Westfall. The thought was frightening. The realization that she regretted the interruption was even more so.

"Out here, Gussie." Riker's voice rose above Leah's head and carried out across the pool. "We're in the shed."

"Well, what are you doing in there? Hiding out?" Gussie called back. "Were these two elves more than you could handle?"

The fainter sounds of Katie's and Marta's voices drifted through the night to reach Leah. Katie, she thought. For the past few minutes, she'd forgotten about Katie. And she'd almost kissed Riker. What kind of mother was she?

In the dark, she felt Riker watching her and she fought the impulse to touch his face and let him know she was as aware as he was of the mistake they'd almost made. And it would have been a mistake. No doubt about—

"Mommy," Katie called softly at the door. "Are you in there?"

"Yes, Katie. Stand back and let Gussie unlock the door."

"It's locked?" Gussie asked. "Where's the key?"

"Look on the ground, Gus." Riker instructed, moving a discreet distance from Leah. "It must have fallen out when the door closed."

"Now, how did that happen?" Gussie's voice faded as if she'd dropped to her knees and had her head bent. "I've never gotten locked in this shed. Have you, Marta?"

There was a guilty pause. Not long, but long enough. "No," Marta said. "Did it lock, Daddy?"

"It locked, Marta." Riker ran a hand through his hair. "Where have you and Katie been all this time, Marta Grace? Didn't you miss me? Didn't you wonder why Mrs. Taylor and I weren't in the house?"

Again the pause. Again the foreshadowing of guilt. "No."

"We were playing," Katie said, raising her voice as if she'd decided she had to be louder to be heard. "Marta has the best toys, Mommy. She has four Barbie dolls. She said I could have one, but I knew I'd have to ask you and—"

"Got it," Gussie's voice cut through Katie's rambling. "It must have fallen out, hit the ground and bounced over here."

No indication of just where the key had bounced, but Leah heard the scratchy noise as it was inserted in the knob and suddenly the lack of information was a moot point. Riker's hand touched her shoulder, squeezed gently, and then dropped away as the door swung open to reveal Gussie's curious expression and the questioning expressions on two identical faces.

"Hi, Daddy," Marta said.

"Are you okay?" Katie asked.

"What's going on?" Gussie put one hand on each girl and moved them out of the way so that Leah and Riker could step out of the dark shed into the light of a million stars and a couple of incandescent porch lamps. "How did both of you manage to get locked in the pool shed?"

"That's a mystery, isn't it?" Riker directed his question to his daughter. Leah fastened a suspicious look on Katie.

Marta broke first under the pressure. "We didn't know it locked, Daddy. Katie said it would be funny and I know we're not s'posed to be around the pool if you're not there, but you were out here, and…and…"

"It was Marta's idea." Katie made a stab at shifting the blame, but when Marta sniffed with her first guilty tear, Katie's shoulders drooped and her chin dropped to her chest. "I helped."

Leah was afraid Riker would weaken with the introduction of the twins' tears and she decided to intervene. "Let's go into the house," she said. "I think you two young ladies have some explaining to do and I, at least, want to be comfortable while you do it."

The confession took ten minutes, maybe less. Riker frowned. Marta cried. Leah shook her head. Katie cried. Gussie tried her best to hide a smile. In the end, the girls were very sorry for misbehaving and promised faithfully that they would not get into such mischief again. There was a moment in which Leah caught Riker's glance and felt his thoughts turn to her. Did she think the girls should be punished or were their guilt and chastisement penance enough? He didn't ask her aloud, but Leah knew he was joining forces with her. Not against the twins, but for their own good. She didn't want to align herself beside him, but under the circumstances, what else could she do?

DURING THE COMING weeks, as May turned toward June and spring toward summer, Leah found herself more and more aligned with Riker in various united fronts *for* the twins. Katie and Marta couldn't seem to get enough of each other and Leah sometimes wondered if she was ever again going to spend time alone with her daughter. Marta always seemed to be around, evenings, weekends, in person or on the telephone. If Marta wasn't at Katie's house, Katie was at Marta's. If Marta didn't badger Riker into letting her call Katie, Katie conned Leah into letting her use the phone to call Marta. Every Friday night was an "overnight." If not at the Taylors' house, then at the Westfalls'. When school let out for summer break, *spending the night* became the main words in Katie's vocabulary. *It's all right with my dad,* Marta said almost as often.

The bond of birth held the two in a relationship Leah and Riker recognized but still didn't quite understand. She and Riker watched together as their daughters moved from being playmates to being sisters. Identical twin sisters.

It was not a comfortable transformation for a mother to witness, Leah thought. Especially when she was mother only to one. She and Riker discussed—endlessly, it seemed—the problems involved in parenting twin daughters from separate homes and separate backgrounds. Leah wondered if some of their lengthy discussions—generally undertaken while the girls played nearby—weren't simply avoidance mechanisms to keep the man/woman attraction between them at bay. It worked, she supposed, because her relationship with Riker had evolved into a friendly with-definite-limits kind of relationship. He didn't sit close to her and she didn't sit close to him and life was easier that way.

Until the ballet ticket arrived in the mail.

Chapter Nine

"You have sighed long and longingly over that ticket for two days now," Susannah said, wiping the table with the edge of her palm and setting the fast-food chain sack square in the middle. "For Pete's sake, Leah. Go to the ballet. It will make you happy. It will make me happy. Who cares where the ticket came from?"

"I don't have a good feeling about going." Leah opened the sack and took out two salads. "Why don't we ever go out for lunch?"

"Because we're under the thumb of Tyrant Tom and he holds us to the thirty-minute lunch. Which means a brought-from-home bologna sandwich or this prepackaged, garden-variety salad from the drive-through down the street." Susannah made a face before taking off the plastic lid and applying two ready-serve packages of salad dressing. "Did I tell you that our boss called me the other night? At home? After ten?"

"He wanted you to do a layout before midnight, right?"

"He asked me to go to the races this Saturday." Susannah popped a crouton into her mouth and chewed noisily. "I think he actually asked me for a date, but I'm not certain, yet. I'll let you know on Monday." She smiled as she took a mouthful of salad. "And you can tell me all about the ballet."

"It's *The Merry Widow* and *Rodeo*," Leah said as she ran the tines of the plastic fork over the lettuce in front of her. "But I can't go. The ticket just came in the mail. No card or note or anything."

"Your fairy godmother sent it."

Leah shot her a cynical look. "It was sent to me by mistake. I just don't know how to return it."

"Okay, you're right, it was a mistake. So use it. Whoever sent it wrote down the wrong address. Their bad luck. Your lucky day." Susannah reached across the table, letting her blondish-brown hair swing over her shoulder before she pushed it back impatiently. "Are you going to use this?" She picked up one of Leah's salad dressing packets and tore the designated corner. "The way I see it, Leah, you're not hurting anyone by using the ticket, you're dying to go, and you're not tied down on Friday night. Katie will be at Marta's. Treat yourself. Please."

It was tempting. Leah had thought about doing just that for two days now. Where was the harm? She couldn't return the ticket. It had been addressed to her, even if she didn't know where it had come from. And she would love to see the ballet. "What if it's a...setup?"

"A setup?" Susannah laid down her fork. "As in a blind date setup, you mean?"

The thought that Riker had sent the ticket had occurred to Leah more than once. She didn't quite have the nerve to ask him. "Tickets to things like *Rodeo* and *The Merry Widow* usually come in pairs," she said evenly, hoping her friend might provide an explanation she herself had overlooked.

"A setup." Susannah shook her head and ate some more salad. "Loosen up, Leah. I'm going to the stock-car races with our boss, for heaven's sake. Can't you drive into Tulsa on the off chance that you'll have a pleasant evening at the ballet, regardless of who might be sitting next to you?"

It sounded sensible enough when put like that, Leah thought. But if Riker happened to be sitting next to her. If he happened to have accidentally on purpose sent the ticket to her...

"I don't know, Susannah."

"It's only Thursday. You have twenty-four hours to make up your mind. And blind dates aren't always so bad, you know. I've had one or two that turned out all right."

Leah laughed. "Oh, yes. I recall. The guy with the toupee and the man who spoke only a dozen words of English. What was it he said? *Will you marry me and be the mother of my children?"*

"That isn't quite the way he said it." Susannah made a face and pushed the depleted salad container away from her. "He always put a *please* on the end. But that's neither here nor there, Leah. The ballet ticket is in your hand. It's fate. Kismet. Live a little."

Leah hadn't said much to Susannah about Riker Westfall. She'd kept most of the information she offered centered on Katie and Marta and their relationship. Susannah had asked, but she hadn't pushed and Leah hoped her friend didn't know just how attractive Riker was. "Well," Leah said. "Maybe you're right. If you can go with Tom to the races on a maybe date, then I can follow the call of adventure to the Tulsa Performing Arts Center and see what awaits me there."

"Good idea." Susannah smiled and leaned her chin on the palm of her hand. "Are you going to eat the rest of your salad?"

The theater was crowded when she arrived. Parking was difficult, but she finally followed a line of cars into the underground garage and found a space. It had felt funny leaving Katie, knowing she, Leah, was going someplace special, someplace adult. Of course, she would have loved to have brought Katie with her. Many of the people entering the building had small children with them.

But there'd been only one ticket. And Katie had been excited about spending the night with Marta. She'd tried in every way possible to help Leah get ready to go. She'd asked question after question. *Mommy, why don't you wear these earrings? Mommy, don't you want to put on some lipstick? Mommy, will you stay out late? Mommy, why don't you put your hair up on top of your head like the ballerinas do? Want some flowers for your hair, Mommy?* Leah had been relieved to drop Katie into Gussie's waiting hands. Riker had been nowhere to be seen and Leah told herself he was probably working late.

Not until she saw the back of his head as she approached the aisle where her seat was located, did she panic. She came within a breath of turning around and walking out. But...well...there was the stage and the orchestra was tuning up and there was an empty seat…and she did want to stay. Lifting her chin, she decided to enjoy the ballet first and tell Riker what she thought of his trick later.

He looked astonished when she slipped into the chair beside him. "Fancy meeting you here," she said and adjusted the hem of her skirt over her knees. She set her evening bag in her lap and then offered him a gently chastising smile. "Thanks for the ticket. I love the ballet."

His lips didn't match the curve of hers, humor didn't quite touch the blue of his eyes. "You'd better thank Marta, not me."

"Marta?" Leah lifted her eyebrows skeptically. "How would Marta have gotten a ticket?"

"From my desk. She was supposed to come with me. She even suggested it. A father/daughter evening out, she called it. I got the tickets. Then she decided it would be more fun to have Katie spend the night. I said no. She fussed. I gave in. And when I got here with what I thought were two tickets in the envelope, there was only one. So here I am. How about you?"

"I got the ticket in the mail."

"What?"

She shrugged. "The mail. No note. Just the ticket. No return address, either. And it was postmarked Tulsa."

Riker nodded solemnly. "The postmark implicates my mother."

"You think Gussie sent the ticket?"

"I expect so. But I don't think she's working alone."

"Katie must have mentioned something to Gussie about how much I wanted to see these ballets."

"Or Marta decided it would be a romantic evening for two."

"Romantic?" Leah's voice almost trembled on the word. "Marta wouldn't think that. Katie certainly wouldn't." Leah turned her head toward Riker, shared a look that asked and answered the question. "Would they?"

"Let's just say I wouldn't lay any money on what the two of them couldn't think up together. They've spent a lot of time on the phone lately."

"And together. But you don't really believe they could plan and pull off something like this, do you?"

For the first time tonight a slow smile tipped his mouth. "You're here and I'm here. Any other questions?"

"But that's so..." Leah searched for what she was trying to convey. "...premeditated. They're only six."

"Nearly seven and obviously going on twenty-one. Face it, Leah. We're here on a blind date, set up by our loving daughters. With some discreet help from my mother."

The orchestra burst into the overture and the lights dimmed. Leah turned automatically to face the stage, aware of Riker sitting tall and straight beside her, aware that she was, for all practical purposes, his date. Could Katie have planned this? Even with outside help? Were the twins up to their pert little noses in matchmaking?

Incredible idea. Silly. Stupid, even. Maybe Riker had sent the ticket and was now trying to cover his tracks in case she got angry.

But that wasn't Riker's way. If he'd wanted to take her to the ballet, he'd have asked her straight out, no anonymous tickets or wild tales about children who tried to fix up one parent with another. Leah would have a talk with Katie tomorrow. Marta, too, perhaps. But tomorrow was several hours away and for the next few hours she was on a date.

A date.

She hoped she didn't pass out from nerves before she had a chance to enjoy it.

"Do you want to go get something to eat?" Riker asked when it was over. He half hoped she'd refuse. He'd hardly been able to enjoy the ballet for all the effort it took to pretend it didn't make any difference that Leah was sitting beside him. She looked startled by the suggestion. Did she think he was only being polite? Was he?

"We could meet somewhere," he said as if there was no question she would agree to go. "Or you could leave your car parked and we could take mine."

"My car's in the covered garage. I don't think I can come

back later and get it." She gripped her bag with both hands, then with a small self-conscious gesture, she tucked it under her arm. "I'm not sure I could eat so late. I'm usually ready for bed by this time of night."

He smiled. "Actually it isn't very late. A little after ten, I believe. And I'm certainly not going to insist you eat anything. But it would be nice of you to keep me company while I do."

Her gaze lifted to meet his, her brown eyes locked with his blue ones in a moment of indecision. He began to hope she wouldn't refuse, even though he knew it was a dumb thing to wish for.

"Well, maybe something cold to drink...?"

It was a question and he immediately answered. "A drink. Good idea, Leah. I'll walk you to your car and we can drive to where mine is parked."

As in everything else, Riker took charge of the situation, leading the way through the maze of hallways to the stairs that connected the lower level parking garage to the theaters and galleries of the Performing Arts Center. Leah ignored as best she could, the random touches of his hand at her elbow or at the small of her back. She appreciated his guidance, his self-assured way of moving through the crowd, but she wished it didn't stir such a fluttery feeling in her stomach.

Awareness. She recognized it, could almost feel it envelop her as they walked toward her car. She shouldn't be going anywhere with this man. For the past month and a half, she'd spent far too much time with him anyway. It was insanity to stroll at his side, just the two of them, as if they were simply a man and a woman enjoying each other's company. Katie and Marta should be between them, a constant reminder of priorities and responsibilities. If she hadn't liked Riker so much, it might not have mattered. If she didn't know he liked her, too, it might have mattered even less.

But she did know. And so did he.

"Shall I drive?" he asked. "Since I know where I parked and how to get there?"

It seemed childish to refuse. She handed him the keys and got in on the passenger side, telling herself she was an adult. She could handle this situation, this attraction. She wouldn't let anything happen. She couldn't. She had Katie to consider. "Where are we going?" she asked, snapping the buckle of her seat belt. She turned to smile confidently at Riker. "After we get your car?"

"I don't know. Anyplace special you'd like to go?"

"You're the world traveler. I hardly ever leave home."

"But you used to live in Tulsa. No fond recollections of dining out? No recommendations, however dated, of places to get a drink and a bite to eat?"

Her throat tightened. "None, I'm afraid. It's been years since I lived here and, when I did, Jonathan favored the country club." She paused. "I don't think I want to go there tonight."

"Of course." Riker felt like an idiot. Jonathan probably had been a jerk long before he moved Leah and Katie to Bartlesville and then left them. Her memories of nightlife in Tulsa obviously weren't special. "I know just the place. Now, if only I can remember where I parked my car."

He knew exactly where it was, but her breath of laughter rewarded his small bit of humor. Relax was the key word tonight. He wanted her to relax and realize he was a nice guy. He had no intention of starting anything. Their daughters had gone to a lot of trouble to get them together tonight, and he wanted Leah to enjoy her evening out. She got few enough of those, he knew. Besides, if she relaxed, maybe so would he.

Twenty minutes later, sitting at a corner table in a noisy pub-type restaurant, Riker found it all too easy to be with Leah without Katie's and Marta's supervision. Leah laughed easily. She smiled at all the right moments. She seemed to know what he was going to say almost before he did. She was a comfortable companion.

She was also very pretty. Sitting there, nursing a glass three-quarters full of blush wine, with her dark hair loose and inviting around her face, she was quite easily the most beautiful woman he'd been with in a long time. She was wearing black, a simple little dress that Riker had tried all evening not to look at too closely. He didn't want to notice the creamy V of skin revealed by the dress's neckline and he thought it best not to notice the way the waistline dropped to fit the slim curve of her hips. For the past few weeks, since the night he'd practically kissed her in the shed beside the pool, he'd been cautious. And now all the things he'd been cautious about confronted him full force. He'd known the minute she'd said the words, banana pepper, that he would like her...a lot. Nothing that had happened since had changed his mind.

If only...

If only Katie was here, Leah thought. Katie and Marta. The atmosphere of the pub was far from intimate. The restaurant was full of talk and laughter, the clatter of dishes... But Leah felt closed in. She was alone with Riker. They were talking as adults talk, interspersing the lighthearted sharing of life's trivial, unimportant, necessary details with deeper moments of exchanging opinions and beliefs. They were friends, a man and a woman, trying desperately hard to pretend there was nothing but friendship between them. If only Katie and Marta were here to remind them they couldn't be anything but friends.

"Did you enjoy the ballet?" Riker asked. "It's the first time I've seen *Rodeo*."

"It was fun, wasn't it?" Leah smiled. "And *The Merry Widow* is such a romantic dance. I loved it."

"So did I," he said simply and she liked him all the more.

"The girls would have loved it, I think. Marta especially, since she takes ballet lessons."

"Oh, I think Katie would have been the one enchanted. She's such a little romantic," Riker said.

"*My* Katie?"

Riker's lips slanted in a wry tilt. "Don't tell me you don't know what a dreamer she is. Her head's always in the clouds."

"Well, I know her imagination certainly works overtime." Leah swept the air with a rueful gesture. "We're proof of that. I wonder what they're doing now? What they're plotting? And what they think *we're* doing."

"Probably best not to dwell too much on that last one. If they've set themselves up as matchmakers, we may have to set them straight fast and ruin their fun."

Disappointment made a little wrinkle in Leah's composure,

but, of course he was right. The girls would have to be set straight. Nothing romantic could happen between her and Riker. They were friends. For their daughters' sakes, they had to keep it that way. "If we say anything, it's probably going to make things worse. Katie, little *romantic* that she is, is hard to discourage once she gets an idea in her head."

"Marta, too. It's always amazed me just how stubborn she can be."

"Two of a kind." Leah said it with a smile and realized how far she'd come since she and Riker had first sat alone at a dinner table discussing their twin daughters. "I have to admit, Riker, that they're getting along better than I'd thought possible. And Katie's grades improved toward the end of the school term. I have to give Marta some of the credit. I know Katie decided that if Marta made good grades, then she should, too."

"Marta is better, too. Since Katie came along, she's not so introspective and I do believe she's becoming more daring every day. Gussie thinks it's the best thing that's ever happened."

Leah laughed. "What? That Marta's more daring? Your mother doesn't know yet how nerve-racking 'daring' can be."

"My mother? You're joking. She invented the dare. Trust me, she'd be pleased to see Katie and Marta try anything. And I do mean, anything."

"Then why are we sitting here, while she's watching them and encouraging Lord only knows what new escapade?"

"We're sitting here conserving our energy so we'll be ready to face the results when we get home."

Leah turned the wineglass between her forefinger and thumb. "I do feel replenished. It's been ages since I attended a ballet. Ages since I—" She grabbed for the words. "I'm beginning to sound like Cinderella, locked in my room and never allowed out except to clean and sweep. My life is not devoid of entertainment or outside activities."

"I know that, Leah. You've made quite a nice life for yourself and for Katie. I'm envious of your ability."

"Envious? Of me?" She couldn't stop the startled arch of her eyebrows or the skeptical note in her voice. "Don't be silly, Riker. You and Marta have everything."

"Not everything. No matter how it may look."

He said nothing else. She didn't ask. She didn't want to know what was missing from his life. It might match too neatly with what was missing from her life. "We'd better get back," she said. "It's late and we still have an hour's drive ahead."

"That's right." He frowned with the words. "And we're in separate cars, aren't we? I wish we weren't. The drive goes faster when there's someone to talk to."

Leah didn't relish driving home alone, either. It would be a letdown after the pleasure of this evening. "Next time, we'll have to tell our matchmakers to work out a better arrangement for transportation."

"*Next time,* we'll bypass the middlemen and make our own arrangements."

Smiling, Leah stood, not wanting to meet his eyes and share the certain knowledge that there wouldn't be a next time. "Too bad I don't have a car phone. You could call me and we could talk on the way home."

"I'll follow you all the way," he said as he placed his hand at her waist and they walked to the doorway. "And I'll think about you. That will be almost as nice."

"All I ask is that you stop and help me change a tire if I have a flat."

"Are you kidding?" he said. "I'll call the Automobile Club on my car phone and let them change the tire while I take you home." He held open the door for her. "I'm a man who plans ahead, you see."

"The girls must take after you, then."

The pause that followed was brief, poignant, sad and sweet. Then Riker laughed. Leah laughed, too. And they headed for home.

He followed her all the way, just as he'd said he would. She didn't know if he thought about her all the way, too, but she thought about him. She thought he'd drop off when they reached Adams Boulevard, but he stayed behind her until she pulled into the driveway of her house. It felt odd coming home to a dark and silent house. Usually, when she went out at night, Katie was with her. Usually, she didn't come home so late. She opened the car door. Riker walked up the driveway to where she stood in the small pool of light from the car's dome light. What was he doing? He should have gone on. "There was no need for you to—"

"I'm going to make sure you get home safely." He said it in a tone that brooked no argument.

So Leah didn't argue. In silence, intimate silence, they walked to the side of the house and she unlocked the door. "Safe," she said as she stepped inside and switched on the light.

He stepped past her. "Let's make sure."

When he was satisfied that she was, indeed, safe, Leah walked him back to the door and waited as he stepped outside. She reached for the screen door to pull it closed, but he stopped, blocking her way. "I had a lovely evening, Leah. I wish I'd thought of asking you to the ballet, myself."

"I wouldn't have gone." Since she wanted him to understand that she would have wanted to go, but she wouldn't have done so, she added, "But I had a lovely evening, too."

"I guess I can't say let's do it again, can I?"

She swallowed. "I guess not."

He nodded and the silence lengthened, winding around the two of them, holding them, midnight still.

"Good night, Riker."

He lifted his head, his gaze caught hers and then he stepped up, put his hands on her shoulders and bent his head to kiss her. Leah had time to stop him. But she didn't. And when his arms went around her, she stepped inside their circle.

His kiss was long and agonizingly sweet. It had been a long time since she'd been kissed by a man. It had been years since she'd enjoyed being kissed. She tried to savor the moment, so she could bring out the memory like a warm, wool shawl, on some future wintry day.

And then, like winter, she was cold again and Riker was stepping away from her. At the edge of the doorway, he paused and offered her a quiet smile. "Good night, Cinderella."

He turned then and walked away, whistling *The Merry Widow Waltz.*

Chapter Ten

"But, Mommy...I really, really, really, really want to go to camp." Katie bobbed up on the side of the pool, brushed the water from her eyelashes, and renewed her assault. "Marta gets to go. It's not fair if I don't get to go, too."

Leah pulled her sunglasses to the end of her nose and gave her daughter a stern look. "Katherine Anne Taylor, if you say the word, camp, one more time, I will pick you up out of the pool and take you home. Do you understand?"

Katie pursed her lips in a stubborn pout. "I understand. But I don't understand why you won't let me go." She flipped backward into the water and dunked out of sight.

Setting her sunglasses back into place, Leah tried hard not to sigh. Katie had been after her for a week now. Ever since Marta had asked if Katie could go with her to a seven-day camp. There'd be horseback riding, canoeing, painting, swimming and bunches of other good things, Katie had been quick to add. It had obviously been a foregone conclusion in Katie's mind and probably in Marta's as well, that Leah would allow Katie to go.

But Leah had said no.

And she'd been hearing about it ever since. Even Riker had joined forces with the Dynamic Duo. *I'll pay her fees,* he'd said. *It's not that expensive.*

Not to Riker, maybe, but Leah couldn't afford the price. Her pride and independence wouldn't let her allow Riker to foot the bill. And under all the rationale about money, was the probably irrational worry that Katie wouldn't be safe away from her mother. It was silly. Kids went away to camp every summer—even kids as young as Katie. Some went for weeks at a time. But the bottom line was...Leah didn't want Katie to go.

"Leah?" Marta bobbed up in the same spot Katie had just vacated, looking exactly as Katie had looked, down to the slicked-back hair and watery eyelashes. Leah was surprised at how quickly it had become natural for Marta and Katie to drop the formality of Mr. and Mrs. and start calling each other's parents by first names. Marta's question was no surprise. "Could Katie come over here and spend a whole week with me?"

"You're together almost every day as it is."

"But she could stay overnight the whole week."

"Why don't you spend a whole week with us, Marta?"

"No." A note of panic crept into Marta's voice. "She wants to spend the whole week over here."

The whole week. Leah wondered if they really thought she was that dumb. "What would you and Katie do for a whole week, Marta?"

"Oh, we'd play and run and stuff."

"Okay," Leah agreed. "I'll leave her for the rest of this week."

"No." Marta splashed and propped her elbows on the side of the pool. "Next week would be better. I haven't asked Daddy yet. But next week would be better."

"Next week you'll be at camp, Marta."

"Oh." There was a splash and Marta vanished into the water. Probably she was joining the other little mermaid to develop a different strategy. Leah wondered if they'd ever give up. Her guilt was growing by leaps and bounds already. Susannah had told her she was crazy not to send Katie. "Take advantage of the opportunity," Susannah had said. "Think of all the things you can do in a week. Think of the books you can read, the television shows you can watch, the naps you can take." At some moments, it was actually tempting. A whole week without worrying about Katie's needs. A whole week to spend on herself.

What would she do?

And there was the crux of her problem. Leah knew she'd be lonely. She didn't even enjoy the nights Katie spent at Marta's house. What would she do for an entire week without Katie to pick up and drop off? Without Katie to cook for, clean for, talk to, laugh with, tuck into bed? Was she really so dependent on her child that the thought of being away from her was scary? Or was there another reason? A more personal one?

Leah stretched out on the lounge chair and tried not to think about that anymore. She'd let the sun bake her. Maybe she'd even drift off to sleep. But, of course, she wouldn't. Because she was the lifeguard. Gussie had asked her to watch the girls swim until Riker got home. Leah had agreed, thinking she'd sit by the pool and read the newspaper. But, with daylight saving time, the sun was still golden warm and in a very few minutes, she'd succumbed to the cool lure of the pool and the twins' invitation to swim with the mermaids. Having her swimsuit in the car seemed a lot like premeditation, but Leah forgave herself for any untoward intentions and now she allowed herself to relax in poolside luxury. If she could only forget all the reasons she didn't want Katie to go to camp.

"Mommy?" Katie was back with a splash and a new plan. "I'll make my bed every morning forever if you let me go. They teach you things like that there. Marta said so."

"Marta's never been before." Leah pointed out.

"But Kristen has and she told Marta and Marta told me. Please, Mommy?"

"Katherine." Leah tried to sound firm and unshaken in her resolve, even though her resolve was wearing thin.

"I'll never ask you for anything else as long as I live." Katie lifted her hand in a solemn vow, splashing droplets of water over Leah's bare legs. "I promise, Mommy. I'll be good for the rest of my life, if you let me go to—" Katie stopped in midbeg, obviously remembering Leah's threat. "If you let me go to *K-A-M-P.*"

"*C.*" Leah closed her eyes behind the dark glasses. "Camp begins with a *c.*"

There was a gasp and then a giggle. "You said the word, Mommy. You said, camp. Does that mean I get to go?"

When had society allowed children to start talking? Leah wondered. Whenever it was, it was a bad idea. "Katie," she said wearily. "For the last time…"

"Hello, Water Sprites." Riker's voice rolled over Leah like a cool wind, opening her eyes and causing a warming ripple under her skin. She lay motionless as he walked from the house to the pool, his shoes clicking on the wooden deck. He stopped beside Leah and loosened the knot of his tie. "And you must be Undine, the lovely spirit of the water."

"And you must be Neptune, come to stir up a storm in the sea." She swung her legs to the side of the lounge and sat upright, trying to behave as if she didn't want to grab a beach towel and wrap it over her suddenly, too-bare body. "Stir it up on the other side, if you don't mind. I'm sun-dried and don't want to get soaked again."

Riker's smile stirred her to nervous excitement. Since the kiss, every time she saw him, every time he spoke her name, or looked directly at her, Leah's heart jumped into a fluttery pattern of beats and her stomach became home to a thousand anxious butterflies. She was too old for this nonsense. She knew it. He probably knew it, too. Probably it even was written in some ancient epistle. She was too old to feel this way. And she was supposed to be too wise, as well.

"Daddy, Daddy," Marta called. "Jump in."

"Jump in, Riker," Katie made a production of splashing and giggling. "Play with us."

"Okay, Water Sprites, let me change into my suit and we'll do battle."

"We always beat you, Riker." Katie teased him as if she'd known him forever. "Marta and I have been planning, again."

"I'll just bet you have." The girls splashed over to the slide and Riker bent close to Leah's chair, came closer to her eye level, came closer to her level of friendly resolve. "What have they been planning this time?"

"How to send me to Shanghai so Katie can go to camp. That's camp with a *k*, in case you didn't know."

Riker glanced at the two girls. "I'm surprised you haven't given in yet, Leah. Camp, with a *k*, seems to be written into their destinies. Marta said she didn't want to go if Katie couldn't go, too.''

"They have to be separated now and then, Riker. They're beginning to act like real twins, afraid to do anything without the other."

"They are real twins, Leah, but I don't think they're afraid. They just want to share a good time."

"You're not making this easy, Riker."

"I know. I'm sorry. It's not up to me to make this decision. You have to do what you think is best for Katie."

Put like that, Leah felt like the last-place contender for Mother of the Year. She was trying to do what was best for Katie, but... "I'm not ready for her to be away that long, Riker. She's never been away from home, other than the nights she's spent over here, and I'm afraid she'll be homesick."

"It's a well-supervised camp, Leah. I went there when I was a kid and, believe me, I was too busy to get homesick. The counselors are great. The emphasis is on fun. She'll have a wonderful time. Especially with Marta there. I know the week of camp runs through their birthday, but the camp goes by age and this is the only time available for Marta's and Katie's age group. We can always celebrate their birthday later." He paused. "And if the expense of sending Katie to camp is a problem for you, I'll take care—"

"The expense is not a problem."

"Good. Then I hope you'll reconsider so these two little urchins will give us some peace." He rose and placed a hand on her shoulder, squeezing briefly, like a consoling friend. "Gussie's taking a trip to the Florida Keys to visit an old friend, so I'll be on my own next week. I have a dozen things I want to get done while Marta's away, but if you let Katie go and things get too quiet for you, we could go to a movie or something."

The "or something" was the other side of Leah's concern. If Katie and Marta were not around to provide boundaries, what would happen to her resolve to keep Riker at arm's length? "I think I can keep myself busy," she said airily, not wanting him to guess how much the thought worried her. She was afraid of becoming dependent on this man. Already they shared responsibilities she hadn't expected to ever share again.

They were together often because of the twins. It had become usual for Riker to pick up Katie from the day-care center on Tuesdays and Thursdays after Marta finished her riding lesson. As often as not, when Leah came to get Katie from a visit with Marta, she ended up staying for dinner. As a matter of routine, Leah stopped by the dance studio on her way home from work every Wednesday to get Marta. Sometimes she took Marta home. Sometimes the child stayed with Katie all evening. Sometimes Riker did, too.

Occasionally Leah allowed Katie to spend the entire day with Marta and Gussie rather than attending day care. It was hard to explain to Katie why she couldn't stay at the Westfalls' every day. She said she hated day care. It was stupid. They had to take rest breaks. Marta didn't have to do that stuff. Leah tried to explain that Riker and Gussie couldn't be responsible for another child twenty-four hours a day. Katie had Leah.

And Leah would take care of Katie. It was her responsibility.

But the pressure of the situation was wearing on her. Through no fault of her own, she was caught in this no-win situation. Katie had a mother, but no on-the-scene father. Marta had a father, but needed a mother. The two girls found security and stability in their relationship with each other. It was great fun for them to be twins, to share secrets and stories…and parents. It might have been great for Leah, too, if she hadn't been so attracted to Riker.

And there, in a convoluted way, was another reason she didn't want Katie to go to camp.

"You can't catch me!"

"You're as slow as a turtle!"

The squeals of the girls roused Leah from her thoughts and she realized Riker had changed into swimming trunks and was approaching the pool. He was bare chested and muscular, broad shouldered and gracefully masculine. His hair lightened to strawberry blond in the sun, his moustache had taken on a deep, reddish hue, and his skin was honey-tan. By rights, he shouldn't have looked so good. And if she'd had a lick of good sense, she'd have learned by now not to look. But still her gaze followed his long strides to the edge of the diving board and then the smooth arch of his body as he jackknifed into the pool. Some long-buried yearning awoke inside her and Leah tasted desire.

"Come on in, Leah." Riker surfaced in the center of the pool. "Help me immobilize these two."

Katie...or was it Marta...jumped him from behind. The other child attacked from the side and the battle was on. Leah smiled, pleased that her daughter liked Riker so much and scared that perhaps she liked him too much. Marta showed signs of wanting to get closer to Leah, too. Leah hadn't discouraged the overtures as often as she probably should. Though she discouraged Katie's tendency to look on Riker as a father figure. It was all becoming more complicated. If only, Leah thought, she and Riker could have liked each other without really *liking* each other. Maybe it was only her. Maybe he didn't feel the same way. Still, he had kissed her. But kissing was different for men. It didn't always mean—

"Come on, Mom," Katie shouted. "We're beatin' Riker."

"No, thanks. I'm going inside to change. I'll be ready to leave soon, Katie."

"Mooommmm." Katie dragged the word into a long protest, but Riker flipped her backward into the water and she came up laughing, forgetting for the moment that the fun was almost over.

Leah forced herself to turn from the cozy little scene, forced herself to turn away from the taboo thoughts of whole families with one father, one mother and two point three children.

"They're really having a fine time out there," Gussie said as Leah entered through the kitchen doorway. The older woman stepped back from her viewing station at the window and smiled at Leah. "It's amazing how much fun they have, isn't it? I suppose if they had to live together day in and day out, it wouldn't be quite so enjoyable."

"They think it would be heaven." Leah padded across the tile floor to the bathroom where she'd changed earlier. "They don't realize how quickly togetherness can lose its charm."

"Yes, they're a little young for reality. But they have a birthday next week, you know. Seven years old." Gussie glanced out the window again, the affectionate smile settling again on her lips. "Their first birthday together. We'll have to have a party."

Leah didn't comment on that idea as she stepped into the bathroom and closed the door. Birthday. She hadn't forgotten, but she hadn't really thought about it, either. Katie would want to share the day with Marta. Marta would want to share the day with Katie. Riker would insist they have the party here. The girls would beg for her agreement. And what possible reason could she give for refusing? Could she say she'd rather have a small get-together at her house just for Katie? And if she did agree, would Katie be unhappy if her presents didn't measure up to the ones Marta received? But next week was camp. Marta would be gone.

But Marta wouldn't go, if Katie didn't.

Leah sighed and faced her reflection in the mirror. Okay, so this was the choice. Either she allowed Katie to go to camp with Marta, which meant robbing the small savings she'd set back as a fledgling college fund, or she insisted that Katie stay home, which meant ruining Marta's week at camp and planning a birthday party to boot. Making a face, Leah turned around and stripped off her swimsuit. She dressed quickly, all the while tossing the pros and cons of each decision and knowing deep in her heart the deciding factor was Riker.

If Katie went to camp, Leah would have a week away from Riker. A week for clear thinking and new perspective. If Katie stayed home, Marta would stay home, and Leah and Riker would be working together on a birthday party. Leah knew she'd have to juggle her finances again to repay the savings account, but it might just be worth it. One week without Riker Westfall looking sexy and attractive in his swimsuit. One week without a phone call from him. One week to pull her mind out of fantasyland and back into the real world.

Leah brushed her hair, smoothed her eyebrows and wrinkled her nose at her mirror twin. One week, she thought. Okay, she could handle that.

ON SUNDAY, just before Riker came to pick up Katie for delivery to Camp Wachatoume, Leah wished she could change her mind.

It was too late, of course. Katie was already bouncing off the walls with excitement. No worry in her mind about being away from home. No regrets about spending her birthday at camp. They'd have a party, later, Katie and Marta had agreed. Camp would be great. Katie couldn't wait to go. Leah was surprised Katie remembered to give her a goodbye hug when Riker's Jeep turned into the driveway.

"You're welcome to drive down with us," Riker said. He'd offered her the opportunity several times, but Leah knew she'd have to ride back alone with him. And if she was going to use this week to regain control of her attraction for him, then she knew she'd better start the way she meant to end. Katie didn't care. She giggled and whispered with Marta and waved goodbye like a happy camper. And then the Jeep and Katie were out of sight. Leah went into the empty house, poured herself a cup of coffee and watched an old movie.

Monday wasn't bad. She prepared for work leisurely, had time to read the morning paper, a luxury she usually enjoyed only on the weekends. Coming home to an empty house wasn't the pleasure she sometimes thought it would be, but she did laundry and cleaned and read a couple of chapters of a book that was overdue at the library.

By Wednesday, she missed Katie so much she could hardly stand it. She missed Marta and Riker, too. Even Gussie. Leah wandered through the house, looking for something, anything to do to keep her from calling the camp and asking to speak to her daughter. She saved Katie from certain embarrassment by weeding the flower beds, something she hadn't done in far too long. She went to bed with a backache and lay there so tired and lonely she wished she could howl at the moon like the big-mouthed beagle across the street.

On Thursday, she tried to talk Susannah into going to a movie, but Susannah was busy. Some kind of racing thing with Tom. Leah was beginning to suspect, despite her friend's protests, that there was something "romantic" going on between Susannah and their boss. Oddly, though, Leah wasn't interested in finding out. She wanted to go to a movie or out to dinner or anywhere, except go home to her achingly silent house. The thought of calling Riker came to her off and on throughout the day, but she didn't call him. She didn't even let herself believe she might. So, after work, she went to the supermarket, bought a frozen dinner and a half gallon of Fudge Ripple ice cream. Life couldn't get much better than that, she told herself.

Riker's Wagoneer was parked in her driveway when she pulled in. She wondered if she could get inside and get the frozen foods into the freezer without him noticing the mediocrity of her purchases. Somehow, she didn't think Riker was the type to console himself by spooning ice cream from the carton while watching syndicated reruns on the television. He'd probably want a bowl. And she'd only bought one frozen dinner.

"Hi," he said as she approached with the sack in her arms. "Are you as lonesome as I am?"

Would he know she was lying if she said no? "Oh, maybe a little." She shifted the sack and ran her a hand into the outside pocket of her purse, looking for the car keys she'd automatically dropped there. "Have you heard from Marta?"

"No. Have you heard from Katie?"

"Not a word, but I really wasn't expecting to hear. Katie would only call if she got into trouble, so I guess her silence is something I can be grateful for."

"When the two of them are together, they don't seem to need us around, do they?"

"Considering we haven't even received the traditional 'Hello, Mother,' 'Hello, Father' letters, I'd say you're right." Leah found her keys and jangled them free from the debris in the bottom of her bag. "Did you get everything accomplished? All those things you were going to get done while your mother and Marta were away?"

"Not everything." Riker reached for the grocery sack, but Leah shifted it to her other hip as she moved to open the door. "Truthfully," he said, "I've been sitting in the middle of that big silent house wondering what I was supposed to do."

She nodded toward the flower bed. "I did some weeding. Something I haven't done in…I can't remember the last time I pulled weeds." The door swung open and Leah stepped inside. Riker followed. She'd half hoped he wouldn't. In the kitchen, vanity debated indifference and won. With a rueful sigh, Leah folded the paper sack in and around the frozen food and stuffed the whole package into the freezer.

"What's in the sack?" Riker asked, as he positioned himself beside the oven and crossed his arms low on his chest.

"Just some food."

"Aren't you going to take it out of the sack?"

"No." She pretended surprise, as if his suggestion made no sense. "It's double insulated this way. Keeps longer. No freezer burn."

He nodded, as if her answer actually made sense. "Have you had dinner?"

He had an unfair advantage, Leah thought. She ought to say she'd eaten on the way home. "I'm not very hungry."

"Neither am I. Let's go to an early movie and get something to eat afterward." He paused, offered a small, persuasive smile. "My treat."

"Riker, you don't have to treat—"

"Dutch treat, then. Just say you'll come along and keep me company. I'm lonely and I don't know anyone else who's a Camp Wachatoume outcast."

"What about Kristen's mom?"

"She has Kristen's dad."

"Oh," Leah said. "One of those couples."

Riker's eyebrows went up, a glint of amusement surfaced in his blue eyes. "One of *those* couples?"

Leah set her purse on the counter and eased her feet out of the uncomfortable pumps she'd worn all day. "Just a turn of phrase. When she was littler, Katie would come home from day care and tell me about a new friend she'd made and, if the child's parents lived together, Katie would invariably refer to them as 'one of those couples.' It got to be a private joke between us."

"I hope she won't mind that you shared the joke with me."

"Are you kidding? Katie thinks you're the greatest thing since popcorn."

"I'm glad. Marta thinks you're pretty terrific, yourself, Leah. I think so, too."

Leah looked up and met his eyes. The room felt suddenly

close. Her breath seemed heavy and too short. He shouldn't say things like that. No matter how innocuous it might sound to an outsider, Leah knew matters were fast moving out of her hands. She needed to get him out of her kitchen, out of her house…even if she had to go with him to do so. "If we hurry, Riker, we can just make the last matinee. Let me grab a different pair of shoes and I'm ready to go."

"Good." He smiled easily, as if he didn't understand exactly what she was doing, as if he were simply glad she'd agreed to go. "Give me your car keys and I'll switch the cars around."

"I'll drive." She slipped past him and headed down the hall to her bedroom. "Riker?" she called. "This is dutch treat, okay?"

"Okay, Ms. Independence. But get a move on. The show starts in seven minutes."

"Which movie are we going to see?"

"The one that starts in seven minutes."

Leah smiled and grabbed her shoes. All right, so she'd only made it four days. So her perspective was still slightly skewed. Going out beat staying in hands down. And what could possibly happen at the movie?

He held her hand.

It wasn't that big a deal, really. He put his elbow on the narrow armrest between the seats and pressed down on her hand accidentally. He jerked his arm out of the way, she pulled her hand into her lap, he reached over to pat her injury. And he wound up holding her hand. Simple.

If only her response had been so simple.

The strength of his fingers wrapped around hers felt nice. Leah couldn't remember the last time someone had held her hand. Someone male, that is, and older than six, almost seven. Funny, the little things one missed after a divorce or a death. A simple touch meant warmth and good feelings, fellowship and that indefinable sense of belonging to the human race. Being single made one separate, somehow. Untouchable, at a time it was most important to be touched.

She knew she probably shouldn't leave her hand resting in his.

She and Jonathan had started out holding hands, too, and look where that had ended.

And there were Katie and Marta to consider. Little match-makers that they were, they couldn't understand the ramifications of a relationship. She and Riker might fall desperately in love and live happily ever after with their beautiful twin daughters. More likely, they'd get involved in a brief affair that would end with pain and disillusionment and it would be Katie and Marta who got hurt the most.

The thought choked Leah. She'd hurt enough already for one lifetime and she couldn't bear the thought of hurting Katie. Marta had already lost a mother. She shouldn't have to lose again. Leah quietly slipped her hand from Riker's and offered a faint upward tilt of her lips when he glanced her way. He answered in kind and returned his attention to the movie. He didn't reach for her hand again.

After the movie, they ate in a local restaurant that Riker selected. It was casual and inexpensive. When Leah paid her half of the bill Riker fought the urge to slip the money back into her purse. She'd have a fit if she caught him, but he wanted to help. He knew she needed her independence and admired her stubborn "I'll-pay-my-own-way" method of holding on to her autonomy. But some holdover chauvinism inside him needed to take care of her problems, wanted to smooth a few of the wrinkles out of her life.

"I'll bet Katie won't have a single stitch of clean clothing when she gets home Saturday," Leah said after she finished her last french-fried potato and washed it down with a drink of water. "Do you think it's muddy at Camp Wachatoume? Dumb question. The camp is right on the Illinois River. So Katie and Marta are bound to have found mud somewhere."

"Marta never has liked mud all that much, but Katie will probably have changed her mind about it." Riker pushed away his plate. Something had happened to his appetite in the past couple of hours. He wondered if it had anything to do with holding Leah's hand. "Do you think they'll have had enough togetherness for a while?"

"I hope so." Leah looked up, her eyes wide and sparkling

brown. "Oh, don't take that wrong. It's not that I mind them being together, it's just that…"

"You don't have to explain, Leah. I know you're still not crazy about this situation and the amount of time you have to spend with me as a result."

"That's not tru—" She seemed to reconsider her denial and he wondered what was going through her head. "It's just that everything is getting so…complicated."

"Complicated." Riker weighed the word, testing its precision, its correctness. "I thought my life could never get more complicated than it was when Jean was ill. Every day there was some new crisis, something traumatic pulling at me. I thought once it was over, once she was gone, things would be simple again. But that didn't happen. The complications of living kept coming. They just wore a different disguise." He offered a smile to ease her distress. "This is only one small wrinkle, Leah."

"Well, I don't want to be the one who has to iron it out."

"Would you stop worrying about the complications of Katie and Marta's relationship? They're going to be fine."

It wasn't Katie and Marta's relationship she was worried about. Riker could almost read the thought as Leah's lips pursed in a rueful frown. But what was he supposed to do? Tell her he didn't find her attractive? Tell her he didn't enjoy her company? Say something stupid like he thought of her only in the most platonic ways? It would be a lie and she'd know it.

"Let's go." She was on her feet, ready to leave almost before the words hit the air. "I have to work tomorrow."

He accepted her excuse with good grace and made inconsequential conversation on the drive home. But he could tell by her white-knuckled grip on the wheel that her tension was building. Leah was feeling the same attraction he felt and the moment was coming when he would have to confirm or deny the fact that they were past the point of being merely friends.

"Thanks, Leah," he said when she'd parked her car in the street to avoid trapping his in the driveway. His arm rested along the back of the seat, his fingers were within touching distance of her cheek. Once in a while, a strand of her hair brushed across his skin. "You saved me from a long and lonely evening."

She looked at her hands as they rested on the steering wheel. The sounds of a spring evening were loud in his ears...the cicadas, the breeze tiptoeing through the treetops, the occasional call of a night bird, and the whisper-soft sound of Leah's breathing. Her sudden sigh was deep and poignant. His heartbeat quickened, sensing an alteration in her mood, preparing for whatever might be coming. Would she tell him to leave her alone? Would she say Katie wouldn't be allowed to see Marta anymore? Would she ask for his help in breaking up the twins' relationship?

Then, Leah lifted her head and smiled at him. Slowly. Like someone tentatively reaching for a light switch in a darkened room. "Tomorrow is their birthday," she said. "I've never been away from Katie on her birthday before. Do you think she'll miss me?"

"I'm sure of it. The question is what are you going to do to keep from missing her?"

"I don't know. See another movie, maybe."

"I have a better idea. Let's go to a baseball game. I have tickets and we may as well celebrate the twins' birthday by eating hot dogs and peanuts instead of sitting home alone wondering what they're doing. The kids are at camp. We'll participate in the great American pastime. What could be more patriotic than that? Are you game?" He grinned. "No pun intended."

Leah frowned slightly, and he imagined the tracks her thoughts were following. A baseball game was public. Lots of people. Lots of noise. About the least intimate setting available for two people looking to avoid intimacy. Safe. And a more attractive option than an evening alone. He knew when the corners of her mouth tipped upward that her thoughts agreed with his. "We'll have to drive into Tulsa," she said as if that might be a problem.

"We'll leave at six-thirty." He lifted one finger and threaded it through a wavy strand of her hair. "And on the drive, we might even plan a birthday party for the twins."

"Katie's suggestion was to have one as soon as they get back from camp. She thought this Saturday night would be a good time, but I told her we'd have to wait until the following weekend."

"Next Saturday would be better, I agree. We'll give them a week to recuperate."

"Give ourselves a week, you mean." Leah laughed. "I'll be doing laundry until next Thursday, at least. And I won't be surprised if we have to pick stick-tights from each and every sock that went to camp."

"You're a pessimist, Leah Taylor. I'll bet they both bring home a bird cage made from popsicle sticks and maybe a braided keychain, too."

"Maybe a plaster-of-paris doorstop, too."

"Painted a beautiful shade of camp green."

She laughed. "Aren't we the lucky ones?"

Riker wanted to kiss her then. The impulse was strong and compelling. The distance between them was negligible. His finger was still involved with that one strand of her hair. Her lips were soft and inviting in the dusky interior of the car. "We're about the luckiest two people in the world right now," he said, his voice going husky with the thought of touching her, tasting her, holding her. "We've been to a movie. We've had a late supper. We've enjoyed the evening. Tomorrow night we have a date with a baseball diamond and a hot dog, and in a little over thirty-six hours, our daughters will be home from camp. What more could we want?"

"Yes," she said. "What more?" The words were a throaty murmur. Her eyes were wide and ebony dark in the stray ribbon of light from the street lamp on the corner. She knew, Riker thought. She knew. He leaned forward, forgetting suddenly everything except the need to reach for her, touch her, pull her into his arms...kiss her.

She came willingly, without even a token resistance, and when she was close enough, he bent his head and took her lips in a long, exploratory caress.

Leah didn't know why she allowed it to happen. She'd seen the look in his eyes, felt her lips part with response, recognized the seduction of the dark night and the mesmerizing effect of his hand gently toying with a strand of her hair. She'd known what he intended to do. There'd been time to sabotage the moment.

Ways to keep this wrinkle from making an irreparable mark. But she did nothing.

And he kissed her.

His mouth opened over hers, testing her control with the tantalizing movement of his tongue. And she kissed him back, matching him pressure for pressure, tempting him to explore deeper, seeking to discover more than she'd known before. Like a child with a forbidden toy, Leah savored the wild pounding of her pulse, the shivery, achy sensations in her body. Her hands drifted from his forearms to his shoulders and her arms curved around his neck.

He released her mouth, only to scatter a line of kisses along her cheek and down to the hollows of her throat. With a low moan, he retraced the path and found again the invitation her lips offered so freely. A shiver coursed down her spine, leaving her feeling needy and confused.

Leah slipped her hands from the thick, textured strands of his hair, placed them against his chest and wedged a small distance between his body and hers. Her lips left his reluctantly, trembling with the yearning to return, to forget responsibility and priorities in his kiss.

His eyes held hers for a breathless moment. It was too late for denial. Too late for regret. But Leah had to tell him, she had to be sure he understood, that it couldn't happen again. No matter how many long and lonely evenings they might have to spend.

"Riker, I… I don't want to save you, Riker. Not from loneliness, or complications, or anything else. I don't have the resources and I can't afford to take the risk. Please understand. It's not just because of Katie and Marta. It's me, too. I…can't. I just can't."

He didn't even pretend to misunderstand, but his heart went out to her in exactly the wrong way. "I do understand, Leah. But I'm not sure we're going to get a choice. This may be one wrinkle that can't be ironed out." He got out of the car and stood for a second by the open door. "I'll pick you up tomorrow night, six-thirty. Bring your Drillers ballcap and a jacket, in case the wind kicks up."

She looked at him, her eyes filled with questions he didn't

want to answer. "We have to think about Katie and Marta," she said.

"Don't worry, Leah. We'll plan a birthday party that will knock the mud right off their socks."

Chapter Eleven

"Yooouu'rre out!" The umpire's voice carried into the grand-stand and Leah jumped to her feet to protest, along with a couple of hundred other fans.

"Did you see that?" She glanced down at Riker, who sat eating peanuts and watching her. "That ball was so far out, the batter would have had to go to Kansas City to hit it."

"Yeah!" The man on Leah's other side agreed with her and thumped her on the back in the fraternal spirit of baseball before he cupped his hands around his mouth and shouted, *"Kill the umpire!"*

Leah sat and leaned toward Riker. "Can people get thrown out of here for yelling at the ump like that?"

"Yes." He patted her knee. "But don't worry, I'll tell you how the game turns out."

She frowned. "*I* didn't abuse the umpire. I just said he couldn't see the Goodyear Blimp if it was hovering in front of his nose."

With a laugh, Riker offered her the bag of peanuts. "Have some peanuts. It's the only way to fight Umpire Frustration."

Leah reached into the sack and grabbed a couple. She cracked and shelled them with a vengeance, ate the meats, then carefully handed the husks to Riker. "I don't want to drop them," she said as she dusted her hands. "The umpire might make me clean up the stands."

Riker dumped the shells into his empty drink cup. "I'll take full responsibility. Never let it be said that I took a litterbug to the ballpark."

"You're a good citizen, Riker." She took a drink from her cup and reached for another peanut. "And just to show my appreciation, I'll let you have a sip of my drink if you get thirsty."

"You're my kind of woman, Leah." His blue eyes teased her, laughed with her, enjoyed her. "Conscientious, generous and a rabble-rouser."

"I'm not a—"

"Did you see that?" The man beside Leah jabbed her with his elbow and she jumped up to see what had happened. "Hey, ump! You couldn't see the strike zone if it kicked you in the stomach! You couldn't see a herd of elephants at first base!"

"That's right," Leah yelled because it seemed to be the thing to do. It felt good to be in the spirit of the game. "You couldn't see a bat in a belfry!" She glanced at Riker, arching an eyebrow questioningly.

He rolled to his feet with a shrug. "You couldn't see a major league hitter if he shoved a bat up your nose."

Leah smiled her appreciation and gave him a hearty slap on the back. After all, this was baseball.

"I KNEW they wouldn't throw us out," Leah said smugly as they drove away from the stadium. "If the fans can't yell, then what's the point in going to a game? You might as well stay home and watch it on television."

Riker decided not to point out that Tulsa was in a minor league and, as such, didn't have many televised games. "I'm glad you had a good time," he said instead. "I didn't know you could get so...loose."

"Neither did I. I think there might have been joy juice in the hot dogs. Or it could have had something to do with the man sitting next to us. He made it hard to sit still and keep my mouth shut."

"Yes," Riker agreed with a smile. "He did."

"Well, you got into the spirit of things there in the last inning, yourself."

"I ran out of peanuts. Yelling at the ump was the only thing left to do."

"So what do we do for an encore, Coach? Too bad there wasn't a doubleheader tonight."

He glanced at her, surprised by her lighthearted banter, by the flirty toss of her head and the dance of laughter in her eyes. "We could always find a bar and rehash the game over a couple of beers."

"Is that what baseball fans do after a game?"

"I don't know, but it sounded like a pretty sporty thing to do."

"It did, but I'm not crazy about beer...or bars. So let's think of something else."

Her tone of voice was companionable, almost coy in its cheerfulness. She didn't want to go home. Riker could figure out that much. But was it because today was Katie's birthday and she didn't want to think about being away from her? Or was it because she'd really had a good time and wanted to be with him a little longer? "How about birthday cake?" he suggested, laying his question on the line. "We really should do something special to celebrate this momentous day in our daughters' lives."

Leah turned toward him. "You know, that's the first time I've thought about Katie since you picked me up this evening. That's funny. I'm usually thinking about her all the time, in one way or another. But today's her birthday, and I'd all but forgotten."

"It's all right, Leah. You can take a few hours off from motherhood every now and again." Riker was sorry he'd introduced the subject and reminded her. On the other hand, he couldn't deny the ripple of pleasure her admission of forgetfulness had brought to him. He was getting to like Leah far too much. At certain moments lately, moments like this one, he wondered if he wasn't a little bit in love with her.

"By all means, let's have birthday cake," she said. "Where do we find one at this time of night?"

"I happen to know a place where we can get a piece of cake, a candle and a Happy Birthday serenade. There's only one catch."

"What's that? I have to bake the cake, provide the candle and sing, too?"

"No." Laughter rumbled in his throat. "The catch is, I'll have to tell them it's *your* birthday."

"Oh," she said. "Why can't we tell them it's *your* birthday?"

"Why don't we tell them it's *our*—"

"—*our* birthday." Leah finished the suggestion with him and matched him laugh for laugh.

"I STILL CAN'T believe you told that waitress such a sob story, Riker," Leah said as she settled her head against the headrest of the car. "Telling her I'd had amnesia for twenty years and just this year remembered my date of birth. Shame on you."

"I don't believe she actually believed me. But we got two pieces of cake and the ultra deluxe birthday song, now didn't we?" He waited for a southbound car to pass in the oncoming lane before he flipped the headlights to bright. "Besides, I didn't see you denying that you'd had amnesia."

"I forgot."

He grinned. "A likely story."

Leah wrinkled her nose. "You're right. I admit it. I'm an accessory to the lie. But I couldn't help myself. Anything called 'Death by Chocolate' is worth a few risks."

"And being serenaded by every waiter and waitress in the place was exciting. You have to admit that, too."

"All right, I will. I enjoyed the rousing birthday chorus." She closed her eyes for a minute, relaxed, happy, and altogether too...loose. "You know, Riker, if we'd committed any real crimes tonight, we'd be in big trouble because I'd probably spill my guts to the ten o'clock news."

"Lucky for us it's after ten and there's not a newsperson in sight."

Lazily she turned toward him. "We didn't commit any crime, did we?"

"I think yelling at the umpire might be a misdemeanor, but that could be only in the major leagues."

"I haven't laughed so much since the day Katie flushed a library book down the toilet."

"That does sound like hilarious entertainment," he said dryly.

"Well, she did it page by page and by the time I followed the gurgling and splashing sounds and found Katie in the middle of it all, there wasn't much left to do but laugh. I wrote in her baby book that she was showing a true discernment about literature at the precocious age of sixteen months." Leah chuckled softly, remembering. "I think tonight was more fun, though. Cleaning up the bathroom and getting the plumber's bill did take away most of my merriment."

Riker's laugh was soft and slow. It flowed over Leah in warm, tingly ripples. She was too comfortable, too easy with his company. His conversation, light though it was, pleased some small discontented corner of her mind. His laughter pleasured her, mixing as it so often did with her own. He liked her. Genuinely liked her. And she found that more seductive than bouquets of roses or tomes of poetry. "You're a nice person, Riker. Thanks for taking me to the ball game."

"It was my pleasure, Leah. Thanks for spending this special evening with me." He paused without glancing her way. "And I didn't mean it was special because it's the twins' birthday."

Thank you, she thought but didn't say. It wouldn't do to acknowledge just how special the evening had been for her. Katie and Marta would be home tomorrow at noon and Leah and Riker would have to go back to being parents once more. There'd be no more evenings spent with just the two of them. He'd be Marta's daddy and she'd be Katie's mommy and that was the way it had to stay. But, oh, she'd enjoyed today and the fleeting sense of being a woman Riker Westfall found desirable.

"You're very quiet all of a sudden," he said. "Did you develop a real case of amnesia?"

"I was just thinking about tomorrow and Katie and Marta coming home."

"We still have a few hours left before we hear someone yelling, 'Daddy' or 'Mommy.'"

She would have liked to spend those hours with him. Her heart and body were in one accord in that respect. How long had it been since she'd been held in the circle of a man's arms? Partaken of the satisfying fruit of passionate kisses and sensual touches? Too long, obviously. Just the thoughts, in and of themselves, were dangerous. She certainly shouldn't think about Riker that way. She absolutely must not....

"We could go to my house and have a midnight swim in the pool." His suggestion was just this side of hesitant, as if he were wary of making it, as if he knew she would refuse.

Leah sighed, wishing the situation were different, wishing she didn't have to consider anyone else, wishing his thoughts didn't so closely parallel her own. "I may have no better sense than to yell at an umpire, Riker, but I do know better than to go for a midnight swim with you."

"I won't dunk you."

"I don't think you could even if you tried. I'm a pretty good swimmer."

"Is that a challenge?"

"Just wishful thinking. There are some things that should never be put to the test."

"Does that mean yes or no for the moonlight swim?"

"No. Definitely no. And I don't think we should tell the girls we've been together the past two nights, either. Little matchmakers that they are, they'd probably get the wrong idea."

He was silent for a minute. The road slipped by at a steady fifty-five miles an hour. "What *is* the wrong idea, Leah?" he asked finally, his tone husky, questioning. "What is the idea we don't want Katie and Marta to get?"

Leah straightened in the contoured seat, slid a sidelong glance at him, wondered if he really needed an answer. "We don't want them to think something...romantic...is going on between us, Riker. That would be devastating for the girls."

"It would? Why?"

She didn't want to talk about this. Not tonight. Not like...this. "We're adults, Riker. Marta and Katie depend on us to put their needs above our own."

"I don't see a conflict," he said. "Do you really think that our spending time together because we enjoy each other's company is somehow detrimental to our children?"

Leah moved restlessly, searching the darkness for familiar landmarks, for the protection of home. "Don't you see the potential for disaster, Riker? What if…what if we…got…involved? And then got…uninvolved? What happens to Katie and Marta, then? They'll still be sisters. But you and I won't be friends. We might not even be on speaking terms. It wouldn't be fair, Riker. Surely you can see that."

"I see, Leah." He said it to soothe her distress, but he didn't mean it. Leah obviously was afraid of a relationship, and he didn't think Katie's welfare was her sole concern. He could think of a dozen ways that two sensible, mature adults could manage a relationship without devastating the two very young children in their lives. Leah had trusted Jonathan and he'd betrayed her and Katie in a heartless and harmful way. She was protecting herself and Katie in the only way she knew…by denying herself another love relationship.

He could understand that. But he could hardly say that to her. He wasn't even sure he wanted a relationship himself. Losing Jean had been the worst thing that had ever happened to him. The remembrance of that pain still scared him. He wasn't sure he had it in him to love someone else and risk hurting like that again. So why had he opened this discussion with Leah? Why not just go along with her and pretend nothing outside of companionship was going on?

You're like a dog with a bone, Gussie always said to him. And maybe she was right. He'd already acknowledged to himself and to Leah that she aroused in him emotions unrelated to friendship and simple camaraderie. He'd enjoyed kissing her. He wanted to kiss her again and probably would at the next opportunity. He hadn't really thought for a minute that she'd accept his invitation for a moonlight swim, but if she had, he wouldn't have withdrawn the offer. It was too late for him to start pretending that he didn't find Leah Taylor attractive, that he didn't want to spend more evenings like this one with her. It had been too late the moment he'd looked at her over that silly banana pepper.

Silence accompanied them the rest of the way home, sitting squarely between them like a jealous child. When he pulled into her driveway and turned off the engine, Leah reached for the door handle. Riker placed his hand on her arm and felt her shiver before she turned reluctantly to face him. Her face was pale, her breath a shaky whisper of sound in the silent, close interior of the car. She lifted her chin, ready for whatever argument he put forth. The darkness felt tight, like a shoe one size too small. He took a deep breath. "Leah," he said softly. "I didn't come looking for you. I'm not even sure I'm ready for another relationship, but something *is* happening between us. Something special. And I'm not going to lie about it. Not to my daughter. Not to myself. Not to you."

She trembled as if he had threatened her. "Good night, Riker, and thank you. It was a lovely evening."

"I'm walking you to the door."

"I'm not going to ask you to come inside."

"I didn't think you would."

"It would be better if we kept our distance from now on. We've already said too much. This whole situation can only get worse."

"That's like expecting to get stuck by a thorn every time you lean down to smell a rose."

"My experience has been thorny, Riker. I'm not willing to offer Katie a rosebud and have her end up with a palm full of thorns."

"Are you so sure that's what will happen?"

She slipped her arm out of his grasp. "Are you so sure it won't?"

"Leah, I—"

"Please, Riker, don't say any more. Just leave me alone. We can be friends, but that's all. Absolutely all. For Katie's and Marta's sake, let's just keep this friendly." She was out of the car before he could answer. She was almost to the back door before he caught up with her.

"We're past 'friendly,' Leah. I know it. You know it. Probably Marta and Katie know it, too. Pretending it isn't so will only confuse them."

"They're only six, Riker. Everything confuses them."

"Seven, Leah. They're seven, going on twenty-one."

"Seven," she repeated softly. "Today. That's the second time you've reminded me. How could I forget Katie's birthday?"

"You're entitled to a life of your own, Leah. Life, liberty, and the pursuit of happiness. The adoption papers didn't say anything about giving up those rights in order to be a good parent."

Her lips curved in a rueful smile. "I think it was written into the divorce papers, though. Katie is all I have, Riker. Her happiness and well-being are more important to me than anything else in my life. Right now, her relationship with Marta is new and exciting. It's fun for the two of them to pretend we're one big happy family. After all, we *look* like a family. But that doesn't make it true, Riker. I lived with illusions all the time I was married to Jonathan. I won't ever do that again."

Riker stood, hands in his hip pockets, gaze steady on hers, wondering if he could act as if she were a friend, a buddy, someone to take to a ball game once in a while, someone to pal around with when the girls each needed a parent in attendance, someone he just liked.

She stood, watching him, searching his expression for understanding. A breath of June breeze fluffed the ends of her hair, lifting it and blowing it in wavy strands across her face. She brushed it back with her hand, a movement he envied and wanted to emulate. The midnight moon tinted her face in soft shadows and made her lips appear wet and inviting.

"I think it's time I went in," Leah said, her voice unsteady and hesitant, as if she wanted to say more, as if she were afraid to say anything else. "I did have a wonderful time."

He had to clear his throat in order to answer. "So did I. Let me hold the door for you. Shall I check the house? Make sure everything is—?"

"No. Everything is…fine. It's just…fine." She should have turned away then. He waited for her to do so, waited for her to go inside and close the door to shut him out, but she didn't move. She just stood as if she had no choice. "Riker? I want you to know that…well, no one ever took me to a ball game before and…I'm glad I went with you tonight."

"I'm glad, too," he said. "I've never had a date who yelled at the umpire before."

It was her smile, her shy, winsome, little smile, that pushed him over the edge of caution. He stepped forward. She didn't back away. Without taking his hands from his pockets, he leaned toward her, brushing her lips with his...once, then again returning for a more satisfying taste. It was odd, he thought, that he could stand there, touching her only with his mouth, holding his body away from temptation, and yet he experienced a yearning, a desire that threatened his control. Jean had been frail and he'd never kissed her without being fully conscious of the care and gentleness she needed. Leah needed care, too. And gentleness. But there was something in her independence, her stubborn courage, that challenged him, dared him to discover her inner strength for himself. He sensed that she would be a passionate, demanding and giving lover. She would enjoy lovemaking as much as she'd enjoyed yelling at the umpire. She would...

Riker forced the images from his mind and straightened. She never took her eyes from his as he took that crucial step backward. "If that was an illusion, Leah, I don't think I could survive the reality."

She opened her mouth, closed it again and turned from him without a word. He watched until she was safely inside the house before he walked back to the car. Instinct urged him to go to the door, knock and demand a showdown. Reason urged him to drive away. Maybe Leah was right. Maybe he hadn't fully considered how a grown-up relationship between him and Leah would affect Marta and Katie.

But he'd be damned if he could see how one relationship truly threatened the other. Marta and Katie were practically inseparable, now. Wouldn't it be easier if he and Leah were practically inseparable, too?

Leah's ball cap rested on the dash and Riker picked it up, turning it in his fingers, finally setting it atop his head. A smile caught him unaware. She'd been charming, delightful and endlessly fascinating. He could have watched her for hours tonight. Watched the way she moved, the way her eyes crinkled with a smile, the way one corner of her mouth tucked in just before she laughed.

He dipped the brim of the cap low on his forehead and glanced in the rearview mirror to check his reflection. Yeah, he thought, they were past the point of "friendly." So what was he going to do about it? Nothing? Or everything?

With a twist of his hand, he started the car and put it into reverse. The twins would be home tomorrow and that would put a damper on romance for the time being. He would have time to think, time to plan. For Leah's sake, for Katie's and Marta's sake, he wanted to be sure of his own feelings before he started tilting at the windmills of Leah's fears. Before he stepped up to bat in front of a blind umpire.

LEAH BACKED the station wagon into a parking space and glanced around the lot to see if she could see Riker's Wagoneer. It wasn't visible from her limited vantage point, so she relaxed against the seat and changed the radio station. Soothing sounds of easy-listening music filled the car and Leah clicked the tuner to another station. Oldies but Goodies lasted thirty seconds before she clicked past. A news report didn't catch her interest and a country and western station barely made it through the announcement of its call letters. She found a Top 40 station, but after one song, she turned off the radio.

She was restless. Deep down, finger-tapping restless. Damn Riker Westfall. It was his fault. She hoped to pick up Katie, grab her duffel bag and make it to the car without running into Riker. Forlorn hope though it was, she thought it could happen. He might be late. The camp bus might be early. There was always the possibility of a solar eclipse.

Chicken. Leah slumped in the car seat, stretched her legs to the mat on the passenger side, and leaned her head against the window behind her. She was a chicken. A bona fide, Grade A coward. Riker had scared her last night. His kiss had been light, nonthreatening, and she had fallen apart.

So now she was hiding, hoping he wouldn't see her, wouldn't come over, smile that lazy, sexy smile, flash that intriguing cleft in his attractive chin and make her forget where her obligations lay.

Katie, she thought. Katie was coming home. She'd be here any minute. Leah had missed her. The restlessness could just as easily be attributed to being away from her daughter, from anticipating Katie's safe return. It might have little, if anything at all, to do with Riker Westfall.

She saw his Jeep then as he turned onto the parking lot and she thought seriously about sinking a bit lower in the seat. But as he drove past the place where Leah was parked, a bus turned the corner at the four-way stop and rumbled and rattled up the hill. Little girls yelled and screamed, tugging at stubborn bus windows and waving frantically at their parents. The big orange Camp Wachatoume bus clattered to a halt and as the doors opened parents and children converged in one huge hug.

Leah scanned the crowd for Katie, looking first for the familiar flyaway ponytail, going up on tiptoe to catch a glimpse of the children still inside the bus. Then Katie, wearing a floppy hat, stepped from the shadowy interior to the sunlit steps of the bus and Leah smiled all over. "Katie!" She jumped and waved. "Katie! I'm over here."

Katie glanced up and Leah waited to be seen. She couldn't have made her way to Katie through the group clustered around the bus steps anyway, so she waved and smiled and waited. Katie glanced over her shoulder and said something to the child behind her. Marta, of course. Leah stopped waving. A rush of unfamiliar panic rippled through her. The child on the steps might have been Marta. Not Katie. Leah realized she wasn't sure which child she'd waved to, which child stood on the steps.

But that was silly. Despite the matching jackets all the campers wore, despite the hat, of course, she knew her own daughter. Leah had never had a moment's doubt as to who was Katie and who was Marta.

Until this moment.

Leah pushed away the irrational doubt and let the glad, welcoming smile return in full force. "Katie!" she said again. "I'm over here."

Katie jumped down the bus steps and minutes later, Leah stooped down and gathered her daughter into a bear hug, kissing her forehead, slipping off the hat to touch her hair. Leah went still, her hand at Katie's nape. "What happened to your hair?" Leaning away, she inspected the short-cropped layers of hair and Katie's guilty expression.

"Marta cut it, Mommy. It was raining and we…played beauty shop in our cabin."

"I see." Leah lifted her gaze, knowing as she did so that Marta would have an identical cut. Short, badly shaped, but identical. Her eyes met Riker's over Katie and Marta's shorn heads. He made a face and lifted his shoulder in a shrug to indicate he wasn't any crazier about the new "do" than Leah was.

"I'm never going anywhere with her again," Katie declared. "I hate my hair." Tears shimmered in the depths of her baby-blue eyes. "Can we go now?"

"Don't you want to say goodbye to Marta?"

Katie wrinkled her nose. "No. Marta's mean and ugly and I…don't like her."

"You're ugly, too. You're the ugliest." Marta stuck out her tongue and Katie replied in kind.

"You're the ugliest in the whole world."

"You're stupid."

Before Katie could answer, Leah grabbed her by the arm and spun her toward the car. "Stop that. You don't talk to other people that way, Katie. You know better."

Katie dipped her head in uncharacteristic remorse and for a second, a fragment of time, Leah experienced an odd sensation that something was amiss. It proved fleeting, though, as Katie recovered and raced to the car, pulling Leah with her. "I can't wait to get home," she said. "They fed us yucky stuff at camp. Are there any cookies at home? Can we have hot dogs for supper? Did Brownie Bear miss me?"

Leah opened the car door, tossed Katie's bag in the back seat and helped her daughter buckle up. "We all missed you, Katie, and we're all glad you're home."

"Riker, too?"

Leah heard the piquant question and wished she could ignore its deeper implications. Ruffling Katie's short hair, Leah smiled. "Yes, Katie, Riker missed you, too."

Katie nodded with satisfaction and a pleased smile settled on her sweetheart lips. "Good," she said. "'Cause I missed him, too."

Walking around to the other side of the station wagon, Leah

thought it odd that Katie had mentioned Riker. Especially since she now hated his daughter. But then, Katie often surprised her. "Tell me all about camp," Leah said as she started the car. "Was it fun? Did you make some new friends?"

Katie leaned forward, peering through the windshield as a string of cars drove past. "It was okay," she said. "Do you see them?"

Them could only mean Riker and Marta and, with a sigh, Leah nodded toward the black Wagoneer two cars back. "There they are."

Katie watched as the Jeep approached and then paused to allow Leah to pull out of her parking space. Leah caught a glimpse of Riker's face and her heartbeat quickened at the sight of him. He wasn't smiling. In fact, he looked rather stern, his moustache drooping into a frown. Beside him, Marta was making a face...at Katie. Leah negotiated the turn and Katie turned in her seat to gaze out the back window. A niggling concern edged through Leah at the wistful look on her daughter's face. "What happened between you and Marta?" she inquired softly.

Katie faced forward again. "Nothing."

"Something must have happened."

"She made me mad." The words were quiet, the tone bland. Not Katie's usual way of expressing anger. She must be tired.

"You haven't told me about camp." Leah tried to coerce a little information. "I thought you'd have bunches of things to tell me."

"Oh." Katie stared out the side window, her face averted from Leah's glances. "It was fun. The food was yucky. Can we have hot dogs for supper?"

"Sure," Leah said with a frown. "We can even stop for a hamburger on the way home, if you're hungry."

"No. I want to go...home."

"We're on our way, babe." Leah promised herself she wouldn't press Katie further. The child was obviously tired, obviously upset by the quarrel with Marta, and obviously not herself. By tomorrow, she'd be rested, relaxed and back to normal. It was, Leah thought, one of those things a mother simply knew.

Chapter Twelve

Halfway through a hot dog, Leah knew the child sitting across the table from her was not her daughter. Oh, she looked liked Katie and she talked like Katie. But she was too quiet, too polite, and too fastidious with her food to be Katie. All afternoon Leah had had moments in which she sensed that something wasn't as it should be, moments when Katie seemed too subdued or didn't respond in the way Leah expected. But, well, her daughter had never before been away from her for so long. It must have been a tiring week. Leah tried to tell herself that Katie just hadn't as yet regained her equilibrium, her natural tendency to bounce from wall to wall.

But over supper, Leah realized she'd only been avoiding the obvious. The child with her was Marta Westfall. And across town, her own Katie was eating supper with Riker. Did he suspect the switch? Had it occurred to him to wonder what energy bug had bitten his daughter? Or was Katie actress enough to pull off the masquerade?

Leah got up to fix herself a glass of water. "Do you want more milk?" she asked Marta. "Another hot dog?"

"No, thank you...Mommy." Marta patted her lips with a napkin, which she subsequently returned to her lap. If she was self-conscious about her role, she didn't show it. In fact, she seemed perfectly at ease here with Leah.

The little scamps, Leah thought. Which one of them had dreamed up this idea? Katie seemed the obvious choice, but then Leah didn't really know Marta all that well. She might be the mastermind, Katie the disciple. Leah dropped ice in her glass and leaned against the counter, observing Marta and wondering what to do.

Her first impulse was to get Riker on the phone and tell him exactly what she now thought of his plan to let the girls be "sisters." Her second impulse was to wait and see what the twins came up with next. After all, they were both safe at home, even if it was each other's home. She decided to finish her hot dog.

"You still haven't told me much about your week at camp," Leah said as she resumed her position at the table.

"I had fun."

"Did…Marta…have fun, too?"

Marta/Katie glanced up and quickly concealed a wary look. "I guess so."

"Did you and Marta get into a fight?"

"No." The child began to fidget, playing with a potato chip. "But we got mad."

"What about?"

"Nothing." Marta slipped from her chair and offered a shy smile. "I think I'll go play in my room. May I be excused, please?"

Leah wondered how long it would have taken her to realize the switch if Marta hadn't been so inherently polite and Katie so naturally unconcerned with manners. It was scary to think what might have happened if they'd been a few years older and better able to conceal their differences. As it was, they'd fooled Leah—and apparently Riker, too—for several hours. The haircut helped, but still Leah couldn't believe it had taken her until now to figure out what was going on.

She finished the last mouthful of hot dog and took another drink of water. Marta waited patiently to be excused. "Let's do something about your hair," Leah said. "I think it needs to be evened up a little. Go get the step stool."

Marta's hand investigated the ragged strands of hair. Her eyes wandered from one corner of the kitchen to the other. "Where's the step stool?"

Leah smiled. "Right where we always keep it."

"Oh."

"In the garage." Leah took pity on the child. "Next to the washing machine."

Marta skipped off to fetch the requested chair and Leah carried the dishes to the sink. Her fingers itched to dial Riker's phone number, but she told herself she'd give Marta a fair chance to confess first. And she'd give herself a chance to discover why the twins had decided to switch places, although she had a sinking feeling she already knew the answer.

Leah trimmed the new haircut into a smooth bob. It was cute. She had to admit the style suited Katie's—and Marta's—pixie face. It would be cool for summer, too.

"There you go," Leah set down the scissors and combed the shiny dark bangs above Marta's serious blue eyes. "You look like a princess. I'm glad you and Marta got scissor happy. This will be so much easier than combing that ponytail into place every morning, won't it? I wonder what Mrs. Cleary at the day-care center will say about your new hairstyle?"

"Day care?" Marta's eyes widened. "But I don't... Couldn't I stay at my...at Marta's house?"

"We've been through that dozens of times, Katie. You know you can't spend all your time with Marta. And I thought you were mad at her, anyway."

Marta seemed at a loss. Katie had obviously told her too many stories about her boring life there. "When do I have to go?" she asked, her voice fatalistic and small. "Will you come and pick me up?"

"Of course. I haven't forgotten you once in all the years you've been going to day care. Why would you be worried about it, now?"

Looking at her feet, Marta seemed at a loss for an answer. "I guess because...I missed you." She lifted her head, but couldn't quite meet Leah's eyes. Then she stepped forward and threw her arms around Leah, hugging as tightly as she could, and burying her head against Leah's side.

Leah stood transfixed for a second, feeling Marta's need, and her own immediate, intense response to it. Slowly she bent and gathered the child into her arms, giving short, maternal pats of reassurance. "I missed you, too," she said. "I missed you a lot, Marta."

Marta kept hugging, but when she slackened her grip on Leah, Leah put her hands on the child's shoulders and waited until Marta met her gaze. "Tell me why you and Katie switched places, Marta. I'm not mad and I'm not going to punish you, but I want you to tell me why."

Distress registered in the child's eyes. "How did you—? I mean, I'm Katie."

Leah smiled. "You look like Katie and you talk a lot like her, but you're not her. You can tell me, Marta. Tell me why you came home with me and Katie went home with your daddy."

Marta drooped. "She'll be mad. Katie said to be careful, but I didn't think you'd believe us. I told Katie it wouldn't work like it did in the movie, but all the kids at camp couldn't tell who we were and we thought… She's going to be mad at me for real."

"So you two were just pretending to be mad? You didn't really have a fight?"

Marta shook her head. "I wanted you to be my mommy for a while and Katie thought it would be fun to live at my house with Daddy and Gussie and so we did this. The twins in the movie did it and it worked."

"You saw a movie where twins exchange identities?"

Marta looked confused, but she nodded. "Katie'll be mad, but I…miss Daddy and Gussie and my own Brownie Bear."

"I know you do, sweetheart. Do you want me to call your daddy now and ask him to come and pick you up?"

With a baby frown, Marta considered that. "I would like to live with you…for a while. But maybe I could do it later. When I don't miss Daddy so much."

Leah's throat went tight around a lump of emotion. What had she and Riker done to these babies? They weren't mature enough to handle the intricate relationships inherent in the situation. "I'll go call him right now, Marta. Do you want to talk to him?"

Marta nodded, then shook her head. "Could you just maybe take me home? That way, maybe Katie won't be mad. Maybe she could even spend the night with me. We're really not mad at each other. We just pretended."

"Yes." Leah straightened. "And as soon as I call your daddy, I'll take you home. Okay?"

"Okay." Marta reached up and squeezed Leah's hand. "You're not mad because I called you Mommy, are you?"

"No, Marta. I'm not mad. We'll leave in a few minutes. Go get your jacket."

A few minutes. Leah groped for composure, fought the sudden, inexplicable sting of tears, wondered why she wasn't hopping mad, and tried to form the words she wanted to say to Riker. Somehow, this was his fault. If he hadn't insisted the girls be allowed to form a relationship... If he wasn't so persistently sure he was right... If he just hadn't kissed her...

When he answered, Leah blurted out the first thing that came to mind. "I have Marta," she said. "And you have Katie."

"What?"

"They switched, Riker. I have Marta here with me and Katie is there with you. We should have known the minute we saw the haircuts."

"What?" he repeated. "The haircuts are bad, I admit, but I don't think—"

"Riker, I'm coming over and bringing Marta. You may as well prepare Katie for a lecture, because I feel a long one coming on." She was beginning to be angry. The whole thing was beginning to seem a little more than irritating.

"Leah, I can't believe—are you sure about this? Could you have made a mistake?"

"Not this time. I worried about the girls being 'sisters' in the first place. I wanted to wait until they were older, mature enough to handle it. But I stupidly gave in and now look what's happened."

"Wait just a minute. Why do I suddenly feel this is my fault? I'm not the one who placed them for adoption. I'm not the one who put them in separate families. And I'm sure as hell not the one who suggested they switch places. Let's deal with the problem at hand, Leah. Not some trumped-up accusations about mishandling the situation."

He was right, but Leah was disappointed by Katie's behavior, disappointed by her own, too. She needed to blame someone. Riker, even though it wasn't entirely his fault. "We've created a monster. And now we're all going to pay the price. You should have listened to me in the first place."

"Listened to your fears and insecurities, you mean. Listen, Leah, we did the only thing we could do. We didn't *let* Marta and Katie be sisters. They were born that way. We're just allowing them to have the relationship they would have had if we hadn't come along and separated them."

"I did no such thing."

"We *did* separate them. Innocently, that's true. But we made two separate families, two individual lives out of one whole. They're twins, Leah. What were we supposed to do once they'd met and figured out that they were identical twins?"

"We should have left them alone. Let them grow up in their separate families, in their individual ways. They could have gotten together later, when we weren't involved."

The words echoed across the phone wires and met silence. "Oh," Riker said. "I think I'm beginning to understand. It's not the *twins'* relationship that bothers you. It's *ours*."

"We don't have a…a relationship, Riker. And even if we did, it wouldn't matter now…" It would matter. She knew it would. "I'm bringing Marta home. I'll be there in fifteen minutes."

"I'll get Katie," he said and broke the connection.

Leah put down the receiver and realized she was trembling. What had Riker done to her and Katie? They'd been doing all right before he'd come along. Maybe life hadn't been perfect then, but she hadn't spent hours daydreaming about things she couldn't have, either. She hadn't missed the companionship, the support and succor of a relationship with a man. She hadn't needed anyone except Katie. And Katie hadn't needed anyone except her. Now all that was changed. Now Katie needed Marta. She wanted a big house, a grandmother, a daddy…like Marta's. And Marta wanted a mommy…like Katie's.

Leah pressed her lips into a thin line of angry concern. She and Riker had created this situation. They'd have to fix it, now, the best they could. And then, right or wrong, Leah intended to bow out of the picture. She couldn't keep the twins apart, but when Riker was around, she wouldn't be. She wasn't going to be in the "family portrait" any longer. She and Katie had had a life of their own before Riker and Marta entered the scene. All Leah had to do was figure out how to get back to that life without losing anything terribly important. Like her independence, her daughter, or her heart.

"I AM, too, Marta." Katie protested stubbornly. "You're trying to confuse me."

The four of them stood in the middle of the Westfalls' living room, Riker and Katie on one side, Leah and Marta on the other. From a safe distance, Gussie observed the scene over her needlework.

"Katie, for heaven's sake, stop that." Leah shoved her hand into the pocket of her skirt to keep from grabbing her daughter out of sheer frustration. "We know you two pretended to be mad at each other and switched places. There's no reason to keep on pretending."

Riker fixed his gaze on the child beside Leah. "Marta?" he said quietly, and was rewarded with a guilty nod.

"Oh, Marta!" Katie stamped her foot. "You told! Nobody at camp knew. You should have kept pretending and *they* wouldn't have known, either."

Leah couldn't stop her glance from sliding to Riker's face. They were pitted side by side now against their daughters. She didn't like it, but then there wasn't much about this situation that she did like. "Marta did not *tell*, Katie," Leah said. "I figured it out all by myself."

Katie lifted her obstinate little chin. "How?"

"She said please and thank you and she asked to be excused from the table, Miss Smarty. Do you see now why you should have paid more attention to minding your manners?"

Riker's eyebrows went up and a hint of a smile courted one side of his mouth. "That's the only way you could tell you had Marta and not Katie?"

"Don't be smug." Leah turned her frown to him. "You didn't have any idea of the switch until I told you."

"They look exactly alike." Riker glanced from one girl to the other. "They did, anyway, until you combed that one's hair."

"I *cut* her hair, evened up the straggly parts."

"Are you going to cut mine, too?" Katie developed a sudden interest in Marta's hair. "I want mine just like hers."

"As soon as we get home, Katie, I'll cut yours."

"Exactly like that?"

Leah sighed. "Exactly. Now let's go."

"Couldn't she spend the night?" Marta looked pleadingly into Leah's face. "It's all right with me."

"It's not all right with me, Marta. I haven't seen Katie all week and I want her at home with me. You'll want to be with your daddy and grandmother, too. Your family should be together and our family should be together. You and Katie can spend the night together some other time."

"Marta and I are family, too, aren't we?" Katie asked, making her way, finally, to Leah's side. "We're twins."

"Yes, Katie," Leah said. "You are twins, but you don't live together. Now let's go."

"But why can't we live together? Why can't Riker by my daddy and you be Marta's mommy? Why can't we do that?"

Too late, Leah saw the trap and she looked to Riker for help.

"We can't do it tonight," he said. "That's for sure."

What kind of help was that? she wondered. Practically setting them up to have this same discussion again. "Katie." She brought to bear all the authority she possessed, putting firmness in her voice and in her eyes. "I'm ready to leave. Get your jacket."

It looked for a moment as if Katie was going to rebel one more time, but apparently she thought better of it because she motioned to Marta and the two girls raced upstairs, whispering all the way. Leah sagged with the effort of dealing with her daughter's willfulness.

"How did they come up with this idea?" Riker placed his hands on his hips and shook his head. "I'd have thought they were sort of young to be playing switcharoos."

Leah pinned a strand of hair behind her ear. "They saw a movie. I guess they showed it at camp."

Gussie cleared her throat as she bent over her needlework. Riker turned, alerted by his mother's self-consciousness. "Do you know anything about this, Gus?" he asked.

"What?" She glanced up, smiled, returned to her needlework. "A movie, you say? I don't know where—" She stuck her finger with the needle and grimaced. "Well, we did rent a video tape one night when Katie was staying over and it was about these twins who wanted to get their parents together and... I never thought *our* twins would take it to heart, though. They must have had some encouragement." She paused. "At camp."

Riker nodded. "At camp. Yes, that must be where they got the encouragement."

"Now, Riker," Gussie began, "I never told them to—"

"Save it, Gus. The damage has already been done."

"*Damage* is right," Leah muttered and Riker spun toward her.

"What is wrong with you, Leah? You're acting as if this were the end of the world. They're kids. They played a trick on us. I think it's pretty darn ingenious of them to have thought of it in the first place." He glanced at his mother. "Even with a little encouragement. And the haircuts. That was a masterful touch, you have to admit."

Leah didn't believe this. He was defending them. "I'll admit that Katie is beginning to look on you as a daddy and Marta thinks she'd like for me to be her mommy. But it can't happen, Riker. You and I have to extricate ourselves from their fantasies. We can't allow them to go on believing that someday we'll all live in some nice little house with a picket fence and two puppies in the yard. It's not fair. Not to them and not to us."

Riker studied her in silence and Leah grew uncomfortably aware of his regard and of his mother's keen interest. "I don't remember either one of the girls mentioning a house or a picket fence. Puppies in the yard I can believe."

"They probably haven't mentioned a house with a fence because they're both visualizing us all in *this* house. *Your* house."

"And that would be bad." He said it without conviction, almost like a question.

"Yes, Riker. That would be bad. It's not going to happen. The four of us are not going to live together in any house. If Jean were still alive, if Jonathan were still around, the question would never have arisen. We have to nip the idea in the bud. And that means right now.''

''I see.'' Riker's gaze never wavered from her face. ''So you think it would be better if I treated you the way I would have if Jean were still alive. And you'll treat me as if you were still married to Jonathan.''

It sounded ridiculous put in those words, but Leah stood firm. ''Yes. That's the way it will be from now on, Riker. If you don't see the harm to Marta in this, then I'm sorry. But you won't stop me from protecting my daughter in the best way I know.''

Gussie had stopped pretending to stitch and her bright green eyes roved from one intent face to the other. Leah was embarrassed and angry at Riker for pursuing the discussion in open forum. She wanted to go home. She just wanted to take her daughter and go home.

A simple and sore quiet descended around her and Leah waited impatiently for Katie to end it. It seemed like forever before the sound of seven-year-old voices drifted down from upstairs, followed quickly by the seven-year-olds in person.

''Mom, Marta and I have an idea.'' Katie tossed the suggestion ahead of her as she walked down the steps. ''We think we all should go on a camping trip so we can show you what we learned at camp.''

Riker turned toward the twins with a hastily composed smile. ''We who?''

Marta frowned at him, as if he were diluting the potency of their suggestion. She directed her heartfelt plea at Leah. ''We learned lots of stuff. We got a 'happy camper' on our cabin before we left. Can we please go camping?''

''Katie and I are going home. I think you've both had enough camping for a while.'' Leah moved to Katie and took the jacket that drooped at her feet. ''Good night, Gussie, Marta, Riker.'' Turning to the doorway, she hoped against hope that Katie would come without a struggle. ''Come on, Katherine.''

''Bye, Marta.'' Katie couldn't have sounded madder, even if she tried. And she wasn't trying at the moment. ''Bye, Grandma Gussie. Bye, Riker.'' In utter dejection, she followed and Leah thanked whatever lucky star had smiled on her. It was a small triumph, she realized, but just getting Katie to the car without having to say anything else to Riker, without having to hear what else he had to say, without having to look at him and wonder…

Katie opened the front car door and climbed into the seat. She fastened her belt in silence. She rode like that, in a solid pout, for several minutes. "You're mean," she said, when they were halfway home. "I was just going to stay there a couple of days. And Marta wanted to stay with you. She doesn't remember what her mommy looked like and she never got to play with her 'cause she was always sick. And you won't play dunk in the pool, but Riker will. And Grandma Gussie lets us mix punch whenever we want to." Katie crossed her arms at her chest. "And I want to go camping."

Leah kept a handle on the impulse to lecture her daughter loud and long. Not that Katie didn't deserve a lecture. Not that she wasn't going to get one later. But Leah knew that if she said anything now, she would say too much. Katie didn't need to hear Leah's fears and insecurities. She was seven-years-old. How could she possibly understand that her mother was desperately afraid she had fallen in love?

SUSANNAH had a new dress, a new hairstyle and a new attitude. She smiled a lot, laughed a lot, and gazed into space a lot. Anytime Tom entered the workroom, she sat straighter, toyed with strands of her hair and talked softly. July was almost over before Leah came to the obvious conclusion.

"What's going on between the two of you?" she asked, half-irritated at Susannah's dreamy expression. "Did you fall in love at the stock-car races?"

"The races, the movies, the trip to Denver, the flea market…" Susannah sighed. "Six months ago if you'd told me I might lose my heart to a bespectacled, short man with a disgusting habit of talking about work at the most inappropriate moments, I'd have sent your name to every mailing list in the country, just to get even. But…" She lifted one shoulder in a magnificent shrug. "I think this is it, Leah. I'm so crazy about Tom it's embarrassing."

Leah agreed there. But she had no right to rain on her friend's parade just because she, herself… She clipped the thoughts and her words as she bent over a layout. "Are congratulations in order?"

"Not from you," Susannah said snippily as she got up to sharpen a pencil. "Honestly, Leah, I'm beginning to see where Katie gets her mouthiness. You used to be kind of nice to work with, but lately…"

"Sorry. I've been tired lately."

"You've been unhappy lately, you mean. Ever since you broke up with Riker Westfall—"

"There was no 'break up,' Susannah, because there was nothing to break up. You're in love and going through that stage where you want everyone else to be in love and to act as nutty as you do."

"Thanks, Dr. Taylor, for that analysis." Susannah plopped herself back on her work stool. "Acting a little 'nutty' would be good for you. You're becoming a real…stuck-in-the-mud."

Leah looked up, smiled a little. "*Stuck*-in-the-mud?"

"Stick, stuck. It's difficult to be precise in the middle of an impassioned speech."

Leah couldn't keep her smile from expanding. "Save the impassioned speeches for Tom, Suz. I'm immune to all that passion stuff."

"You're not immune, Leah. That's your problem."

"Oh, please—"

"No. I haven't said anything for weeks, now. Part of it, I admit, is that I've been a bit…self-involved. But the truth is, Leah, for a while you looked really good. Happy, I mean. You had this kind of…glow. I thought something really nice was happening for you. Then Katie went off to camp and wham! You're acting like somebody took away your birthday…cake, ice cream, and all."

"You're imagining things, Susannah. I'm fine. Katie's fine. Nothing's different than it was before."

"Uh-huh." Susannah bent over her sketch.

"It's true," Leah persisted even though she knew she was protesting too long and too loudly. "Katie and Marta have settled into a more reasonable schedule. They don't have to be together night and day like they did before. Since they went to camp, everything is better.''

Susannah's glance was frankly skeptical. "I'd like to hear Katie say that. Somehow, when I've been around her lately, I haven't gotten the idea that everything is better from her point of view.''

Leah bent toward the sketch board. "She's a child. Barely seven. She doesn't know what's best for her.''

The comment met the incredulous silence it deserved and Leah was ashamed of herself. For nearly six weeks, she'd pretended that nothing *was* different than it had been before Riker and Marta had entered her life. It was a lie, of course. Nothing was the same. Even though she'd tried to keep her life and Katie's separate from Marta's and Riker's lives. Even though she'd stayed away from Riker and any hint of the "one big happy family" scenario…

Tom walked into the room and Susannah lit up like a firecracker. Leah pretended not to notice their secret glances and the casual brush of one hand against another. So what if a silly remnant of romanticism teased her into longing for that same kind of closeness with a man…with Riker. She could and would live without it.

For Katie's sake.

Chapter Thirteen

"Please come in with me, Mommy. You can swim with us and everything." Katie hesitated before closing the door and Leah felt the now habitual twinge of guilt.

"Katie, you know I can't. I have to—"

"But, Mommy, Riker isn't here."

"That doesn't make any... Where is he?"

Katie shrugged. "Somewhere. I think it might be Texas. I don't know. But he's not here. So you can stay this time, Mommy. Please? Please?"

Was she so transparent, Leah wondered. Did everyone, including Katie, know she was afraid to be near Riker Westfall? "No, Katie, we've been over this and over this—"

The slam of the car door pretty much indicated Katie's feelings about the subject. Leah sighed as she watched Katie turn her back and head toward the house. Marta was waiting on the front deck, leaning on the rail and observing the exchange. She seldom came out to greet Leah anymore when Katie was dropped off. And when she visited at their house, Marta kept her distance. Nothing had been said, but Marta had gotten the message that Leah was not, and would never be, her mother. Katie wasn't so easily convinced about Riker, or maybe Riker just hadn't made it clear enough.

Leah hated the situation. If anything, it was worse than it had been before and it was all her fault. No one seemed eager to share the blame, least of all Riker. Six weeks hadn't simplified her life and it hadn't made much of a dent in the uneasy suspicion that she loved Marta and was in love with Marta's father, too. She tried to refer to him that way as often as possible, thus keeping her priorities constantly in view. But there were moments, like now, when Riker filled her thoughts and she couldn't think of him without aching all over.

She'd missed him a great deal during the past lonely weeks. Gleaning bits of information from Katie and Marta wasn't easy and Gussie was almost as stingy. But Leah told herself it was for the best. She didn't need to know where Riker was or what he was doing or if—by any chance—he thought about her. It was easier like this. She was doing the right thing. Leah had to be certain of that.

She put the car into reverse and prepared to back into the turnaround so she could get a running start on the sloped driveway. With a glance, she checked to make sure Katie was safely inside with Marta. The girls stood on the deck, talking to each other, and Gussie stood in the front doorway, waving her arms frantically. With a frown, Leah put the car in park, turned off the engine and opened the door. "Is something wrong?" she called to the older woman.

"Yes," Gussie yelled, cupping her hands around her mouth as if she were a mile away, instead of a few feet. "I've got a problem. Will you help?"

What now? Leah debated the wisdom of entering the Westfall home...even if Riker *was* in Texas. Or somewhere. "What is it?" she asked Gussie.

Gussie shook her head and moved her hand to cup her ear, as if she couldn't make out Leah's words. What an actress, Leah thought as she slipped the keys from the ignition and closed the car door. If this was another twin trick... If Riker was really inside the house instead of being somewhere else...

"Oh, thank goodness." Gussie said by way of greeting as she led Leah into the house and directly to the kitchen. "I was afraid you'd drive off and I'd never figure out what to do."

"What are you trying to figure out?" Leah asked cautiously, still not entirely sure Gussie was being honest. "Some new recipe?"

Gussie looked back over her shoulder, arched a coppery eyebrow and shook her carroty curls. "I gave up cooking weeks ago, Leah. I've never been good at it. Now, I'm working on tie-dye T-shirts for the girls. And I need some assistance."

"Tie-dye?" Leah looked around the kitchen, but Riker was not there. She pretended not to notice her disappointment. "Didn't you do tie-dye in the sixties?"

"I did protests in the sixties, Leah. I wasn't a college student, you know. I could afford to *buy* my clothes."

"Can't you afford to buy them now?"

"I'm doing this for the fun of it, Leah." Gussie frowned at the pots and paraphernalia clustered on the center island. "Anyway, I think it will be fun, as soon as I figure out how to do it. Won't the girls look cute in little tie-dyed shirts and shorts? I'm even thinking of tearing some material scraps and letting them make tie-dye ribbons for their hair."

"Pretty ambitious." Leah glanced in the pots, sniffed the pungent odor of hot-water dye, and heard Katie and Marta running upstairs. "Did you say you're going to let *them* do this?"

"Of course, I'm going to let them do it. It isn't any fun for me if they don't help." Gussie made a face. "I'm their grandmother, for Pete's sake. I'm supposed to help them make messes."

Leah decided not to address the *their* grandmother issue. Katie loved Gussie and felt more comfortable with her than she'd ever felt with Mildred, her own grandmother. The fact that Katie had a relationship with Gussie didn't seem threatening to Leah. It was only Riker who—"I don't know much about tie-dye," Leah said, as much to distract her own thoughts as to answer Gussie. "But it looks like you've got everything under control. What's the problem?"

Gussie smiled. "The problem is I was lonesome for you, Leah. We haven't talked in ages. And it does take two people, two adults, I mean, to do this."

Leah hesitated. "I'll bet you could manage on your own, Gussie."

"Maybe. Maybe not. But Riker's gone for the weekend and I may as well get some enjoyment out of being cooped up in this house." She nodded toward the refrigerator. "There's crab salad for lunch."

"All right, you talked me into it." Leah capitulated without a fight. After all, Riker was the problem and if he was gone, then there was no reason for her not to stay. Maybe it would make Katie happy. Maybe it would do wonders for her own dismal state of mind.

And she'd kind of like to have a tie-dye T-shirt, herself.

THREE HOURS, four successful dye operations and two ruined shirts later, Leah sank onto the lounge chair beside the pool and stretched out with a glass of iced tea in her hand.

"Come in with us." Katie and Marta called at intervals, begging as they always did, for more attention. "We won't dunk you. We promise."

Leah adjusted her sunglasses. "You'd dunk me before I got completely wet," she said. "Besides, I didn't bring my swimsuit."

"You don't need it, Mommy. You can borrow one of Gussie's."

"Now, wait a minute." Gussie spread a beach towel on the other lounge and prepared to sunbathe. "I might want to swim. I can't go loaning out my swimsuit."

"You're wearing your swimsuit, Gussie." Marta gurgled with a laugh. "And you have more than one, anyway."

"Yeah," Katie added. "And you never get in the pool with us, anyway."

"Never?" The older woman picked at her red curls before tying them away from her face with a strip of fabric. "I do other nice things for you all the time, Marta Grace. I just don't swim in pools. I prefer the ocean."

"Take us to the ocean, Gussie," Katie said, paddling to the edge of the pool. "I've never been."

"You should see it, Katie." Gussie began to relate the wonders of the sea as she stretched her body into the heat of full sunlight. Katie quickly tired of descriptive phrases and splashed Gussie.

"Thank you," Gussie said. "Keeping the skin moist is important at my age. But if you splash me again, I will lock you in the laundry room for three days. Understand?''

With a giggle, Katie dived out of sight and surfaced beside Marta. Leah allowed herself a small smile of enjoyment. For the first time in quite a while, she relaxed. ''Thanks for talking me into helping with the shirts, Gussie. I have really enjoyed the afternoon.''

''You should come around more often, Leah. We'd all have more fun.''

''I can't do that, Gussie.''

Silence, broken occasionally by the twin voices in the pool, settled around Leah.

''Riker's in Texas,'' Gussie said out of the blue. ''On business. He's going to Missouri next week. He's talking about buying a store in St. Louis.''

''He's a busy man.'' Leah hoped that would be the end of the discussion. Talking about Riker, like everything else about Riker, made her nervous.

''Yes.'' Gussie reached into the pool and dribbled water over her bare legs. She really had a nice figure. Leah hoped she would look half as good when she was Gussie's age. ''Next week,'' Gussie continued, ''while Riker's gone, Marta and I are going to Kansas City to visit a friend of mine. Would you allow Katie to go with us? We'll leave on Thursday morning and be home Monday.''

''Oh, I don't think—''

''Leah.'' Gussie opened her eyes and frowned. ''Just because you're uncomfortable with the idea that Katie and Marta are twins, is no reason to make Katie uncomfortable with it. I'm inviting her because I feel she's as much my granddaughter as Marta is. Regardless of who her parents are. I'll take good care of her. You know the two of them together are less trouble than either one alone. Don't deny her the pleasure of this trip. We're going to Six Flags and the water park and anywhere else it pleases us to go. You don't really mind, do you?''

Put like that, Leah thought she'd have to be an ogre to say no. ''I guess that would be all right. I'd planned to take off a couple of days next week to take Katie shopping for school clothes, but I guess that can wait.''

"I'll take them shopping in Kansas City. They'll love it." Gussie lifted her hand to ward off any argument. "Don't deny *me* that pleasure, Leah. I can afford to buy them both a few school clothes and I'm afraid I'm not going to be a huge success at creating fashions for them. The tie-dye wasn't too bad, though, was it?"

"It looks fine. In fact, I'm going to wear my shirt as soon as it dries.''

"You'll look great in it. If you want, I'll give you one of my famous tie-dye hair ribbons, too."

"Thanks. We can all be twins."

Gussie repositioned her psychedelic sunglasses on her nose. "Good idea," she murmured sleepily. "Just do me one more favor.''

Leah stretched lazily and sipped her drink. "What's that?"

"Stay for supper tonight. I feel a nap coming on and these girls need supervision.''

"Yes," Leah said, feeling relaxed, lazy and utterly at home. "They certainly do. I'll wake you when it's time to turn over."

Gussie said nothing as the sun beat down and the girls splashed and swam in the water. Watching them, Leah wondered if their biological mother ever thought about them, ever wondered where and who they were. Silently Leah thanked the woman, whoever and wherever she was, for giving a gift of love so precious. If only she hadn't split the two....

Leah smiled as one of the girls scampered up the slide and slid, belly down, into the pool. Katie? Or Marta? From here it was really impossible to tell. Whatever reason the biological mother had had for separating the twins, Leah had to acknowledge a feeling of relief that they were separated no longer. Even though the situation was fraught with emotional danger. Even though she herself was drowning in it.

Katie's happiness was worth the sacrifice.

IT SOUNDED like fun. A trip to Kansas City. Shopping. Sightseeing. Playing. Katie could hardly contain her excitement. Leah was open to an invitation to tag along, but Gussie was oblivious to hints and when Thursday morning rolled around, Gussie and the twins drove off without a backward look. It seemed silly to feel left out, Leah thought. She had a four-day weekend to spend as she chose, considering nothing and no one except herself. It was a single mother's dream.

So why did the day seem to stretch before her in a monotonous flow of dreary minutes? Had she become one of those mothers who was lost when her child wasn't around? No. Definitely not. She'd think of something to do. Something different. Something she'd always wanted to do, but hadn't as yet had the opportunity. Maybe she'd go somewhere. Maybe she'd take a trip to Oklahoma City. Or Wichita. Maybe she'd call up an old friend and go out for lunch. Maybe she'd...clean Katie's room.

Ten minutes into the toy chest, she was rescued by a phone call.

"Leah?" Riker's voice caught her by surprise and her heart flew to her throat.

"Riker? I thought you were out of town."

"I am. I've been trying to call home for the past hour, but I can't get an answer. Do you, by any chance, know where Gussie might be?"

"She's on her way to Kansas City. She picked up Katie less than a half hour ago."

"Damn! I was afraid of that." He drew the words into a slow groan. "She told me she wouldn't forget, but I should have trusted my gut instinct and called yesterday to remind her. She's certainly thrown a monkey wrench into my plans."

Leah knew she shouldn't ask, but suddenly the question was just there. "Is something wrong?"

"Nothing earth-shattering. Just inconvenient." He paused. "Damned inconvenient."

She didn't know what to say. "If I'd known, maybe I could have..." The words trailed into conjecture.

"There's no way you could have known Gussie would forget she was supposed to meet me at the airport later this morning. It isn't as if you talk to me often enough to know my schedule.

We haven't really talked to each other since the great twin switch.''

Her breath became shaky and uncertain. "No," she said.

"We probably ought to speak to each other more often," he said, his voice gentle and somehow sort of wistful. "For Marta and Katie's sakes."

Leah didn't like the way she was feeling. She didn't like the deep-down yearning that twisted her stomach into knots. Riker had no right to make her feel that way. "I'm sorry you missed your mother, Riker. I hope you get your problem worked out."

"I don't suppose you would consider…? No, never mind. You're probably on your way to work right now."

It would have been smart to agree, but Leah was honest. "I have a couple of days off. I'd intended to take Katie shopping for school clothes, but when Gussie invited her to go to Kansas City, my promise of a shopping trip fell out of favor."

"The water park was probably the deciding factor. You know how the twins love to play in water."

"You knew they were going?"

"Yes. Gussie told me all about it, but she wasn't supposed to leave until after I got there. I'm on a tight schedule today, trying to make it from the Dallas market to a meeting in St. Louis this afternoon. To simplify things, Gussie was supposed to meet me at the airport in Bartlesville and bring some papers that I need for this meeting."

"Couldn't one of your employees take care of it?"

"Ordinarily, yes. But my attorney couldn't get away to come with me because he had a trial this week, so he drew up a proposed contract and took it out to the house a couple of days ago. I know he delivered the papers to Gussie. What I don't know is what she did with them."

"I guess that means you'll have to search your house, then, huh?"

"And if I do that, I'll miss the meeting anyway." He sounded tired. "Maybe I can reschedule the damn thing without making the guy too nervous. He's been skittish about the sale and I really thought I had him committed to deal this time." Riker sighed. "But there isn't much else I can do…under the circumstances."

"Where do you think Gussie put the contract?" Leah asked, knowing she was probably going to regret offering to help. "Could I find it? Could I even get into your house to look?"

"You'd do that for me?" His tone picked up hope and energy. "I can get you in, no problem. The lady who cleans the house will be there in another hour and I'll call and tell her you're coming by. I don't want you to feel like you have to help, Leah, but if you would…"

"Tell me where you think the papers will be," she said in a voice that had a buoyancy she couldn't explain.

"*If* Gussie didn't take it with her—which is possible—my best guess is that she'd have put them on the counter in the kitchen. The same spot where she keeps her purse. If they're not there, try on top of her dresser in her bedroom. And if not there, she might have put them on the dresser in *my* bedroom. Last place to look would be the desk in the study." He waited a moment, as if considering other places the contract might be. "Don't worry if you can't find it."

"What am I supposed to do if I find it?"

"Would it be too much trouble to bring it out to the airport? That would save me almost an hour."

"No trouble," Leah answered, trying to sound like a generous neighbor, running a simple errand for the guy next door. She hoped Riker couldn't detect the eagerness she felt at being able to help, at knowing she would see him in a couple of hours. "I'll be at the airport, with or without your papers. That way, even if I can't find them, you'll know. What time will you arrive?"

"I'm at the Dallas airport now and I've filed my flight plan, so as soon as I can get out to the plane and in the air, I'll be there within an hour and a half. Let's say two hours from now. Is that okay with you?"

"Don't forget to call the cleaning lady," Leah said. "And I'll see you in two hours."

"Leah? I really appreciate this."

"That's okay, Riker. I don't mind."

There was a small hesitation, as if he wanted to say more. But he merely cleared his throat. "Okay. I'll see you…in two hours."

"Yes."

He broke the connection then without saying goodbye and Leah wondered if he was afraid she would change her mind if he kept talking. She wouldn't have. It was, after all, only a small favor. One she'd have done for almost anyone in her acquaintance. It didn't mean anything.

Never mind that her heart was pounding like a kettledrum at the mere thought of seeing him. Never mind that her palms were sweaty with nervous anticipation. Never mind that her day seemed suddenly filled with possibilities.

WHEN RIKER STEPPED out of the plane, Leah was caught off guard by the ripple of gladness that washed through her. He walked toward her with an easy gait, arms swinging at his side, mouth widening with a smile directed only at her. Her heart skipped a beat and then settled into a reckless rhythm. The late-morning sun picked out the reddish highlights in his hair and burnished his skin to a deep, end-of-summer tan. He was wearing his favorite cotton-knit shirt and a pair of navy slacks. Leah wished she'd changed into something more attractive than faded jeans and her tie-dyed T-shirt, even though she'd stylishly knotted the hem of the T-shirt with one of Gussie's famous fabric ribbons. She'd thought she looked nice enough for a trip to the local airport, but she suddenly felt self-conscious and awkward.

"Leah," Riker said when still a few feet from her. "I was afraid you wouldn't come."

She swallowed the impulse to tell him nothing could have kept her away. "I have your papers." She extended the legal-size manila envelope toward him. "They were on Gussie's chest of drawers. No telling why she put them there."

His smile encompassed her in soft pleasure. "No telling," he said. "I wouldn't have been surprised if she'd taken the whole thing with her to Kansas City. She's a terrific lady, but she can be the most forgetful person in the world."

"And she's in charge of our daughters for the weekend."

"A scary thought, but we'll take solace in the fact that she couldn't lose Marta and Katie if she tried. The two of them are more than a match for Gussie."

Leah let her expression melt into a replica of his smile. "Katie was so excited about this trip, she could hardly sleep last night. She kept saying she'd never been to the *City*, as if she were going on a pilgrimage."

He nodded his understanding and reached up to take off the sunglasses he wore. His eyes met hers and Leah was aware that no matter what they said aloud, their hearts were exchanging information on another level.

She'd missed him. And she'd thought she'd done such a good job of pretending she hadn't. But here he was and here she was and the emotions she'd been running from bloomed inside her like a wild rose, untended and neglected, but still beautiful and brave.

"You look...great." Riker's voice conveyed sincerity and genuine delight at seeing her again. "I like the shirt."

Leah glanced down at her clothes, made a small and unnecessary adjustment to the ribbon-tie. "I made it myself," she said. "With a little help from Gussie and the twins."

"I heard about the tie-dye project. I'm sorry I wasn't there to make one for myself."

"It was fun." The words felt thick and heavy on her tongue, but Leah kept on talking, hoping he couldn't sense her tension, hoping she sounded normal and unaffected by his nearness. "It was Gussie's idea."

"Yes."

The drone of an engine cut through the conversation and Leah turned to watch as a light plane taxied from the ramp to the runway. She was aware of Riker standing behind her and the thought crossed her mind that if she took a single step back, she would be practically in his arms. And if she turned around and took that single step...

But she wouldn't, of course. She couldn't. For Katie's sake.

Then, suddenly, unexpectedly, she felt his hands on her shoulders, his body strong and straight against hers, his breath seductive and warm in her ear. "Come with me, Leah."

Her breath fluttered frantically in her throat, a throat that was tight with conflicting emotions. She struggled for composure and settled for a shocked whisper. "What?"

He turned her to face him. "I said, come with me."

She swallowed hard, fought against a wave of longing that urged her to agree. "That's...crazy."

"Yes," he agreed.

"Riker, I—" She searched for some word, some light way of turning away the invitation. "You know I can't."

"You can, Leah. Just say yes."

"Riker, you can't be serious." She could tell by the look in his eyes that he was and thoughts on the insanity of his suggestion rose to her lips. "I can't just get on that plane and go to St. Louis. I don't have any clothes or anything. And...well, it's just completely irresponsible."

"Is your house locked?"

"Yes, of course, but—"

"Then you're free of responsibilities for the weekend. I own a clothing store and I have some samples in the plane right now that I picked up at the Dallas Market. Something in there will probably fit you, so you'll have at least a change of clothes. And there are plenty of shops in St. Louis. There's really no valid reason not to go. Didn't you say you'd love to travel? Go somewhere outside the state of Oklahoma?"

"Yes, but—"

"This is your opportunity. Your opportunity to go to the *City*, as Katie would say. Why not take it?"

It was wrong even to listen to his argument. She couldn't simply go with him. Impulsive actions always brought regrets. "Riker, you know it's impossible. There are just too many reasons not to go."

"And one good reason that you should." His hands tightened on her shoulders, his eyes darkened with intensity. "Just once, Leah, do something for yourself. Something impulsive and crazy, maybe, but something you'll remember for the rest of your life. For one weekend, you can relax. You don't have to be anyone's mother. You don't have to be the sole support of your family or someone's employee. Please, Leah, come with me. Let me show you that Jonathan was wrong about you."

The last words weighted the scales in his favor. It had been a perceptive and masterful stroke on his part to have hit her most vulnerable point. Jonathan had left and, deep inside, in dark places of her heart where the sun of logic couldn't reach, she'd always felt it was her fault. And now, out of the blue, Riker asked for the chance to prove to her that Jonathan had been wrong. Leah had no control over the quick tapping of her pulse and she knew, in that instant, that she was about to do it. "What about Katie?" she asked. "What about the girls?"

"We were people before we became parents, Leah. Katie and Marta are well taken care of this weekend. We don't have to worry about them. We can call Gussie and let her know where to reach you in case of emergency, if that's what you're worried about. And the girls don't ever have to know."

"But…" She wanted to go and even the beginning of her protest sounded weak and artificial. "I don't know."

Riker dropped his hands from her shoulders. "You think about it, Leah. I'm going inside to call the weather service and check on conditions in St. Louis. Then I'm going to file my flight plan. If you're not here when I come back, I'll understand. But…I hope you'll wait."

She watched him walk away and told herself to turn and walk in the opposite direction. But somehow, she couldn't get her feet moving. What she was considering was insane. It defied logic and every sensible cell in her body. It was impulsive, reckless, dangerous. To go to St. Louis with Riker was tantamount to admitting that she was in love with him. And she couldn't afford to be in love. Not with him. Not now.

But she kept standing there, waiting for him to return, eyeing his plane and wondering what it was like to fly in a plane that size. And what was St. Louis like? She'd never been there, not even in passing. She'd never seen the Mississippi River or the barges that floated upon it. She'd never seen the St. Louis Arch or a riverboat. And St. Louis was home to a major league baseball team, the Cardinals. Leah sighed, wanting to see those things, wanting to experience something new, wanting—needing—to be alone with Riker.

Would it really be so awful to go? She could manage without extra clothes and hair curlers and makeup for a day or two. Those weren't, after all, necessities. In fact, at the moment, she couldn't think of one thing she *absolutely* needed.

Except Riker Westfall.

Therein lay the danger and the adventure. Riker wanted her to go. She was a grown woman. Couldn't she take this one journey without her whole world falling apart? Katie would never know about this small indiscretion, this tiny deviation from the usual routine.

One weekend, Leah promised herself. One long weekend. And then, she'd go back to her old sensible, responsible way of living.

Chapter Fourteen

"Comfortable?" Riker asked over the steady drone of the engine. She lifted skeptical brown eyes and he smiled. "I guess comfort doesn't exactly describe this, does it? But we'll be in St. Louis in another forty-five minutes. Then you'll get a chance to stretch your legs and talk without having to shout."

"I don't mind the noise," she said loudly. "I'm enjoying the flight, even though I'm a bit nervous. It's my first time in a small plane."

"Good thing you chose to fly on a reliable plane with a hot-dogger pilot."

"Hot-dogger?"

"If I'd been born a hundred years earlier, I'd have been a match for the Red Baron."

She laughed, but the hum of the engine ate the sound. "If you'd told me that ahead of time, I wouldn't be here now."

"Where's your spirit of adventure, woman?"

"The spirit is right here," she said. "But the flesh is having a hard time understanding why." Her upper teeth closed over her bottom lip for an uncertain moment, then she offered a tentative smile. "I still can't believe I'm actually halfway to St. Louis and I can't even remember whether I turned off the coffee maker this morning."

"I'm sure you did, so don't worry about it. We're going to have a wonderful time."

"Oh, I know." She sounded unconvinced, even through the above-normal pitch of the voices they had to use in the confines of the small plane. Riker wondered what he should say to put her at ease. She was nervous, but not because of the flight. He knew the situation was awkward, impulsive, and probably not wise. It started things they'd have to finish. And there was no telling where it would end. Leah had to be having the same up-and-down thoughts. He wanted to be with her, was so very glad she'd come with him, and he planned to do everything in his power to ensure her enjoyment and pleasure.

But…well… He was nervous, too. Nervous because she was so special. And so vulnerable. And right now her happiness depended on him.

"We can fly home this evening, if you want." He made the offer reluctantly, because he knew it had to be made. "It might be late, but I'm certified for night landings. If it would make you feel safer…"

"I haven't felt safe since I met you, Riker. I don't suppose a couple of days more is going to change that, one way or another."

"I'm no threat to you, Leah." The words lost some of their impact as the plane hit a pocket of air and bounced for several uncomfortable seconds. This was not a good time to have a serious conversation, Riker realized. Maybe there wasn't a good time. He was kidding himself if he thought he could be with Leah for the next two days and not want to kiss her, hold her in his arms, make love to her. She'd occupied his thoughts for hours on end during the past few weeks. Oh, he'd honored her decision to keep her distance and he'd told himself she might have a point about creating a make-believe family hurting Marta and Katie. But the time away from her had only pointed out how much he'd come to love her. Marta had missed her, too. And Gussie. Leah had become important in all their lives. He didn't intend to simply let her walk out, now. He'd lost Jean. He wasn't going to lose Leah, and maybe Katie, too.

WHILE RIKER had his meeting, Leah wandered through the shops and stalls of Union Station. She'd called Gussie and told her she could be reached at the number Riker had supplied. Now she was enjoying the luxury of "just looking." It was something she thought she could become accustomed to. Usually she had Katie claiming her attention, tugging her in another direction, asking endless questions and generally making shopping a headache, not a pleasure. But now she had the time to spend and nothing else— oh, the incredible indulgence of being able to say those words— *nothing else* she had to do.

By the time Riker caught up with her, she was enjoying a frozen daiquiri at an open area on the upper level and watching the shoppers walk past. "Hi," she said as he pulled out the chair on the other side of the small round table. "Are you the proud new owner of Robey's clothing store in St. Louis?"

Riker loosened the knot of his tie. "*Mr.* Robey has taken the contract I offered under consideration. He's just not sure he's ready to sell."

"Maybe he's hoping you'll come up with a better offer."

"That's not likely to happen. In fact, I'm almost to the point of rescinding the offer I've already made. It's a good investment, but I'm not sure it's worth the hassle. If he does come around, I'll have to spend a lot of hours traveling back and forth. And that means time away from home, not to mention the extra responsibilities of managing a store in another state." He shrugged and grinned. "Of course, if you'd consider a career as my travel agent and companion, it might not be so bad."

"I'm afraid my career as a mother takes precedence. This weekend will have to be my one and only contribution to your business."

"Then we'd better make it one hell of a weekend, hadn't we?" He eyed her frozen drink. "Where did you get that and do you want another?"

She indicated the booth where she'd purchased the drink. "No more for me, thanks, but try the Tropical Fruit flavor. I couldn't make up my mind between that and this strawberry-pineapple daiquiri. If you get the Tropical Fruit, I can taste both."

"You're a manipulative woman, Leah, but because I like you and because I'm as dry as the Sahara, Tropical Fruit it will be." He rose, walked to the beverage counter, and returned a few minutes later with a hurricane glass filled with frosty, frothy, apricot-colored ice. He offered Leah a sip and she rolled the pungent taste on her tongue before she said she'd trade her drink for his.

"Not a chance. Yours is almost gone." He shielded his glass and took a couple of long drags on the straw. "I'll tell you what, though. As soon as I've finished this concoction, we'll shop around and see what else there is to see in this place. Have you been to all the shops, yet?"

"I haven't even made it to the lower level of the mall," Leah admitted. "I spent a wonderful hour going through the hotel lobby and looking at the railroad memorabilia."

"It's great, isn't it? I think that's one of the reasons I'd like to own Robey's store. It's here in Union Station and I'd get atmosphere for no extra expense." Riker glanced around, observing the mall traffic. "Busy place, too. Robey's store does a good business here."

"Why does he want to sell?"

"He's almost seventy. He has no one to take over and he's tired." Riker stirred his daiquiri. "Do you think Marta and Katie will be waiting to take over the management of Westfall's when I retire?"

Leah shifted uneasily in her chair. "I don't know about Marta, but Katie's ambitions don't include retail merchandising. She's going to be an animal trainer in the circus or maybe an ice-cream truck driver."

He smiled. "I'd forgotten. And Marta plans to be a nurse or a circus clown. I won't count on either of them to step into my shoes at the store."

"They do have minds of their own, even at seven years of age." Leah twisted the base of her nearly empty glass and decided she didn't want to challenge the way he'd included Katie in his and Marta's future. She and Riker simply didn't see the situation in the same light and Leah had to wonder what she was doing three hundred miles from home with a man for whom she had too many conflicting emotions. She wanted to be here…because he was here. She wanted to be with him. She wanted to experience that elusive sense of being free to do anything she wanted without considering someone else's happiness. And just when she'd managed to rationalize her impulsive actions, just when she'd begun to relax, Katie and Marta entered the conversation and she was torn once more between being a mother and being a woman…and reminded that they were two very different things.

"Are you ready?" Riker set his glass on the table, aware of Leah's sudden apprehension and determined to dispel it. "After we're through shopping, we can either catch a ride on a riverboat or go up to the top of the Arch. There are shops and restaurants down by the river, too. I'd hoped the Cardinals would have a home game this weekend, but I'm afraid you won't get to yell at a major league umpire this trip."

"I'm out of practice, anyway," she said with a soft smile.

"You're a natural, Leah. It will all come back to you as soon as you hear someone yell, *'You're Out.'*" Riker offered a grin and hoped he could overcome the obstacles he'd set for himself. Leah was tense, unsure and uncomfortable. Maybe he should simply admit that this wasn't working and take her home. He'd thought a weekend alone, without familiar surroundings, without the constant reminders of their roles as parents, would allow Leah to see how much he cared for her. Not as Katie's mother. Not as a possible mother for Marta. But as a woman in her own right. And what was the first thing he did? Mention the twins and send Leah's thoughts spinning back toward home. He didn't know if he could rectify the mistake, recover the ground he'd lost. Was it even worth the effort?

"If you'd rather go back home…" He left the sentence to hang, knowing even as he spoke the words how much he wanted to pretend they didn't have to be said.

"Home?" Leah was surprised by his suggestion, following so closely behind the suggestions of things they could do during the rest of the afternoon. Was her tension so obvious? Or was Riker regretting the invitation? "I'd really hate to leave without seeing St. Louis," she began. "But if you…?"

His jawline tightened before he formed a slight smile. "Leah, let me tell you something. I've missed you. Really missed you these past few weeks." He leaned forward, clasping his hands on the tabletop, holding his blue eyes steady on hers. "I appreciate the complications of our situation, and I understand your concerns. But I want to spend this weekend with you...the woman I met in the grocery store, the woman who took the last banana pepper right out of my hand. There's nowhere I'd rather be than right here, no one I'd rather be with than you, but if you're having second thoughts and you really don't want to be with me, then I'll take you home right now."

She was touched by his words and by her own increasing need to stay with this adventure to its conclusion. It had been crazy and impulsive to come with him, but she'd done it and now...well, she wasn't going to run away. "The day's getting away from us, Riker," she said with a tentative smile. "We can't sit here gabbing and drinking daiquiris all day. I'm ready if you are."

THE SUBJECT of sleeping arrangements didn't arise for a couple of hours. It occurred to Leah as they browsed through the shops at Union Station that she had nothing to wear to bed. And while they toured the museum at the base of the Arch, she did think it had been a long time since she'd spent the night away from home. But it wasn't until she sat, scrunched close to Riker inside the small capsule that carried them to the top of the Arch, that she fully accepted the fact that the two of them would be spending the night in a hotel...together. And from that point on, she thought of little else.

Riker treated the question of where they would sleep as a practical matter. "I made a reservation at the hotel I told you about, here on the waterfront," he said as they waited in line to buy tickets for a riverboat cruise. "As soon as we've got the tickets, we probably should walk over and check in. We'll need to be back here, ready for the evening dinner cruise in a little less than an hour, but that should give us plenty of time."

"Check into a hotel," she repeated in a breathless, but steady voice. "I...guess we should do that, unless we want to spend the night on a street corner somewhere," she said in a lighter tone.

Riker stepped up to the counter and purchased two tickets for the evening dinner cruise. Then he tucked the tickets into his wallet, put the wallet in his hip pocket, captured Leah's hand

and led her across the wobbly planks that connected the *Dixie Queen* to solid Missouri ground. Out of earshot of several passing tourists, he turned to Leah. "The hotel is over there." He indicated a tall, modern building on the other side of the renovated warehouses that lined the waterfront. "I have one room reserved for the night. I'd like for you to share the room with me, but if you're uncomfortable with that, tell me and I'll take care of it. And street corners don't figure into this."

A wave of hot and cold emotion swept through Leah. She had thought about this moment, this decision, for most of the afternoon. She'd started out telling herself she wouldn't sleep with him because that would be just too—well, just because. But now, suddenly, it seemed so personal, so intimate, so important.

She had to ask. "You're not just offering a bed, are you, Riker?"

"No, Leah."

He'd put it straight. There were no roses or music or candlelight. But there was desire in his eyes and gentleness in his touch.

Suddenly Leah felt awkward and unsophisticated. She thought she'd already weighed the question in her mind and decided on a course of action. But, all of a sudden, she was unsure of that decision, uncertain of Riker's reasons for asking, fearful of what she risked by doing what she really wanted to do. "It'll be a mistake," she said slowly. "I'm not—I haven't been—it's been so long for me."

He stared at her for a moment before he drew her toward him. Her heart skipped a beat and then another as he bent his head and brushed her lips in a tender kiss. "You don't have to decide this instant and there's nothing to say you can't change your mind later. This is our weekend, Leah. We can do anything we please and it's just between you and me. Okay?"

She searched his expression and found only sincerity and...desire. Yes, she could see that in his eyes, hear it in his voice. He wanted her and he wanted to please her. That was an unfamiliar, but nice feeling. She hadn't felt desirable since...the last time he'd kissed her. "Okay," she said in a steadier voice. "Okay."

HE BEGAN making love to her as the riverboat left the dock and cruised down the river.

Oh, he did nothing any of the other passengers might note or object to—a meeting of hands, a long, slow smile, a tone of voice, a sweet story about the first time he'd stumbled into love and broken his heart, gentle touches, tender looks, the way he used her name over and over again, weaving it through his conversation like a silken thread of seduction. He talked about Jean and the long, heavy days of her illness. She talked about Jonathan and the anger and helplessness she'd experienced when she'd realized he wasn't coming back. They spoke of the twins, but lightly, as parents do, wistful for the future and the easing of responsibility, but cautious of wishing away the years of childhood, too.

By the time the boat docked and they walked, hand in hand, brushing arm against arm, through the darkness to the hotel, Leah felt serene. As they strolled past the closed shops and noisy clubs of LaClede's Landing, she inhaled the sights and smells of the waterfront and felt the weight of air, humid and hot, against her body. She wanted a shower and the thought was followed, unbidden, by the image of Riker standing beneath the steamy spray and beckoning her to join him. Closing her eyes for a bare second, she enjoyed the thought. It was immediately followed by another sensual image and she missed a step.

Riker's hand moved to grasp her elbow, steadying her. "Whoa," he said. "Watch out there. I don't think this is the best spot in town to twist an ankle."

"Sorry, I wasn't watching where I was going."

He stepped ahead of her and opened the door of the hotel. "I'm glad to be inside. Some of those kids who were hanging around outside of the clubs made me a little nervous. Did you see that one girl—or it might have been a boy—who was wearing at least a dozen chains around her—or his—waist?"

Leah shook her head and wondered how she'd missed a spectacle like that. But, of course, she knew how. She'd been seeing quite a different spectacle in her own mind. She followed Riker into an elevator as if she had not a care in the world.

And suddenly, the apprehension returned. This wasn't right.

What had made her think she could discard reality along with responsibility? She'd never been very good at sex. Jonathan had certainly told her so, time and again. So what was she doing in a hotel room with Riker? She wouldn't be good enough for him, either, and then he'd leave. She couldn't handle that.

He unlocked the door of their hotel room and opened it for her. She walked in, knowing she had to let him know she'd changed her mind. She wasn't a tease. She hadn't meant to lead him on. But facts were facts and—

"Leah?" His voice broke through her frantic thoughts and she looked at him through a world colored by guilt. "Do you want something to drink?"

"What? A drink? No. No, thank you."

He nodded as he closed the door, shutting them into privacy and a thousand possibilities. She twisted the single birthstone ring she wore on her right hand. "Riker, I—I'm sorry. It's not that I don't...like you or want..." Her voice trailed into an uncertain silence. "I should never have let this happen."

For a moment, he stood still, head bent, eyes on the carpet, his lips pursed with thought. Then he lifted his eyes and locked her gaze with his. "Leah, nothing *has* happened. Nothing *has* to happen. I'll get another room. I am not a threat to you, please believe that. Just tell me what you want."

She started to say she didn't know, but that would have been a lie. "I don't want you to get another room. Or another bed. It's just that...I've tried so hard to keep some distance between us, to keep from telling you..."

"Then maybe it's time to stop trying."

He made no move toward her. Not by a single gesture did he coerce her into taking that fragile step forward. Leah took it unaware and stopped before she got too close, before she was well and truly in his arms. "Riker, I'm not good at this. Jonathan never..." She couldn't finish the thought she'd never before allowed herself to voice. "It just won't be...what you expect."

His hands were on her shoulders then, giving a tiny shake, forcing her to look at him. "Jonathan Taylor was a fool from every angle, Leah," he said firmly. He claimed her lips in a long and devastating kiss. All her fears, all her doubts rose in one swift surge of panic and were put down by the sudden rush of yearning that overwhelmed her. Desire whispered to her senses, fear vanished beneath a veritable flood of pleasurable sensations. A moment later, he swept her up and into his arms and carried her to the bed. Protests forgotten, she curved her hands on either side of his face and held him, bound to her through the kiss they shared.

It might have been a moment, it seemed like hours, before she could bear to release her hold and let him lift his lips from hers. Immediately, though, he rained kisses along her cheek and down past the sensitive hollow of her ear to the base of her throat. Shivers of delight raced through her and she sighed a surrender she could no longer contain.

There had been no man in her life since Jonathan. She'd promised herself there wouldn't be one. What did she need a man for? But the question, the self-made promises now seemed obscene and pointless as Riker worked a serious and tender magic on her body. Sex had never been a high point in her life. But, oh, to feel the seductive persuasion of a man's hands and to know the sweet ache of tension low inside her…it felt good at the moment. It felt better than good. And even if this was all she received from Riker, it would be enough. For the first time in years, she remembered how it felt to be a woman, a desirable, attractive woman, and right now, that feeling was worth whatever regrets she might have tomorrow. She only hoped she could make it worth it to Riker, too.

"Leah." His mouth came back to her ear and warmed her with a whisper, as his hand slipped beneath her shirt and caressed her stomach. "Don't hide from me. Concentrate on us."

So he wouldn't let her retreat behind a veil of sensation and dreamy thoughts. He wanted her to participate with her mind as well as her body. He wanted all of her and Leah was afraid he'd be disappointed, no matter how hard she tried. "But, Riker, I don't…"

"Yes, Leah. Oh, yes, you do." His hand found her breast and his lips, once more, laid claim to hers. The tip of his tongue stroking the corners of her mouth and creating a tingling excitement along her spine. His thumb nuzzled her nipple, coaxing it into an achy pout. His free hand spread fires of longing as he caressed her denim-clad thigh. Nerve endings she hadn't even known she possessed came to sudden, demanding life and Leah trembled with the richness of the new sensations.

Maybe this would be all right....

Riker got rid of clothes—both hers and his—the way he did everything...efficiently, purposefully, and with a minimum of problems. Leah felt a moment's strangeness when she first felt the length of his long, bare legs pressed up close against her. But the moment disappeared beneath a rush of strong emotion when he pulled her tightly against him and began another slow and tempting assault of her senses.

She lost the ability to concentrate somewhere along the way and she hoped he wouldn't notice. But how could she think when his every touch sent her reeling through a haze of sensual delights? Somewhere, too, on the journey, she lost her fear of failing, of being less than perfect in his eyes. How could she be afraid when his kisses told her he was hungry for her, when the trembling of his body spoke of emotions deeper than mere physical desire?

When he poised himself above her and slowly, gently rocked his way inside her, she clung to him, closing her eyes and believing for this one precious moment that she could belong to him, fully, completely, with no holds barred, nothing withheld. The feeling lingered, long after he had taken her through one rapturous fulfillment to another.

She lay in his arms afterward, sated and full of the knowledge that she loved this man. For now, she would not deny the beautiful gifts he had given her. She'd been empty before. Unsure of herself. But Riker had given back some of the things Jonathan had stolen from her.

And no matter what happened after this weekend, she would always love him for that.

That and about a thousand other things.

Chapter Fifteen

Leah awakened in Riker's arms, fathoms deep in love.

Her dreams had been sweet ones, sprinkled with sweeter interludes of reality. He was tenderly demanding, gentle and needy and she felt as if she were in love for the first time in her life.

The night had slipped into a gorgeous, hot day and Riker insisted they see more of the city. Leah appreciated his thoughtfulness, but she would have been content to stay in the hotel room for the rest of the weekend. He, however, insisted that since it was her first time in St. Louis, he wanted to show her everything that could be packed into the short time available. So today they did more sight-seeing, traipsed through the tourist attractions and ended up exploring each other with a heady and thorough delight.

She refused his offers to buy things for her and she tried to dissuade him from purchasing matching sundresses and sunshades for Marta and Katie. She finally caved in and let him *lend* her the money to buy a few souvenirs.

Riker was amused and just a little annoyed at her insistence on "paying her own way." He wished Leah would allow him the pleasure of giving something to her. He still could hardly believe she was here with him. It seemed even more impossible that she'd accepted him as a lover. But that part of his fantasy was undeniably true.

Leah. Leah. He couldn't stop the litany that ran through his brain. Leah. She was special, someone he would have loved at anytime during his life, but now...now she was here when he most needed someone special. And he could hardly believe his luck in finding her at that all important "right" moment in time. Now, everything was perfect. For him, for her, for their beautiful twin daughters. He didn't think he could have been more in love with Leah if she'd actually given birth to Marta and he certainly had no hesitation about sharing his life and his daughter with her. Just as he planned to share her life and Katie's.

Things were going to work out great. Simply great.

THEY WERE ALMOST HOME before it occurred to Riker to mention Jerry Hillman.

"You've found him?" Leah asked, pitching her voice above the whine of the engine. The expression in her eyes registered immediate alarm and consternation.

Riker wished he hadn't brought up the subject. "No, not yet, but I did hire a private detective to track him down."

Leah sat still and quiet for several minutes. Her distress was obvious and the carefree atmosphere of the past two days slipped away. "We don't need to know what happened to Jerry Hillman, Riker. I mean, it isn't as if he's of any importance to us now."

"He handled the adoptions, Leah. We have to make sure he handled them correctly."

"You're just asking for trouble. If you find him and something wasn't done properly, well…" Her voice dwindled as she faced the unspeakable possibility that she might lose Katie. "You should have talked to me first."

Riker tried to inject a light, amused tone into his voice. "You'd just have said what you're saying now, Leah."

"Because it's worth saying." She squared her shoulders in the confines of the airplane cabin. "There could be all sorts of complications with the adoptions if Jerry really did something illegal, like separate the twins without the mother's consent. You could have set in motion a chain of events that will jeopardize Katie's future. Marta's, too. Oh, Riker, I wish you had left well enough alone."

"If left up to you, Leah, Marta and Katie would still be separated," Riker said, irritated by the way her fear stirred his own.

"If I'd left things up to you, you and I wouldn't have had a wonderful weekend together."

"It shouldn't have happened, Riker. You know that as well as I do. I shouldn't have gone with you. I shouldn't have…slept with you. And you shouldn't have hired a private detective."

He was stunned by her admission. He'd thought the weekend had been perfect. He'd believed she thought so, too. "What's really wrong, here, Leah? I want to ask Jerry Hillman a few questions. If he really did profit from the adoptions of our daughters, then he at least owes us a few answers. And what does any of that have to do with you and me?"

"Everything. If you want to ask a man a few questions, you go out and hire a detective to find him. If you don't like his answers, you'll hire an attorney to sue him. If Marta's adoption is challenged, you'll go to court and fight tooth and nail to keep her. I don't have your options, Riker. Oh, I'd fight just as hard for Katie, but I don't have your resources. Katie's adopted father didn't die, he *deserted* her. Legally, Jonathan is still her parent. What if the judge sees that as neglect? What if he sees that I can't make up to Katie for what she lost? What if…?"

"Leah, for Pete's sake. None of that is going to happen. No court in this country is going to take Katie from you. And, *if* the adoption was ever challenged, I'd fight just as hard for you and Katie as I would for myself and Marta."

"That's easy enough to say, Riker."

"What does that mean?"

"If you had to choose between Marta and Katie, you wouldn't hesitate. You'd choose Marta. I'm not saying that's wrong. I'm just saying that's the reality of this situation."

The sting of her words went deep and wounded him. He loved Katie. How could Leah think he wouldn't fight just as hard for her as he would for Marta and himself? "You are eaten up with fear, Leah. You let Jonathan Taylor rob you of more than a husband. You let him take every bit of trust you had. And now, you're awfully close to robbing Katie of something precious, something real and worthy of her trust."

"Oh, sure. *I'm* robbing Katie," Leah said. "Katie depends on me to protect her from harm, Riker, and—even including my unconscionable slipup this past weekend—I've done a damn good job of it. I don't know what you want from Katie and me, but from now on you'd better leave us alone. And we'll do the same for you.''

"Damn it, Leah. You don't have to protect Katie from me or from my daughter. I care about Katie. I love her. I love you, too. But you obviously do not feel the same way. Not about me and not about my daughter.''

"My first loyalty has to be Katie. She doesn't have anyone else.''

"No, Leah, you're the one who has no one else and one day you're going to wake up and find out that when Jonathan walked out on you, he was able to steal your whole life—past, present, and future—right out from under you.''

She turned away from him and hoped the flight would soon be over. He didn't understand, she thought. He never had. Riker liked to think they could all just be one happy family. He'd said he loved her. For a minute, she'd almost believed him, but it wasn't true…no matter how convincing his kisses had been.

Riker didn't love her. He loved Katie's mother. He loved the role she could fulfill in Marta's life. He loved the idea of having twin daughters. But it was all an illusion and sooner or later he'd grow tired of it. Just like Jonathan. And then, what would she and Katie do?

Throughout the landing, Leah maintained a stony, unforgiving—and frightened—silence. She acknowledged that it was a means of surviving the remaining minutes in Riker's company. The only means she had. She couldn't bear to admit that he was right about her being afraid, deathly afraid of giving her heart to him and risking another rejection. She couldn't take the chance. For Katie's sake or her own.

It made sense, she told herself. If she stayed away from Riker and Marta—as she'd wisely done until this impulsive trip had come up—she kept hers and Katie's lives intact. Independent, secure, protected. That was the smart thing to do.

Smart? Yes.

Easy? Maybe not, but not impossible, either.

Satisfying?

Well, the solution to a problem was hardly ever perfect.

KATIE was sick.

Gussie dropped her off at the house late Sunday afternoon. "I don't know what happened," Gussie explained. "Unless it was too much fun and too much sun. We spent Saturday at the water park and she seemed a little droopy that night. And then this morning, when she got up, I knew she had a fever." Gussie ruffled the pixie cut of Katie's bangs. "You're home with your mama, now, Poppet, so I guess I'll get Marta on home, too."

"Are you going to be all right?" Marta quietly asked Katie, her childish voice soft and mature with concern. "I won't leave if you want me to stay."

Katie shook her head as she clung to Leah, one arm wrapped around a leg, the other hanging listlessly at her side. "I'll call you," Katie told her twin and, for the first time ever, Leah felt that Katie was happy to see Marta leave.

"What seems to be the problem?" Leah guided her daughter to the rocking chair, sat and pulled Katie onto her lap. "What hurts?"

Katie pulled at her left ear, confirming what Leah already suspected. "An ear infection. I'll take you to the doctor first thing in the morning. Since Gussie gave you some medicine less than an hour ago, we'll just have to sit here, rock and tell stories. Okay?"

With a listless nod, Katie snuggled against Leah. "Where were you Mommy? Gussie said you'd gone away. We called and called on the way home to see if you were back, but you weren't here."

"I...was gone, honey. I'm sorry."

"But where were you? You never go places."

"Well, this time I did. But I'm home now."

Katie was unimpressed with that explanation. "Were you with Riker? He was gone, too."

Asked point-blank, Leah sighed. She'd never lied to Katie, and she wasn't going to start now. "I was with Riker, Katie. I—had to help him with his business."

"Oh." That seemed to satisfy the child's curiosity for the

moment. Then, out of the blue, she asked, "Are you and Riker married?"

"Married? No, Katie."

"I'd like it if you and Riker were married, Mommy. Then I could live in Marta's room and go to the school she goes to. Private schools are better than the one I go to. And I could have lots of pretty clothes, like Marta does. And maybe take ballet lessons or tap dance. Wouldn't that be neat, Mommy? And Gussie would be my grandmother, too, and not just Marta's."

Leah's throat closed tight as Katie outlined the material possessions that would be hers if Leah married Riker. She might have been listening to Jonathan, who all those years ago had cataloged all the "good things" he would bestow upon his child…as soon as he had one. But then Katie was there and within months, Jonathan was gone, along with every one of his promises.

"You have nice things, Katie. And there's nothing wrong with your school. It's a good school. Remember how much you liked Mrs. Hawkins last year?"

"But I got in trouble all the time," Katie said in a tired voice as she began to trace the outline of Leah's buttons with a fingertip. "I wouldn't get in trouble at Marta's school. And it's not fair that Marta gets to live there and I have to live here. We're supposed to live together with our mother and daddy. Marta and I are *twins*." She gave the last word a dignity, a meaning far beyond the simple explanation of a seven-year-old.

"You're twins, Katie, but you belong to different families. You belong to me and Marta belongs to Riker. And even though the two of you can be together sometimes, we can't all live together. It wouldn't be right."

"Why not?" Katie whined. "It would be fun. You'd like it, Mommy. You would."

Leah shifted the child in her arms and hoped that sickness and the healthy dose of cold medicine she'd had would close Katie's big blue eyes in sleep. "Lie still, honey, and I'll tell you a story of—what story do you want to hear?"

"Why won't you let us live with Marta and Riker, Mommy? Why can't we stay at their house and swim and play all we want to?'' Katie's tone picked up a quarrelsome note, not unusual for a sick child, but definitely not anything Leah wanted to deal with at the moment.

"Let's not talk about that anymore, Katie. You might not like living with Marta day in and day out, either. No matter how much fun you think it would be.''

"I would, Mommy. I'd like it. And you like Riker. I know you do. He'd be nice to us, Mommy. He'd be like my real daddy. Only he wouldn't run away.''

"Shhh." Leah stroked Katie's hair and held her close. She was only seven. She didn't know what she was saying or the complications of what she asked. She wasn't old enough to understand.

Leah began to recite Katie's favorite bedtime story, *The Three Bears*, but her mind kept playing Katie's innocent words back to her. *He'd be nice to us, Mommy. He'd be like my real daddy. Only he wouldn't run away.*

But what if he did? What if Riker left—after carving out a place in Katie's heart? Katie wouldn't be able to think he'd been nice. She'd be hurt too badly by that rejection.

No, Leah thought as she described how naughty Goldilocks had eaten Baby Bear's porridge. She was doing the right thing. The only thing she could do to ensure hers and Katie's continued happiness and well-being.

And that was, after all, her job.

"LEAH? It's Riker. How are you?''

Her fingers went slack on the receiver and Leah had to swallow twice before she could answer. "Riker? Hi. I—I'm fine.''

"Good. We're all fine, too. I guess Marta keeps you informed, though, doesn't she?''

"Yes. Yes, she does." Leah's throat tightened with a thousand emotions. She hadn't talked to him since the day they'd returned from St. Louis. She'd asked him to leave her alone and he had. Gussie had handled all the contacts since then, all the arrangements for Katie's and Marta's visits with each other. Leah hadn't even caught a glimpse of Riker during the past few weeks. And

Marta hadn't been overly effusive with details, either. "Is something wrong?"

"No." He sounded uncomfortable and Leah came within a breath of inviting him over to her house so they could talk. "Look, Leah, I thought I should call and let you know that the detective I hired finally found Jerry Hillman. He's in Texas, selling real estate. He was disbarred a few years ago for unethical conduct."

"Oh," was the only comment she could manage.

"I talked with him on the telephone, but couldn't get any answers about Katie's and Marta's adoptions. With all the things he wouldn't say, I think it's very likely he did profit illegally from the procedures. We're probably not the only ones who got taken in and I certainly have no proof, but—"

"Oh, Riker, please don't do anything else. Drop it. For Katie and Marta's sakes."

The silence stretched into an endless pause. "I'd already decided not to pursue the matter further, Leah. Not because I believe it would cause problems for Marta and Katie, but because I know how agonizing any kind of action would be for you."

"Thank you." Leah let out the breath she'd been holding. "Thank you, Riker."

"Don't mention it. I just thought you'd want to know."

"Yes, thank you."

"Goodbye, Leah. Take care of yourself…and your daughter."

He hung up then, before she had a chance to say goodbye or anything else. He'd been cool, she thought, and polite. Which was exactly what she'd wanted.

It was mystifying, though, now that she had exactly what she wanted, she felt more miserable than she'd ever felt in her life.

"I WANT YOU to be in the wedding," Susannah said one afternoon in mid-October. "It'll be at Christmas, so both of our families can be here. I'm going to use red and green colors and I want Katie and Marta to be flower girls. Won't they be cute in matching outfits with little red hats? Or maybe I'll put one in red and one in green. What do you think?"

"I think maybe I should look for another job." Leah picked

up a lettering tool and brandished it at her friend. "I'm not sure I can work for you *and* Tom. He's a workaholic and you're a workhorse and the two of you together—"

"Oh, please," Susannah said with a laugh. "We both have a big soft spot in our hearts for you, Leah. You know that. Besides, my being married to the boss won't change anything. Tom will still expect everything to be perfect. You and I will still be wage slaves."

Leah smiled, but said nothing. Of course, things would change once Susannah and Tom married. Everything changed at some point or another and a love relationship between two people in one office had to affect a third person in that office. She'd felt very much the extra wheel around Tom and Susannah lately, anyway. Their calf eyes and soft sighs would have made anyone else head for the door. Leah had simply kept her head down and her attention focused on her work. Maybe a change of employment wasn't such a bad idea.

"So, do you think the twins will want to be flower girls in my wedding?" Susannah got up and walked to the small refrigerator in the corner. "Do you want a soda?" she asked.

"No," Leah answered. "And you'll have to ask Katie and Marta about the wedding. They're pretty independent these days. At least, Katie is."

"Ah, yes, what mischief has our little angel been into this week?" Susannah popped the top of the can and sauntered back to her drafting table. "I'll bet it's not as good as last week when she decked that little boy for calling her a pixie."

"She did not *deck* him," Leah said tiredly. "She pulled his chair out from under him."

Susannah smiled and gave a wry shrug. "Close enough. What has she done this week?"

"Mercifully, nothing. I thought she'd settle down this year, but so far second grade is not going too well."

"She has too much energy, Leah. Why don't you enroll her in some extra activities? Maybe some dancing lessons?"

"She'd love to take dance, but I can't afford extras like that. And she plays soccer. That's an extra activity."

"Obviously, Leah, she needs more than you're giving her. I've never seen a child with so much energy. Maybe you made a mistake in limiting the amount of time she can spend with Marta.''

So spoke a woman who'd never had any children of her own. Why were single people always sure they knew more about raising a child than a parent? "I did what was best for Katie," Leah said coolly. "She'll survive without dance lessons and expensive clothes and toys."

"I'm sure you're right."

Leah glanced up to see if there was any underlying meaning in the statement, but Susannah was drinking her soda straight from the can and didn't seem inclined to carry the conversation any further. "Susannah?" Leah began hesitantly, feeling suddenly guilty for being so unenthusiastic about…well, about everything. "I'd love to be an attendant in your wedding. And Katie will be ecstatic when she finds out she gets to be a flower girl. Especially since Marta gets to be one, too."

Susannah's happy smile was worth the effort. "Thanks, Leah. I wouldn't want to be married without you there. And don't worry about afterward. Tom couldn't run this place without you. Especially lately. I've been kind of distracted."

Leah grinned. "Love happens to the best of us…despite our good intentions."

"Yes." Susannah propped her elbows on the table and held the soda can as if it were a priceless gem. "I'm really sorry things didn't work out for you and Riker. It seemed so perfect with the twins and all. But I guess you were right. He hasn't exactly been beating down your door with ballet tickets and marriage proposals, has he? Is he dating anyone? Do you know?"

Leave it to Susannah to plunge into a taboo subject, Leah thought. "Riker and I agreed to keep our lives as separate as possible for the girls' sake," she said stiffly. "It's better all around."

"I suppose so." Susannah turned the soda can with the palms of her hands. "Still, it's such a shame. Katie and Marta could have been together. Katie wouldn't be such a handful for you. And you could have had some real happiness for a change. You know, I don't know if Tom and I will have children. It seems like all sacrifice and headaches."

"That's not true." Leah certainly hoped she wasn't responsible for Susannah's opinion. "Having Katie is the single greatest thing that's ever happened to me."

"And the *only* thing, too." Susannah set aside the can of soda and bit her bottom lip. "I'm sorry, Leah. It's none of my business. It just seems like you should have so much more. I guess I can't understand since I don't have any kids."

"No," Leah said, stung by her friend's words. "You can't."

"Okay. I'm an idiot, but—"

"Who's an idiot?" Tom stood in the doorway, his mouth curving into a smile as he looked at Susannah.

"I am." With a gesture of her hand, Susannah called him forward. "Leah and I were having this discussion about being in love and having children and—"

"Wait a minute," Tom interrupted. "Those are two separate discussions. Anyone who lumps them into one *is* an idiot."

"Well, you see I asked Leah about..."

"It isn't necessary to tell Tom everything that was said, Susannah." Leah offered Tom a small smile and an equally inconsequential shrug. "We weren't talking about anything important. And congratulations. Susannah says the date is set for during the Christmas holidays."

Tom was easily distracted and the talk turned to wedding plans. Leah tried to join in the conversation to show that she was paying attention, but in actuality her thoughts were far away. On Katie. On Marta. And, as always, on Riker. Susannah just didn't understand, Leah told herself again, reaffirming her own position. She *was* doing the best thing for Katie. She was protecting her by not letting herself love Riker. It was the only way.

Even though she missed his friendship.

Even though Katie wasn't at all happy with the arrangement.

But when had children ever liked what was best for them?

THE CALL CAME late Friday afternoon. Tom motioned Leah to the telephone with a frown. "I don't think it's the principal of her school this time," he said as he handed her the receiver.

"This is Leah Taylor," Leah said, her heartbeat going staccato in alarm.

"Leah. Riker." His voice was crisp, urgent and irritated. "I think you'd better get down to the store as soon as possible."

Her heart stopped altogether. "Has something happened to Katie?"

"Not yet."

"Is she...is she all right?"

"She's not hurt. Just get down here, Leah. Before I take your daughter and mine and send them both off to military school." The receiver went dead in her ear and Leah looked at it oddly before replacing it in its cradle and heading for the door.

Chapter Sixteen

It didn't take long to get from the printing shop on Adams to Westfall's Department Store on Greystone. Finding a parking space proved much more difficult. There was some kind of commotion in front of Riker's store and the traffic was backed up to the corner. Leah could just make out the camera crew from a Tulsa television station making their way through the crowd gathered in front of the store. She couldn't hear any sirens or see any flashing lights. But what was going on?

She drove to the end of the block and, when she couldn't find a place to park, she did what any frantic mother would do...she parked in the fire zone. It was still tough going, getting through the crowd, but her child might be in danger and that thought gave her the strength—and the voice—of someone much bigger.

"Get out of my way!" she commanded a stout woman who blocked her path.

"I've got to find my daughter!" she told a policeman who was lackadaisically performing crowd control.

He grinned at her. "If she's one of those two little cuties on the door, you've found her."

Leah's gaze shot past his shoulder and her panic disappeared in relief. It was Katie...and she was laughing. A man held a video camera a few feet away and a news reporter held a microphone under her nose. Leah couldn't hear what her daughter said, but the ramifications of the situation began to settle into place. Katie was standing in front of the double doors that led into

Westfall's. Next to her, stood Marta. They were leaning against the door at an odd angle, and it looked like—

"They're handcuffed," someone behind Leah said. "Those two little girls are handcuffed to the door."

Leah glanced over her shoulder, wondering where that lunatic idea had come from. Handcuffed to the—

She pushed past the grinning policeman and walked briskly to center stage. "Katherine, what are you doing?"

Katie gave her mother a look of trepidation before she lifted her chin in her best stubborn pout. "I'm on television, Mom. Can we talk later?"

"Are you her mother?" The news reporter, a cute, fresh cub of a man, shifted the microphone out from under Katie's nose and placed it squarely in Leah's face. "What do you think of this sit-in your daughters are staging? Can you give us the inside story?"

Leah blinked as she realized the video camera was recording her every move. "I don't know what's going on. I just got here. Could I have a moment of privacy with my daughter, please?"

The reporter backed off maybe as much as a half inch and Riker stepped up behind Leah. "It's about time you showed up," he said. "The twins have been here for almost an hour, waiting for you."

She glanced from him to Katie, from Katie to Marta, and from Marta to Gussie, who sat protectively in front of the two girls and the door. "Hi, Leah," the older woman said. "Too bad you weren't here earlier. We had the mayor and the police chief here cheering us on."

"Cheering you—?" Leah turned to Riker for some idea of what was happening. "What are they doing?" she asked. "And why haven't you made them stop?"

"I have the employees scouting the town for a key to the handcuffs. What else am I supposed to do?"

"Key? Handcuffs?" Leah's gaze swung back to the girls and the way their arms were looped through the door handles and then fastened—Katie's wrist to Marta's wrist—with a pair of toy handcuffs. "How on earth—?" She turned back to Riker. "How did this happen?"

"Beats me," he said with a shrug. "I was in my office and all of a sudden someone from the building across the street called and wanted to know where I'd gotten the idea for this particular advertising gimmick."

"If this is a gimmick, Riker, I don't find it effective."

"Oh, I don't know. Marta and Katie seem to be having quite an effect, which I believe is just what they intended."

Frustrated by his amused tone of voice and apparent acceptance of the twins' atrocious behavior, Leah focused her attention on the glint of silver around the girls' wrists. "Those are *toy* handcuffs, Riker? Just take them off."

He lifted his hands, palms outward, in a shrug. "They may be toy, but they're stout enough to hold those two together. And I'm not going to be the one to chance breaking a child's arm trying to get off a silly pair of toy handcuffs."

"This is ridiculous." Leah moved purposely toward the door and the handcuffs. "Let me—"

Katie and Marta came alive, grasping each other around the shoulders with their free hands and blocking any effective way, other than causing bodily harm, of ending their bondage. "Mommy, no!" Katie exclaimed. "We're having a sit-in. You'll have to arrest us first."

"Katie, this is crazy. You're too young to be arrested. Now you take those off right now."

Katie held her ground and met her mother's stare. "Are you sure I'm Katie?" she asked. "I might be Marta."

"Don't start with me, Katherine Anne. You're—" Leah's confidence wavered a bit when Marta lifted her chin in an identical challenge. She *might* be Katie. No. Leah pulled her imagination into line. Side by side, she could always tell the two apart. Even when they were dressed in identical sundresses, with identical sandals, with identical sunshades, pushed into identical positions on top of their identical haircuts. Oh, bother, Leah thought. She wasn't sure which twin was which, but she'd be damned if that would stop her. "You're going to get into a lot of trouble over this," she warned whichever one was Katie. But her threat met double resistance.

"I've already tried reason and threats," Riker said calmly, the thread of amusement still lining his voice. "They're determined to have their say...regardless of intimidation techniques."

Leah shifted her purse to the crook of her arm and put a hand on her hip. "What is it they have to say?"

Riker made a face, which wasn't entirely displeased, and directed her attention to the girls.

"We want to be a family," Marta—or Katie—stated clearly. "We don't like living in different houses and going to different schools. We're twins. We're supposed to be together."

"Yeah," said the other child. "And we want our mommy and daddy to stop fighting and make everything happy like it was before."

Leah's heart sank. Why this? Why now? Why her?

"Would you care to comment now?" The reporter and the microphone were back in her face. "Your daughters obviously want you two to patch up your differences and be a family again. Is that the message you're getting—Mommy and Daddy?"

Leah searched for some means of escape and her gaze landed on Riker's mother. "Gussie, was this your idea?"

"No, absolutely not." Gussie adjusted the knot of her tie-dyed headband and smoothed the rumpled peace symbol stitched on the front of her hippie-style, gauze shirt. "But I have to say, Leah, that I wish I had thought of it. I haven't had this much fun since the time Riker and I staged a sit-in to protest—" Her green eyes switched to Riker. "What *were* we protesting that time we sat in the middle of the highway and held up traffic on the Interstate?"

"The building of a nuclear plant, I believe." Riker didn't smile, but Leah thought he might as well have done so. He obviously wasn't concerned about this spectacle by their daughters and his mother.

The reporter swung the microphone to Gussie. "Did you participate in the peace marches of the sixties?"

As Gussie preened and prepared to dazzle the television audience, Leah whirled to Riker and lowered her voice to an irritated hiss. "This is embarrassing, Riker. I can't believe we're allowing two very stubborn seven-year-olds to put us in this ridiculous position. Isn't there anything we can do?"

"I, for one, find I have more and more sympathy for Marta and Katie. They don't like the 'ridiculous position' their very stubborn parents have placed them in and they've come up with an imaginative and resourceful way of stating their objections."

"Objections? They can't even spell the word. They're children, Riker, and we're their parents. It's our job to protect them and to keep them from thinking we endorse rebellions like this one."

"This isn't a rebellion, Leah. This is the only recourse they had after you and I decided to *protect* them. And made us all unhappy in the process."

"I can't believe you're taking their side."

"Who else is going to?"

Leah sighed in aggravation. "Everyone, apparently. Can't we discuss this in private somewhere?"

He lifted his shoulders in a wry shrug. "I suppose we can ask the girls if they're ready to negotiate."

"Negotiate? I'm ready to—"

"We've decided to do a live telecast for the five o'clock news." The reporter left Gussie and turned to Katie and Marta. "Is that all right with you two? We'll ask you a few questions and you'll need to speak directly into the microphone when you answer. Okay?"

"Okay."

"Okay."

"Okay." Gussie's voice followed the twins and a delighted grin curved her lips as she indicated Riker and Leah with a jerk of her thumb and turned the reporter's attention to the other two participants in the drama. "Ask the mommy and daddy some questions, too. You might win the Pulitzer for this."

"Gussie," Riker groaned.

"Gussie." The name grated past her lips as Leah spun on her heels and grabbed Riker's arm, urging him back to an inconspicuous corner of the building. "We've got to stop this, Riker. I'm not going to let my daughter go on television and say that she thinks I'm unfair because I won't get married so she can finally have a father and go to private schools and have truckloads of toys. You're going to have to do something—"

He reversed their positions and took her by the arm, guiding her away from the front of the store and the crowd gathered there. "Come on. It's about time we talked about this."

"We can't just leave Katie and Marta handcuffed to the door," she said. "Even though, right now, I wouldn't mind handcuffing them to a train on its way out of town."

"You have to admit they chose a pretty ingenious way of calling attention to their problems."

"I'm not going to admit any such thing. Just show me where I go to resign as mother and you can have Katie, bag and baggage."

Riker pulled open a side door and ushered Leah inside. "Now," he said. "We're making some progress."

"What?"

"Come on. We'll go up to my office and see if we can't reach some sort of arrangement that will be acceptable to our daughters."

"Riker, this is crazy. I was joking. I'm not negotiating Katie's future, no matter how many doors she chains herself to."

He said nothing else, just led the way through the store at a brisk clip. When they reached an office marked Executive, Riker opened the door and motioned Leah inside. An attractive secretary looked up from her desk and acknowledged their entrance with a question. "Did you get the key? is it over?"

Riker shook his head. "No. The twins are just about to go live on local television."

"You're kidding." The secretary's pretty mouth formed a delightful smile. "Can I leave, now? You're here to answer the phones and I'd really like to see this for myself."

"Go ahead," Riker said easily. "Just don't tell anyone where we are."

"Mum's the word," the secretary said as she bolted out of her chair, grabbed her purse, and whipped past Leah on her way out the door. "Thanks, boss. You're terrific."

The door closed behind her and Leah offered Riker a severe frown. "You just sent your secretary down to gape at our children? Doesn't this situation bother you at all?"

"Bother me? Hell, yes, it bothers me, Leah. It bothers me that

I sat around doing nothing about this *situation* until Katie and Marta took matters into their own hands. How you and I, two supposedly mature adults, could let our children get to the point they're desperate enough to handcuff themselves to a door is beyond me. But, yes, I'm bothered. And I'd be happy to say so on the five o'clock news, if that's what it takes.''

Leah was beginning to feel confused. ''If that's what it takes for what? Do you want to set up a household for Katie and Marta? Then they can live together, day in and day out, and maybe Gussie will be housemother. Then they could pull stunts like this once a week.''

''Gussie may have her moments, but she, at least, listens to the girls, which is more than you and I can say lately.''

''That's not true, Riker. I listen to Katie, endlessly.''

''But you don't hear a word she's saying. She and Marta are upset over these new rules you've imposed. One night on the weekends, one two-hour visit during the week. They don't like it, Leah.''

''It's the only way to keep some separate identity in their lives.''

''It's the only way you can avoid dealing with your feelings for me.''

Leah tossed her purse on the secretary's desk and faced Riker with arms crossed obstinately at her chest. ''All right. I knew this would get personal. My feelings for you are not at issue here. My feelings for Katie are.''

''I happen to think those feelings overlap. I happen to think your fear for Katie is the same as your fear for yourself.''

''And what, O Great Oracle, is that?''

''You're afraid I'll leave you.''

Leah's heart lodged somewhere near her throat at the accuracy of his remark. ''Considering my experience with Katie's father that's not a particularly enlightening bit of wisdom, Riker. After Jonathan, I have good reason to keep my distance from you or any other man.''

''It goes deeper than that, Leah. You're afraid that if I left, I'd take Katie with me.''

''You couldn't do that.''

"I know that, but I'm not sure you do."

Leah shook her head and examined the leather of her black pumps. "This is pointless, Riker. I told you from the beginning that Katie was my first and only priority, that I wasn't going to allow anyone to interfere in her life. You've tried every way you can to get past that and to make Katie your daughter and Marta's sister. But I'm not going to let you do it, Riker. I'm not."

"Katie *is* Marta's sister by birth. You can't change that, Leah. She is my daughter by choice. You can't change that, either. Katie won my heart a long time ago. How could I not love her, when she's so delightfully imaginative, so full of life, and so much like and unlike Marta? I may never have any legal claim to Katie, but there's no one, anywhere, who can stop me from loving her. And I know you feel the same way about Marta."

"All I want is to be able to raise my daughter." Leah forced the words past the knot of tension in her throat. She didn't like this discussion. She didn't like being in this room alone with Riker. Knowing he was right about her feelings for Marta made her feel so...so torn. "All I want is for you to leave Katie and me alone."

"I've done that for the past several weeks, Leah. It hasn't made Katie happy, it hasn't made Marta happy, it hasn't made me happy, and it certainly hasn't done much for you."

She looked up, met his intense blue gaze, and felt herself sinking into a swamp of despair. "That doesn't mean any—" With a shaky sigh, she gave up trying to argue. "What do you want from me, Riker? I can't give you my daughter. She's all I have."

"No, Leah. Katie's just on loan. She doesn't belong to you. She's her own person. She'll grow up, and one day she'll leave. And you'll let her because that's what children are supposed to do. I love you, Leah. Please stop pushing me away and give me the chance to prove to you that I'm not Jonathan. I'll do my damnedest to make you happy, while the girls are still at home and long after they've left to make homes of their own."

"I'm not a big believer in promises, Riker. I've seen too many promises broken."

"All right, Leah. If that's the way you want it, live the rest of your life making sure no one makes a promise to you. Take Katie and teach her not to trust anyone because her father broke his promises to her and to you. But in my opinion, that's not living, Leah. That's hiding. And I can't see it doing you or Katie any good. I was hurt, too. Jean left me, even though she'd promised to share my life forever. Maybe I had a little more warning and maybe the fact that Jean died was easier to take than Jonathan's unexplained disappearance. But the fact is, she broke a promise. Just like Jonathan broke his promise to you.''

''So we're both martyrs,'' Leah said, trying hard to sound cool and indifferent, if only to keep her composure from falling in scattered pieces at her feet. ''That's hardly reason enough to expose our daughters to the risk of yet another broken relationship.''

''Damn it, Leah. Our daughters are outside this building right now announcing to anyone who will listen that they want to be together, they want to have a real family life, with two parents who love them and each other.''

''You only want Katie, Riker. I'm just the baggage you have to take to get her.''

Silence descended in the room and throbbed in Leah's ears. He looked stunned as he stood there, a few feet away, staring at her in profound amazement. ''Is that what you—? Leah, I love you. How could you think I'd...?''

His question was lost in a choking wave of emotion and she thought she might drown in the aftermath. ''But Katie and Marta are twins. You'd never even have met me if it hadn't been for that chance meeting in the grocery store.''

''A chance meeting over a banana pepper, Leah. Before I knew about Katie. Before you knew about Marta. I like to think you and I were guided by fate or a higher power. I like to think we would have met and fallen in love anyway...with or without the help of our perfect pair of girls.''

''But, Riker—''

''But, Leah—'' He took a step toward her. ''I love you. I want to spend the rest of my life with you. We deserve this shot at happiness, Leah. Don't deny it to us. We might just all live happily ever after.''

Was that possible, Leah wondered. Could she simply lift her hand and grab happiness? Would Katie be all right if she did? Would Katie be all right if she didn't?

There was a timid tap on the door and at Riker's command, Gussie pushed it open. "We got the handcuffs off," she said, her gaze tripping eagerly from Leah's face to Riker's. "The girls have something they want to say."

Katie and Marta, at Gussie's insistence, moved to stand side by side in the doorway. Heads bent, shoulders stooped, chins at a conciliatory level, they raised matching pairs of innocent blue eyes. "I'm sorry," one of them murmured.

"Sorry," muttered the other. "Gussie said we should 'pologize."

"We just wanted..."

"...to be together."

"Sorry."

"Sorry." Two pairs of eyes dropped in unison, but one set returned to Leah. "Are you mad at us?"

Leah knew she ought to be, but her mother's heart just couldn't be angry. "No, I'm not mad."

"Can we get an ice cream, then?"

Gussie bustled the two out of the doorway and shielded them with her body. "I'll take them home," she said. "They've had a long day."

"Wait a minute," Riker stepped toward his mother. "Give me those handcuffs...and the key."

Gussie gave them to him dutifully, but she showed some reluctance when he motioned her out from in front of the twins. He went down on his knees to face the girls eye to eye. "What did you tell the reporter?" he asked.

Katie looked at Marta. Marta looked at Katie. They batted their ridiculously long eyelashes at Riker. "We told him we wanted you guys to get married so we can live together. We are twins, you know."

"Yes, I believe I've heard that before." Riker got to his feet. "Leah and I will see the two of you in a little bit. And we will talk about this afternoon's performance."

Two sets of shoulders drooped at the threat of impending punishment. Then Katie—Leah knew it was her daughter by the fearless disregard for punishment in her expression—lifted her chin. "Well, will you at least talk about getting married? We went to a lot of trouble today and it's just not fair if you won't even—"

Gussie hurried the two girls out the door, effectively ending Katie's exasperated words. "We're leaving now," Gussie said. "See you two later." The door closed, then opened again so Gussie could toss in the last word. "She's right, you know. The least you can do is discuss it."

This time when the door closed, Riker released a throaty chuckle. "We don't stand a chance, Leah. If those three want us to be together, we may as well get married right now."

"Mar-ried?" The word stuck and came out in a two-syllable squeak. Leah cleared her throat. "Because it's in the best interest of the children?"

"It's certainly in my best interest and I think it's in yours." Riker closed the distance between them and cupped Leah's face in his hands. "At the moment, I really don't give a damn about anyone else. I love you, Leah. I want to live with you, today, tomorrow, for the rest of my life. And you know what? I don't care whether Katie or Marta or Gussie think it's a good idea. They asked for it and it sounds like heaven to me."

"But what if it's not…heaven?"

"It will be," he said, his lips coming closer to hers. "We both like baseball, and ballet, and banana peppers."

"You're sure? It's not just because of Katie being Marta's twin? You don't just want to complete your family?"

"Leah, no. You're all I want, all I need. Getting Katie, too, is just a bonus. Please believe that because I've never meant anything more sincerely. I love you. Will you or won't you marry me?"

"I'll…think about it."

He raised his head and frowned. "In that case, I have no choice." He slipped the handcuffs from his pockets and secured them around Leah's and his wrists. "Take all the time you need. As soon as you say yes, I'll unlock these handcuffs and set you free."

Leah looked in astonishment at her wrist, then brought her gaze up to his. "I can't believe you did that. You're as bad as the twins."

"Yes," he said unrepentantly. "But they did go to a lot of trouble this afternoon trying to get us together and it seems to me that the least we can do is...appreciate their efforts."

"What, uh, kind of appreciation did you have in mind?"

"Ice cream, cake, all the movies they can watch, trust funds for college, maybe even a brother or a sister?"

Leah was caught off guard and speechless.

"Don't let that last suggestion overwhelm you," Riker said, grasping her fingers and giving them a squeeze. "I know we'd probably have to adopt, but we did so well the first time, it might be worth a second try, don't you think?"

She'd never dared to hope for another child. She'd never thought it might be possible, but now, suddenly, possibilities were opening up all around her. "I'm not sure Katie and Marta would appreciate a brother or a sister."

"Sure they will. How can they complain when they're getting what they want?"

"A mommy and a daddy who live together?" Leah asked.

"A mommy and a daddy who are *married* and live together."

Leah put aside her fear, knowing she hadn't conquered it for good and all, but that she was ready to take this first step. An exciting step in the right direction.

"Put like that, I don't see how I can refuse." She lifted her eyes to his and jangled the bracelet that bound their hands together. "Especially since we're connected by much stronger bonds than a pair of toy handcuffs."

"The twins, you mean?"

"Love," Leah said. "And trust. A perfect pair, Riker. Don't you agree?"

From the way he kissed her, she knew that this time they were in perfect accord.

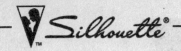

SPECIAL EDITION™

Emotional, compelling stories that capture the intensity of living, loving and creating a family in today's world.

Modern, passionate reads that are powerful and provocative.

nocturne

Dramatic and sensual tales of paranormal romance.

Romances that are sparked by danger and fueled by passion.

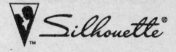

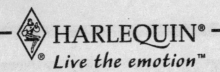

HARLEQUIN®
Live the emotion™

American ROMANCE®

Heart, Home & Happiness

HARLEQUIN®

Blaze™

Red-hot reads.

HARLEQUIN®

EVERLASTING LOVE™

Every great love has a story to tell™

Harlequin® Historical
Historical Romantic Adventure!

HARLEQUIN®

HARLEQUIN ROMANCE®

From the Heart, For the Heart

HARLEQUIN®

INTRIGUE®

Breathtaking Romantic Suspense

Medical Romance™...
love is just a heartbeat away

Ne
xt™

**There's the life you planned.
And there's what comes next.**

HARLEQUIN®
Presents~

Seduction and Passion Guaranteed!

HARLEQUIN®

Super Romance®

Exciting, Emotional, Unexpected

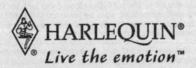

REQUEST YOUR FREE BOOKS!

2 FREE NOVELS PLUS 2 FREE GIFTS!

HARLEQUIN®

INTRIGUE®

Breathtaking Romantic Suspense

YES! Please send me 2 FREE Harlequin Intrigue® novels and my 2 FREE gifts. After receiving them, if I don't wish to receive any more books, I can return the shipping statement marked "cancel." If I don't cancel, I will receive 6 brand-new novels every month and be billed just $4.24 per book in the U.S., or $4.99 per book in Canada, plus 25¢ shipping and handling per book and applicable taxes, if any*. That's a savings of close to 15% off the cover price! I understand that accepting the 2 free books and gifts places me under no obligation to buy anything. I can always return a shipment and cancel at any time. Even if I never buy another book from Harlequin, the two free books and gifts are mine to keep forever.

182 HDN EEZ7   382 HDN EEZK

Name	(PLEASE PRINT)	
Address		Apt. #
City	State/Prov.	Zip/Postal Code

Signature (if under 18, a parent or guardian must sign)

Mail to the **Harlequin Reader Service®**:
IN U.S.A.: P.O. Box 1867, Buffalo, NY 14240-1867
IN CANADA: P.O. Box 609, Fort Erie, Ontario L2A 5X3

Not valid to current Harlequin Intrigue subscribers.

Want to try two free books from another line?
Call 1-800-873-8635 or visit www.morefreebooks.com.

* Terms and prices subject to change without notice. NY residents add applicable sales tax. Canadian residents will be charged applicable provincial taxes and GST. This offer is limited to one order per household. All orders subject to approval. Credit or debit balances in a customer's account(s) may be offset by any other outstanding balance owed by or to the customer. Please allow 4 to 6 weeks for delivery.

Your Privacy: Harlequin is committed to protecting your privacy. Our Privacy Policy is available online at www.eHarlequin.com or upon request from the Reader Service. From time to time we make our lists of customers available to reputable firms who may have a product or service of interest to you. If you would prefer we not share your name and address, please check here. ☐

HI07

REQUEST YOUR FREE BOOKS!

Harlequin® Historical
Historical Romantic Adventure!

2 FREE NOVELS PLUS 2 FREE GIFTS!

YES! Please send me 2 FREE Harlequin® Historical novels and my 2 FREE gifts. After receiving them, if I don't wish to receive any more books, I can return the shipping statement marked "cancel." If I don't cancel, I will receive 6 brand-new novels every month and be billed just $4.69 per book in the U.S., or $5.24 per book in Canada, plus 25¢ shipping and handling per book and applicable taxes, if any*. That's a savings of close to 15% off the cover price! I understand that accepting the 2 free books and gifts places me under no obligation to buy anything. I can always return a shipment and cancel at any time. Even if I never buy another book from Harlequin, the two free books and gifts are mine to keep forever.

246 HDN EEWW   349 HDN EEW9

Name _____ (PLEASE PRINT)

Address _____ Apt. #

City _____ State/Prov. _____ Zip/Postal Code

Signature (if under 18, a parent or guardian must sign)

Mail to the Harlequin Reader Service®:
IN U.S.A.: P.O. Box 1867, Buffalo, NY 14240-1867
IN CANADA: P.O. Box 609, Fort Erie, Ontario L2A 5X3

Not valid to current Harlequin Historical subscribers.

Want to try two free books from another line?
Call 1-800-873-8635 or visit www.morefreebooks.com.

* Terms and prices subject to change without notice. NY residents add applicable sales tax. Canadian residents will be charged applicable provincial taxes and GST. This offer is limited to one order per household. All orders subject to approval. Credit or debit balances in a customer's account(s) may be offset by any other outstanding balance owed by or to the customer. Please allow 4 to 6 weeks for delivery.

Your Privacy: Harlequin is committed to protecting your privacy. Our Privacy Policy is available online at www.eHarlequin.com or upon request from the Reader Service. From time to time we make our lists of customers available to reputable firms who may have a product or service of interest to you. If you would prefer we not share your name and address, please check here. ☐

HH07

REQUEST YOUR FREE BOOKS!

2 FREE NOVELS PLUS 2 FREE GIFTS!

HARLEQUIN®

EVERLASTING LOVE™

Every great love has a story to tell™

YES! Please send me 2 FREE Harlequin® Everlasting Love™ novels and my 2 FREE gifts. After receiving them, if I don't wish to receive any more books, I can return the shipping statement marked "cancel." If I don't cancel, I will receive 4 brand-new novels every other month and be billed just $4.47 per book in the U.S. or $4.99 per book in Canada, plus 25¢ shipping and handling per book and applicable taxes, if any*. That's a savings of about 15% off the cover price! I understand that accepting the 2 free books and gifts places me under no obligation to buy anything. I can always return a shipment and cancel at any time. Even if I never buy another book from Harlequin, the two free books and gifts are mine to keep forever.

153 HDN ELX4   353 HDN ELYG

Name _____ (PLEASE PRINT) _____

Address _____ Apt. _____

City _____ State/Prov. _____ Zip/Postal Code _____

Signature (if under 18, a parent or guardian must sign)

Mail to the **Harlequin Reader Service®**:
IN U.S.A.: P.O. Box 1867, Buffalo, NY 14240-1867
IN CANADA: P.O. Box 609, Fort Erie, Ontario L2A 5X3

Not valid to current Harlequin Everlasting Love subscribers.

Want to try two free books from another line?
Call 1-800-873-8635 or visit www.morefreebooks.com.

* Terms and prices subject to change without notice. NY residents add applicable sales tax. Canadian residents will be charged applicable provincial taxes and GST. This offer is limited to one order per household. All orders subject to approval. Credit or debit balances in a customer's account(s) may be offset by any other outstanding balance owed by or to the customer. Please allow 4 to 6 weeks for delivery.

Your Privacy: Harlequin is committed to protecting your privacy. Our Privacy Policy is available online at www.eHarlequin.com or upon request from the Reader Service. From time to time we make our lists of customers available to reputable firms who may have a product or service of interest to you. If you would prefer we not share your name and address, please check here. ☐

HEL07